Murder on the Run

Lesley Cookman

Published by Accent Press Ltd 2016

ISBN 9781786154422

Acknowledgements

Once again, I have to thank my son Miles for the idea of setting a story within the world of runners and running, but most thanks are due to my friend Rachel Priston, who patiently answered what must have seemed like many inane questions. And my usual apologies to the police forces of Great Britain, whom I misuse shamefully.

Thanks to my editor Greg Rees and all at Accent Press for their unfailing enthusiasm as usual, and to my happy band of regular readers who make sure I keep to the straight and narrow.

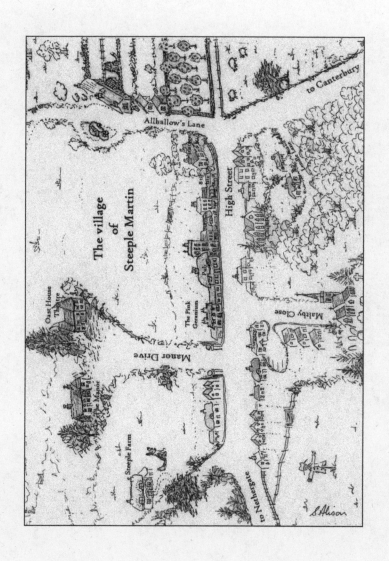

The village
of
Steeple Martin

Allhallow's Lane

to Canterbury

High Street

Oast House
Theatre

The Pink
Geranium

Maltby Close

Manor Drive

The Manor

Steeple Farm

to Nethergate

S Alison

WHO'S WHO IN THE LIBBY SARJEANT SERIES

Libby Sarjeant

Former actor, sometime artist, resident of 17 Allhallow's Lane, Steeple Martin. Owner of Sidney the Cat

Fran Wolfe

Also former actor, occasional psychic, resident of Coastguard Cottage, Nethergate. Owner of Balzac the cat.

Ben Wilde

Libby's significant other. Owner of The Manor Farm and the Oast House Theatre.

Guy Wolfe

Fran's husband. Artist and owner of a shop and gallery in Harbour Street, Nethergate.

Peter Parker

Ben's cousin. Freelance journalist, part-owner of The Pink Geranium restaurant and life partner of Harry Price.

Harry Price

Chef and co-owner of The Pink Geranium and Peter Parker's life partner.

Hetty Wilde	Ben's mother. Lives at The Manor.
DCI Ian Connell	Local policeman and friend. Former suitor of Fran's.
Adam Sarjeant	Libby's son.
Sophie Wilde	Guy's daughter.
Flo Carpenter	Hetty's Oldest Friend
Lenny Fisher	Hetty's brother. Lives with Flo Carpenter.
Reverend Bethany Cole	Vicar of Steeple Martin.
Reverend Patti Pearson	Vicar of St Aldeberge.
Anne Douglas	Librarian. Friend of Reverend Patti.
Ali and Ahmed	Owners of the eight-til-late in the village.
Sir Andrew McColl	Acclaimed theatre actor.
Max Tobin	Director and choreographer, Tobin Dance Theatre (TDT).

Chapter One

'And what exactly *is* the Nethergate Five K?' Libby Sarjeant asked her friend, Fran Wolfe.

'A five-kilometre run round Nethergate,' said Fran, handing over a mug of tea.

'Is Nethergate that big?'

'Apparently.' Fran sat in the big Windsor chair by the fireplace, opposite her friend. 'Anyway, Sophie's doing it. And she wants sponsors.'

'Ah.' Libby sipped her tea. 'And that means me?'

'If you would. I've got a form here, or you can go online. She's got a Just Giving page.'

'A ...? Oh, I know. That site that makes it easy to give money to good causes. Or any causes, come to that.'

'Don't be such a cynic, Lib. Anyway, I think she may be going to persuade Adam to do it with her.'

'Adam?' said Libby. 'My son hasn't done any exercise since gym at school. He hates sport.'

Fran quirked an eyebrow. 'Really? How come he's been going to Nethergate FC with Sophie for the whole of last season?'

'Has he?' Libby was thunderstruck.

'Well, of course it may simply be that he wanted them to get back together and he's been trying to impress her.'

'I thought they were back together.'

'It worked, then, didn't it?'

Libby laughed. 'Do you really think he might do it?'

'I suppose it depends on when it is, and what work

he's got on,' said Fran.

'It'll be a weekend, surely?' Libby frowned 'And that's when he works at the caff, Saturday and Sunday lunchtimes.'

'Harry would let him off, surely?'

'On the other hand it would be a great excuse not to do it.' Libby grinned. 'I can't believe Ad would actually run a hundred yards, let alone 5K.'

'Well, we'll see. Do you want a sponsorship form?'

'I'll do it online,' said Libby. 'Now, are we going to see Jane before I go home?'

They left Fran's Coastguard Cottage in Harbour Street and walked up to Cliff Terrace, where their friend Jane Baker, editor of the *Nethergate Mercury*, lived with her daughter Imogen and husband Terry in Peel House.

Seated in Jane's sitting room overlooking Nethergate bay, Libby broached the subject of the 5K run.

'The Nethergate run? Oh, yes, we've been doing it for years,' said Jane.

'You?' said Libby and Fran together.

'I meant the town,' giggled Jane. 'Can you see me running?'

'Well, you're younger than we are. And Sophie's doing it,' said Fran.

'Is she? Of course, she's a member of the Harriers, isn't she?'

'Harriers?' repeated Libby.

'The Nethergate running club,' explained Jane.

'I don't know much about it,' said Fran, 'except that she occasionally pops in to Coastguard Cottage to have a bath because she's only got a shower in the flat.'

'I never knew any of this,' said Libby. 'It's a different world.'

'It certainly is,' said Jane. 'They're always galloping past my windows and a more unattractive sport I've yet to see. The clothes are so unflattering.'

'I don't think any sports clothes are flattering,' said Libby. 'Except possibly tennis.'

'They run down Harbour Street, too,' said Fran. 'In fact, I think we're both on the route of the run, aren't we, Jane?'

'Where does it actually go?' asked Libby. 'Is it circular?'

'Not quite.' Jane stood up and went to the window. 'Look. It starts at the car park.' She pointed. 'Then down Victoria Place, turn left up the High Street, right to the top, then turn right opposite Canongate Drive, on to the St Aldeberge road. Along there on the right there's the entrance to a footpath down the cliffs which brings you out behind The Sloop and the Blue Anchor. And they finish on the jetty.'

'So they've got to go up quite a steep hill on the High Street,' said Libby.

'Even worse going down the cliff path,' said Jane. 'We've walked that, and it's really steep, not very well maintained and through loads of trees and bushes.'

'They'll have marshals all along there, though? In case anyone gets hurt or anything?'

'Oh, yes,' said Jane. 'And refreshment points where they give out water.'

'Do lots of people come to watch?' Libby was beginning to get interested.

'Loads. *Kent and Coast* send Campbell along to cover it usually.'

Campbell McLean was a reporter for the local *Kent and Coast* television station and had met Libby and Fran at the same time that Jane had made their acquaintance.

Fran was looking amused. 'Why don't you come and watch it with us? We can actually see the finish line from ours.'

'When is it?' Libby was cautious.

'May bank holiday,' said Jane. 'A lot of runs that day. Most of them longer than ours – usually ten K.'

'Steeple Martin does have a fun run,' said Fran.

'It does?' said Libby, surprised. 'How do you know?'

'Sophie told me. She thought she might do that this year, too.'

'When's that?'

'I'm not sure. Possibly the following weekend.'

'They'll all be online,' said Jane. 'Now, what did you want to see me about?'

'Nothing! Just the pleasure of your company. We haven't seen you for ages,' said Libby.

'No productions coming up? No publicity needed?'

'Not at the moment. We've got a few one-nighters, but then nothing really until The End Of The Pier Show.' This had become an annual event, which Steeple Martin's Oast Theatre company put on at The Alexandria, the ornate Edwardian pavilion that stood just below Victoria Parade.

'Will Susannah be doing the music again?' asked Jane, Susannah being her sister-in-law.

'I hope so,' said Libby. 'I wouldn't trust anyone else now.'

'Are you waiting to see Imogen when she comes home, then?' asked Jane.

'She comes home on her own now, does she?' said Fran in surprise.

'No, Mother goes to collect her. It's become a bit of a ritual. It started because I was often working, and now she does it whether I'm working or not.'

Jane's mother, the redoubtable Mrs Maurice, lived in

the self-contained semi-basement flat in Peel House.

'She's certainly mellowed,' said Libby. 'I was scared stiff of her when Fran and I went to see her in London.'

'Yes. I don't know how I turned out so normal,' said Jane with a grin.

When Libby got home to number 17 Allhallow's Lane, she called Adam's mobile.

'Are you working?' she asked.

Adam sighed. 'Yes, Ma. What do you want?'

'Sorry to interrupt. I just wanted to ask about the Nethergate 5K.'

'*What* about it?'

'Whether you were doing it.'

'Yes, I expect so. Look can we talk about it some other time?'

'Yes, yes, of course. Sorry.'

'It's OK – I'll call you later.'

'So,' Libby said to Sidney, the silver tabby. 'Adam's turned to sport. What love will do, eh?'

Libby had never enjoyed any sporting activity, either as a participant or a spectator, except horse riding. As a child she had had free access to the riding stables owned by two of her parents' friends, and had ridden regularly until motherhood intervened. A recent meeting with another of her parents' old friends had rekindled her interest in riding, and over the past few months she had tried out a few local stables. She'd managed to evade school sports in the main, particularly hockey. Running? Never.

'Well,' said her partner Ben, when she told him over dinner. 'I suppose we all ought to get fit.' He patted his stomach. 'I don't get anywhere near as much exercise as I used to.'

Libby made a face. 'I think it's a fad. If you're active

in your job, your daily life, that's one thing, but going out to deliberately make yourself out of breath with all your muscles hurting, that's daft.'

Adam, when he called later in the evening, disagreed.

'Once you get used to it, it's great,' he said. 'And you've no idea how addictive it is!'

'Really?' said Libby dubiously. 'But I would have thought your day job made you as fit as a fiddle.' Adam worked with his friend Mog landscaping gardens.

'I suppose so, but it doesn't give you the high that running does.'

'A high, eh?' Libby was sounding more and more dubious.

'Oh, Ma! It's not drugs!' Adam laughed. 'Anyway, I shall be doing the Nethergate 5K on May Day with Sophie, and the following Saturday the Steeple Martin Fun Run.'

'Oh, yes, Fran mentioned that.'

'So you'll be able to see us dashing up the high street.'

'Oh, I'm coming to see you dashing down Harbour Street, too!'

'You are? That's very supportive of you.'

'I know.' Libby was smug. 'And I hear you've been supporting Nethergate FC, too.'

'Ah – yes.' Adam sounded slightly ashamed.

Libby laughed. 'Just because we've never been a sporting family doesn't mean to say *you* have to conform.'

'No, well – Sophie supports them, you see.'

'So I understand. You're an item again, are you?'

'Mum! Item, indeed. Hate that word. Sounds like something in a shop.'

'All right, all right. You're going out together again.'

'Yes.' Adam sighed. 'Not sure where it's going, but OK so far. No talking about it to Fran, though.'

'All right,' said Libby, crossing her fingers. 'If I don't see you before, I'll see you on May Day.'

'Unless I see you at the caff,' said Adam, who also worked as a part-time waiter at The Pink Geranium, the vegetarian restaurant in Steeple Martin owned by their friend Harry Price.

'Maybe,' said Libby. 'If I can persuade Ben.'

May Day Bank Holiday dawned, thankfully, bright and rather breezy.

'That's good,' Libby said to Ben as they drove to Nethergate in his Range Rover. 'If it was really hot they'd be sweltering, wouldn't they?'

'You're always hearing of people collapsing in marathons,' said Ben. 'They give out water on the way round, don't they?'

'Yes, but they have to be very careful about drinking it,' said Libby, who had been looking it up online. 'It can make you sick.'

Ben pulled a face. 'The more I hear about all this, the more I'm inclined to agree with you. It's a mad way to spend a day.'

'But Ad's right, you know. It is addictive. I had a look at some running groups on social media, and there are scads of people posting every day about how far they've gone. There's some app or something that they can use to plot their route, and up it comes "6K this morning. Must do better." It's quite ridiculous.'

'Oh, so this 5K one isn't particularly special?'

'I think it's more for beginners and charity fundraisers,' said Libby, 'as far as I can gather. I've sponsored Sophie and Adam. They're doing it for one of the homeless charities.'

'I'd better do it, too, then,' said Ben. 'Here we are.

Where are we going to park? The whole town seems to have been closed to traffic.'

'Canongate Drive and walk down,' said Libby, and Ben turned right at the top of the high street.

It appeared that many other people had had the same idea, but luckily Ben knew the owner of a large bungalow right at the end, who allowed him to park on his drive.

'We'll have walked nearly 5K by the time we get to Fran's,' puffed Libby, as they walked back along Canongate Drive.

Crowds were beginning to line the high street as they walked down, and there were already food stalls and balloon sellers in the square at the bottom. Bunting hung across the ancient front of The Swan Inn, and a couple of yellow-jacketed policemen chatted with members of the public.

Ben and Libby turned left along Harbour street, cleared now of parked cars, past the shop and gallery owned by Guy Wolfe, Fran's husband. He waved from behind the counter.

'You made it!' said Fran, opening the door of Coastguard cottage. 'Where did you have to park?'

She led them inside.

'I've prepared a sort of buffet lunch that we can pick at,' she said. 'They start at midday at the other end of town, so we won't see the first runners arrive until about twenty past, if that. Sophie tells me that on the flat people can do it in fifteen minutes, but we've got a steep hill to run up in the high street, and then that descent down the cliff path, which will hold them up.'

'So it doesn't take long, then?' said Ben in surprise. 'It would take me hours to walk that far.'

'You'd be surprised,' said Fran. 'How long did it take you to walk here from Canongate?'

'Twenty minutes?' Ben looked at Libby for confirmation. 'Perhaps a bit longer. We weren't hurrying, and the whole place was getting crowded.'

'There, you see.' Fran was setting out food on the coffee table. 'Guy and I walked the route the other evening, and not hurrying, it took us about an hour and twenty minutes.'

'Golly,' said Libby admiringly. 'Look, it's almost midday. Shall we go and stand at the end and watch as they come through the square?'

Chapter Two

They stood and watched the stream of runners pass through the square, strolling back to Coastguard Cottage after they had seen Sophie and Adam, somewhere in the middle of the field.

Sure enough, as Fran had said, it was barely twenty-five past twelve when the first runner appeared at the finishing line outside The Sloop Inn. This time, the three of them walked along Harbour Street to see if they could spot Adam and Sophie as they came through.

Most people seemed to have accomplished it within three quarters of an hour.

'The worst bit,' said a perspiring Adam, as Ben handed him a beer bottle, 'was that cliff path. It's covered with vegetation and rocks. Several people fell, or twisted an ankle. And there weren't always people nearby. Although we started in a pack, by that time we'd sort of strung out.'

Sophie, looking remarkably fresh with her fair hair pulled back in a ponytail, came over to them. 'Adam did really well,' she said, 'but we appear to have lost a couple of people on the way, so some of us are going back along the route to see where they've got to.'

'Does that often happen?' asked Libby.

'Sometimes.' Sophie frowned. 'People who aren't used to running give up and just drop out. It makes things very difficult because they don't tell the organisers, who then have to go and look for them, just like we're doing now. Although I didn't think Lisa would do that.'

'Who's Lisa?' asked Libby.

'Lisa Harwood. She's a member of the Harriers, and very dedicated. Runs every day, and has practised this route loads of times. She would have been one of the front runners, I'd have thought.

'I'll come with you,' said Adam with only slight reluctance, handing his bottle back to Ben. 'We'll call in at Coastguard later to see if you're still there.'

'Oh, we will be,' said Ben. 'We've got a table booked at The Sloop and we're staying the night.'

'Oh, well, definitely see you, then.' With a farewell wave, Adam set off behind Sophie and a few others wearing the purple sash of the Nethergate Harriers.

After most of the onlookers had gone, Guy closed the shop and came back to the cottage to hoover up what was left from lunch.

'Did Sophie say what time she made?' he asked, through a mouthful of sausage roll.

'No, we hardly saw her,' said Fran. 'She and Adam and some of the others went off to look for some of the runners who had fallen by the wayside.'

'I didn't think they did that,' said Guy. 'I'm sure they don't in the big marathons.'

'I suppose it's because it's a relatively small field and they check everyone off,' said Libby. 'And Ad was saying how bad the cliff path was. Some of them fell and twisted ankles.'

'It's not that easy to walk down, let alone run,' said Fran. 'I think they should have chosen a different route.'

Somewhere, a mobile phone began to ring.

'Mine,' said Fran, and went to find it. 'Sophie?'

She listened for a moment, frowning, then looked over

at the others. 'Hold on, I'll ask Libby and Dad.'

She cradled the phone in her hand. 'They can't find any trace of that Lisa they mentioned. She was seen at the water stop at the top of the cliff path and nothing since. None of the other runners passed her and she never emerged at the bottom. They want to know if they should call the police.'

'Heavens, I don't know!' said Libby. 'Why ask us?'

'She said because we've got experience with dealing with the police.' Fran gave a rueful grin. 'I suppose we have.'

'But not this sort of experience,' said Libby. 'What do you think?' She turned to Ben.

'I think they should probably wait to see if she turns up at home. And surely it's the organisers' problem, not Sophie's.'

'Sophie's on the Harriers' committee,' said Guy, 'so it probably is her problem.' He turned to Fran. 'Tell her what Ben just said.'

Fran repeated the advice and ended the call. 'I think she was rather hoping we'd say we would get in touch with Ian,' she said, as she returned to her chair.

Detective Chief Inspector Ian Connell was, by now, an old friend who had figured largely in some of the adventures Libby and Fran had stumbled into over the years.

'I thought that,' said Libby with a grin.

'I'm sure he'd be delighted with a missing persons enquiry,' said Ben.

'All the same, I wonder what's happened to her,' said Guy. 'You said there were a couple of people who'd failed to turn up. What about the others?'

'She didn't mention anyone else, so I suppose she's the only one they can't find.'

Later that evening, Sophie and Adam joined them at The Sloop.

'Any news?' asked Libby as they sat down.

'No.' Sophie frowned down at the table.

'What about her husband? Hasn't she come home?'

'She lives on her own. Bishop's Bottom I think. Or possibly Shott. Anyway, no landline, as far as we know, and her mobile's switched off.'

'Has someone been to check at her address?' said Ben. 'How do you know she hasn't come home?'

'Another member went to check when they got home,' said Adam. 'Not there.'

'What about her car?' asked Guy. 'Did she drive over this morning?'

'Still in the car park at the top of Victoria Place,' said Sophie.

Libby and Fran exchanged glances.

'In that case, Sophie,' said Fran, 'yes. I really think you should inform the police.'

Sophie turned an imploring face to her father. 'Couldn't you do it, Dad?'

'Not a chance, sweetheart.' Guy patted her hand. 'It's nothing to do with me.' He looked round the table. 'Or with any of us. You need to tell your chair, or race director or whoever, and they should report it.'

'I thought –' began Sophie.

'No!' said four voices together, and Sophie grinned, rather unwillingly.

'Oh, well, it was worth a try.' She stood up. 'Come on, Ad. Let's beard the ogre in his den.'

'Can't you ring the ogre?' asked Libby.

'He and some of the committee are eating up the road at the Indian,' said Adam. 'We're supposed to be joining them.'

'Off you go, then,' said Guy. 'Good luck.'

'Poor kids,' said Fran as they left. 'They do look worried.'

'Hardly kids,' said Ben, 'although I do find myself wanting to ask Adam why he isn't wearing a coat sometimes.'

Libby laughed. 'I thought that was my job?'

The following morning Fran served breakfast in her tiny backyard, where Balzac the cat kept a benevolent eye on the kippers, bought as a treat for Ben and Guy.

'Police up at the quay,' said Guy emerging from the house. 'Think it's about that Lisa?'

'Oh dear,' said Fran. 'I do hope not.'

'So do I, in a way, but if she really is missing, then it's a good job they're looking into it.' Libby picked up her mug of tea. 'And we're not.'

Ben, Guy and Fran looked at her sharply.

'What do you mean?' said Fran.

Libby shrugged. 'It's a good job we aren't looking into it. That's all.'

Ben frowned uneasily. 'Nothing to look into, surely.'

'Of course there is,' said Libby. 'Anyway, I'm sure the kids will tell us when we see them.'

It was just as Libby and Ben were preparing to leave Coastguard Cottage that Adam and Sophie arrived.

'She's disappeared,' said Adam flatly. 'The police are all over the place.'

'They sent someone over to ask questions last night,' said Sophie. 'And they're coming back this morning.'

'Are they sure she's properly disappeared?' said Fran.

'Her car's still in the car park – or it was. I think they're taking it away. And she didn't go home.' Adam shook his head. 'I would have thought she might have gone off with someone, but Sophie says not.'

'And the police have given you no idea why they're convinced she's missing?' said Libby.

'No.' Sophie sank down on the arm of an armchair. 'I'd forgotten what it was like to be tangled up with something like this.'

Sophie had been helpful in one of the previous cases in which Libby and Fran had been involved.

'You're hardly involved with this one, darling.' Guy patted his daughter on her shoulder.

'Stay out of it as much as possible,' said Ben. 'Leave the police to get on with it.'

'Oh, we are,' said Adam. 'I'd like to forget all about it.'

'Aren't you just a bit worried?' asked Sophie.

'I didn't know her, did I?' said Adam reasonably. 'I'm not sure I even know what she looks like.'

'I didn't know her, either, really,' said Sophie. 'I don't think anyone did. She just turned up and ran.'

'Well, it's nothing to do with you, so I really would try and forget about it,' said Libby. 'We all know what police investigations are like and they aren't pleasant for anybody.'

'I can hardly believe I'm hearing that,' said Ben. 'From you of all people.'

'Well, they're not,' said Libby, ignoring the laughter. 'Don't forget there's usually tragedy of one sort or another involved.'

The laughter stopped.

'Absolutely,' said Guy. 'Let's remember that and hope the police find Lisa safe and sound.'

Libby was unusually quiet as she and Ben drove home to Steeple Martin. Eventually, Ben gave her a sideways glance and a tap on the knee. 'What's up, Lib?'

'I was just thinking about that poor woman. I do hope

16

nothing's happened to her.'

Ben sighed. 'Look, you were the one who said to stay out of it. Don't start dwelling on it now.'

'I know.' Libby shifted in her seat. 'But we've been involved in so many murders now I can't help feeling that this is one, too.'

'That's *because* you've been mixed up in them. It's your default position. But it really is nothing to do with any of us, so just treat it as you would a news report.'

Libby nodded and returned to a contemplation of the countryside, which soon gave way to the hill that led into the village.

'Where do you suppose they run here?' she said. 'There isn't a circular route to follow.'

'I expect they start at a certain point, turn at another point and run back again,' said Ben. 'It's not a serious thing, is it? Not like yesterday's.'

'I don't think that was all that serious,' said Libby. 'It was a very short run compared to most. People do more than that every morning, apparently.'

'So I believe,' said Ben. 'I can understand people wanting to keep fit ...'

'Adam says it can get addictive and give you an adrenalin high. Regular runners actually feel bad if they don't run every day.'

'Bad?'

'Ill and grumpy.' She shivered. 'It all sounds most unpleasant.'

'Let's hope Ad and Sophie don't get that addicted, then.' Ben turned into Allhallow's Lane. 'Bugger. I meant to collect Sidney.'

Sidney often went to stay with Hetty, Ben's mother, at the Manor, the Wilde family home. Hetty had lived there alone since the death of her husband Greg, although Ben still had the Manor Farm Estate office there and went in most days. It was also next door to the oast house, which had once been a working one. Ben, a former architect, had converted it into a theatre, which he, Libby and Ben's cousin Peter ran between them.

'We're going up to lunch, aren't we?' said Libby. 'We can collect him then. I'll take the cat basket.'

'And I suppose I can carry it back?' said Ben with some amusement.

'Or,' said Libby, ignoring him, 'we could leave him there overnight and go and get him in the morning.'

'Or, I could drop you off, turn round and go and get him now,' said Ben. 'Go on, hop out.'

Libby let herself into number 17 and tripped down the step even though Sidney wasn't there. The landline was ringing.

'Libby! I tried your mobile number, but you didn't answer.'

'I was in the car,' Libby replied cautiously. 'Is that Campbell?'

'Of course it is. You were there, weren't you?'

'I – what? Where?'

'At the Nethergate 5K. I saw in the list of runners that your son and Fran's step-daughter were there, so I guessed you would be.'

'Why do you want to know?'

'What you know about Lisa Harwood's disappearance, of course! And the poisoned cup.'

Chapter Three

'Poisoned –? Oh, don't be so melodramatic, Campbell. Poisoned cup indeed!'

'Well, it was. One of those plastic drinking cups. The stewards were handing out cups of water if anyone wanted one.'

'So?' Libby's heart was sinking.

'The police have found one somewhere on the cliff path. At least,' Campbell hesitated, 'I think that's where they found it.'

'And you know how?'

'They've issued a missing person alert. I thought you'd know more about it.'

'Why on earth should I?' Libby found herself growing exasperated, as she often was with Campbell.

'Because you usually do, you and Fran.'

'Well, this time, we don't,' said Libby. 'Yes, I knew Lisa Harwood had not completed the run because some of the other runners went to look for her, but that's about all.'

'Oh.' Campbell sounded disappointed. 'Oh. Well, if you do hear anything ...'

'I know,' said Libby. 'But I won't.'

'Won't hear anything, or won't tell me?'

'Both,' said Libby with a grin.

Campbell chuckled. 'I should have known. Bye, Libby.'

Libby's grin faded as she ended the call. Poisoned

cup? She called Fran.

'I've just had Campbell on the phone. The police have put out a statement about Lisa Harwood, and he said something about a poisoned plastic cup being found.'

'How did he know that? The police wouldn't mention that in a statement to the media.'

'That's what I thought. Do you think he was just fishing?'

'He usually is,' said Fran. 'You didn't tell him anything, did you?'

'I never do,' said Libby. 'Let me know if you hear anything.'

Ben appeared, looking flustered and carrying a struggling Sidney, who shot off in a blur of fur as soon as he was put down. Libby repeated Campbell's phone call.

Ben frowned. 'Just trying to stir things up, I should think. You know what he's like. And where did he get the poisoned cup from?'

'No idea. I thought he might have made it up.'

'Odd thing to make up,' said Ben. 'Now I'd better go and change. I seem to have Sidney all over me.'

Hetty cooked a traditional English Sunday lunch every week, to which Ben, Libby and Peter were bidden regularly. If Harry hadn't opened the Pink Geranium, he was invited, if Fran and Guy were up for the weekend, they came too, and any of Libby's, Fran's or Guy's offspring were included if they were around. Flo Carpenter, Hetty's best friend, and Flo's partner Lenny, Hetty's brother, occasionally turned up, especially if anything was going on that Flo might be interested in.

Today, it was only Libby, Ben and Peter.

'So,' said Hetty, basting potatoes, 'you ain't going to look into this missing woman, gal?'

Peter raised his eyebrows.

'A runner went missing yesterday,' explained Ben.

'Yes, Adam told us.' Peter stretched his elegant legs in front of him, neatly crossed at the ankles.

'Oh, he turned up at the caff, did he?'

'Yes. I was merely surprised that you aren't going to look into it,' said Peter, looking innocent.

'Oh, stop it.' Libby laughed. 'It's nothing to do with me, is it? Even that blasted television journalist phoned me thinking I'd know all about it.'

'You've got a reputation,' said Peter. 'Shall I fetch the claret? Or will you make do with my offering?'

Since Peter's offering was a very decent Rioja, they all voted for that, although Ben fetched a bottle of claret in case they ran out.

It was just as Hetty was offering brandy at the end of the meal that Adam came in.

'Sorry to interrupt, Hetty,' he said, 'but I wanted to see Mum.'

'What's up, darling?' Libby was aware of a feeling of foreboding.

'Sophie just rang. They've found one of those energy drink shot things.'

'So? Don't a lot of runners use those?' said Libby.

'They seem to think it's important, so –' Adam began.

'At least it wasn't a poisoned cup. That's what that TV reporter told me it was. I hoped it wasn't true. How does Sophie know?'

'It was one of the running club who found it. They all went out looking again this morning.'

'I bet the police were pleased with them tramping over the scene,' said Libby.

'It's not exactly the scene,' said Adam. 'They don't know where that was, do they.'

'Where was it, then?' asked Peter.

'On the cliff side, but away from the path, apparently.'

'And how did he know it was Lisa's?' asked Libby.

'He didn't. He just picked it up because it was the sort of drink that had been given out. He gave it to the police and I suppose they'll do some tests on it.'

'I wonder how Campbell knew?' mused Libby.

'At a guess, he was probably hanging around just to see what he could pick up,' said Ben.

'Hmm.' Libby thought for a moment. 'I don't think he's supposed to know. This isn't general knowledge, and if the can, or bottle or whatever it was, was only found this morning, they couldn't have analysed it before they sent out the statement to the media.'

Ben and Peter were frowning. Hetty gave a deep sigh.

'What's the matter?' asked a bewildered Adam.

'She's starting again,' said Peter. 'Look at her face.'

Everyone looked at Libby's face, which began to turn a delicate pink. 'What?' she said.

'Just don't, Lib,' said Ben. 'Remember? It's nothing to do with us, and you were never going to get involved again.'

'I wasn't!' Libby sounded indignant.

Her phone began to ring.

'Excuse me,' she said, looking at the screen. 'It's Fran.' She stood up and walked out into the hall.

'Libby? Ian's just been to speak to me.'

'Ian? Why?'

'He's been put on to the Lisa Harwood case. He saw Adam's and Sophie's names on the list of runners and came to ask me if I knew anything about it.'

'What did you say?'

'I told him exactly what happened yesterday, and what Ad and Sophie had told us.'

'Did you tell him about Campbell?'

'No, should I have?'

'Adam just arrived here at Hetty's –'

'Oh!' said Fran, 'I forgot. Did I interrupt lunch?'

'No, we'd finished. But Ad said Sophie phoned him to tell him a similar story.'

'That doesn't sound right,' said Fran. 'How would he have known?'

'Exactly what I said.' Libby beamed in triumph. 'And they all had a go at me about getting involved.'

'Well, they would. To save you the embarrassment, I shall call Ian now and tell him. It just may be relevant.'

Libby went back into the kitchen.

'Ian's been put in charge of the case,' she informed the others casually, 'and he's just been to see Fran.'

A collective groan went up from those gathered around the table.

'It was because he saw your name and Sophie's on the list of runners,' Libby said to Adam. 'I think he leapt to the same conclusion that Campbell did – we must know something about it.' She sighed. 'And we don't. All the same, I could bear to know how anyone – runner, police or TV reporter – knew that drink was relevant.'

'I don't suppose anyone will tell you, Lib,' said Ben.

'No, and I can't ask,' said Libby. 'Never mind. I just hope they find the poor woman.'

A murmur of agreement rustled round the table.

'I'm going back to Nethergate, Mum,' said Adam. 'I think Sophie would like me to be there.'

Forbearing to say that Sophie had her father and stepmother to support her if she needed it, Libby nodded and patted her son's hand. 'Of course she would.'

When Adam had gone, a half-hearted offer was made to wash up.

'You can load the dishwasher,' said Hetty, 'and I'll do

the pots after I've had me rest.'

As this was what she always said, Peter, Ben and Libby grinned and got to their feet. Hetty gave them a half-salute and disappeared towards her own quarters.

'We'd better go and put Hal out of his misery,' said Peter, as they loaded the last cutlery into the dishwasher. 'He'll be dying to know what Ad told us.'

'I expect he knows that,' said Libby, 'but he won't know Ian's on the case.'

'Will he have finished in the caff?' asked Ben, as they started down the drive.

'Not sure – we'll have a look,' said Peter.

In fact, they found Harry, still in his chef's whites, sitting on the sofa in the left-hand window of The Pink Geranium, his feet on the coffee table and a glass of wine in hand.

He cocked an eye at Libby. 'I suppose you're going to tell me you're off on the trail of the missing runner?'

Libby endeavoured to look shocked. 'Of course not. But Ad obviously told you Sophie had called?'

'Yes, saying they'd found an old tin can or something.' Harry swung his feet off the table. 'I suppose you want more alcohol unless you're full of Hetty's?'

When they all had full glasses in front of them, Harry waved an imperious hand at Libby. 'Carry on.'

'There isn't much really,' said Libby, 'just that Ian's called on Fran.'

Harry's eyebrows shot up. 'About the runner?'

'Yes.' Libby frowned. 'And I can't see how they think an energy drink bottle or tin can be relevant to a missing runner. Any one of the field could have thrown it there.'

'Didn't Ad say it was a way off the cliff path?' said Ben.

'Those energy drinks can be dangerous,' said Harry.

'Why?' asked Libby and Ben together.

'They contain caffeine in much higher concentrations than you would normally have. Bad for the heart.'

'Especially if you're a runner, I'd have thought,' said Peter.

'I didn't know that,' said Libby, looking thoughtful. 'That could be it, couldn't it?'

'Could be what?' asked Peter.

'Could be why the police thought it was a clue. High caffeine content drink found, runner not found, ergo, runner could be lying somewhere dying from a heart attack.'

'They'd have found her by now if that was the case,' said Ben.

'So they would,' said Libby, and sighed. 'Good job this is nothing to do with me. I'd be very disappointed.'

Chapter Four

Fran rang later in the evening, sounding miserable.

'What's up?' asked Libby.

'Ian's asked me to help with this search.'

'Has he? Why?'

'They're concerned about the girl.'

Libby wrinkled her brow. 'Yes – well, she's disappeared.'

Fran gave a gusty sigh. 'They're worried because she hasn't turned up anywhere near the route – or anywhere else at the moment – and her husband apparently told the police she has a slight heart defect of some kind. And the energy drink could have triggered a heart attack. He said she never took them for that reason.'

'Blimey! And what husband? I thought Sophie said she lived alone.'

'They're separated.'

'Oh. And what does he want you to do? Ian, I mean.'

'See if I can pick up any what he calls "traces" of her along the cliff path. To be honest, I think he'd be grateful for anything just now.'

'What have you got to do?'

'Walk along the path, I suppose. I wish he wouldn't do this! He knows that part of my brain's gone off the boil. I can't force it.'

Fran had been known to help the police in this somewhat unconventional way in the past, but was very uncomfortable with it. Even when she had been employed

27

by a large London firm of estate agents to "psych out" properties, she'd remained doubtful about her "moments", as her friends called them.

'Humour him,' said Libby. 'Maybe you'll pick up a physical clue instead.'

'They've been over the ground with the veritable toothcomb already. I doubt if there's anything left to find. Look, I was going to ask you, would you come with me?'

'Would I?' Libby was delighted. 'When?'

'Tomorrow morning. Could you get here by ten? Ian's picking me up and driving me up there.'

'I expect I could,' said Libby, who was not known for early rising habits. 'See you then.'

The following morning, Libby had to park right at the end of Harbour Street by Mavis's Blue Anchor cafe, and arrived on Fran's doorstep at exactly the same time as Detective Chief Inspector Ian Connell. He looked down at Libby, one dark, winged eyebrow raised.

'I might have known she'd ask you to come along.' His voice still held the faintest trace of a Scottish burr, which Libby found tremendously appealing.

'Do you mind?' she asked, as Fran opened the door.

'Would it make a difference? Good morning, Fran.'

'Good morning,' said Fran, looking from one to the other of her visitors with slight suspicion.

'I was just asking Ian if he minded me coming along,' said Libby brightly.

'I asked her,' said Fran. 'Are we all ready?'

Ian drove them back along Harbour Street, round the square and up the High Street, turning right on to the St Aldeburgh road. At the top of the cliff path, blue and white tape still fluttered, and a lonely police officer in his hi-vis jacket stood guard.

'Do we need to put on those blue shoe protectors?' asked Libby, eyeing the path dubiously.

'No, we've been over the ground as thoroughly as we can,' said Ian. 'And after yesterday's find it was practically stripped bare. Come this way.'

He led them a little way off the path, where the undergrowth was considerably thicker. Libby grimaced as thin, whippy branches snatched at her top and bare arms, thankful, at least, that she was wearing jeans.

Fran, ahead of her, stopped.

'Is this where the drink was found?'

'Near enough.' Ian, at the head of the procession, turned round.

'Was it in a can?'

'No.' Ian looked interested. 'Why?'

'I just wondered. I didn't know if it was a can, or a bottle or what. I thought at first it would be one of those plastic cups.'

'You were right,' said Ian.

Both women gasped.

'Did Fran tell you what Campbell McLean said?' asked Libby.

'She did. I've got someone trying to find out what he had heard and from whom.'

'It was too early, wasn't it?' said Libby. 'You wouldn't have released anything about "a poisoned cup". And how did you know?'

'That it was poisoned?' Ian shook his head. 'We didn't. Don't either of you let any of this out, but what happened was the running club – The Harriers, isn't it? – decided to do their own search outside the parameters we had drawn. Some of them were searching the cliff side here, although officers had already gone over it, and one of them spotted a plastic cup the same as those handed out at the refreshment stops. Why the officers hadn't seen it, we don't know. It had liquid in the bottom, and the runner and a couple of his friends thought it smelt like a popular energy drink. So they brought it to us.'

'And somehow, Campbell got wind of it and jumped to conclusions?' said Fran.

'It looks like it.' Ian nodded. 'So, any thoughts?'

Fran paced the ground slowly, looking down.

'Were there any tyre tracks?' she asked, looking up.

'Not here,' said Ian, looking surprised.

'But there were some?'

'Yes, but further across.' Ian was frowning. 'Why?'

'I don't know.' Fran shook her head. 'I was expecting to see them, somehow.'

Ian turned and led the way through more shrubbery to a clearing, and pointed. 'There. We took casts. But it's rather a long way from the path.'

'Well, it wouldn't be any nearer, would it?' said Fran reasonably. 'It would have been seen.'

'There was no vehicle here on Monday afternoon,' said Ian. 'The runners have all been questioned about it.'

'Where was she between the afternoon and when she was put in the car, then?' Fran said, staring into the distance.

'What?' said Ian and Libby together.

'Well, she was, wasn't she? Or she would have been found. She might have been left somewhere by the side of the path at first, but ...' She stopped. 'Again, she would have been seen when the runners went back to look for her.'

'Unless one of the runners moved her,' suggested Libby.

Ian and Fran looked at her in surprise.

'I don't see how,' said Ian. 'They were all together.'

'Yes, we saw them go,' said Fran.

'Oh, yes,' said Libby, crestfallen. 'Unless,' she brightened, 'one of them got to where she was first and covered her up, then said there was no sign of her.'

'What would they cover her with?' asked Fran.

'Oh, I don't know,' said Libby impatiently. 'You work it out.'

'We're trying to,' said Ian, his mouth twitching. 'What could you see, Fran?'

'I couldn't *see* anything.' It was Fran's turn to be impatient. 'You know, it's as I've always said – as if I know something for a fact. Without any idea how I know it.'

'All right, all right,' Ian soothed. 'Just so that we're clear, you think it's possible that she was driven away in a car that night. But you don't know where she was the rest of the time?'

'No. She could have walked away herself, of course.'

'I should have said, there are signs that she fell, not far from the path.' Ian led them back to where they had originally stopped.

'And she could have had a heart attack,' said Fran.

Ian narrowed his eyes. 'Could have?'

'You told me her husband said she had a heart defect.'

'Caffeine,' said Libby. 'She didn't drink energy drinks.'

'She wouldn't have drunk this one, then, would she?' said Ian.

'If she was handed a cup by someone she trusted, like a race official, she might start drinking it before she realised,' said Fran. 'Do you know who gave it to her?'

'The team are asking now. There were so many people involved, stewards as well as runners and organisers, we're having trouble tracking them all down.'

'Social media?' suggested Libby.

Ian smiled, 'Yes, Libby, that's being done. In fact, we've posted on the Harriers' group pages, and several people have got in touch.'

'You haven't denied the heart attack,' said Fran.

Ian sighed. 'No. I really can't tell you any more, though. And if McLean comes back to you again, tell him to call me.'

He began to walk back to the cliff path.

'Was I any help?' asked Fran.

'I think so.' Ian held up the police tape for them to go under. 'We must try harder to find the vehicle.'

He drove them back in silence to Coastguard Cottage.

'Have you time for coffee?' asked Fran.

'Sorry, no. Got to go and peer through my magnifying glass.' Ian gave them each a brief smile and drove off.

'He didn't even say thank you!' said Libby indignantly.

'I think he was a bit preoccupied,' said Fran. 'Are you coming in for coffee?'

'Yes, please.' Libby followed her friend inside. 'What did you really think out there?'

'Exactly what I said.' Fran filled her new cafetière. 'Have you got one of these yet?'

'No. I'm not that fond of coffee. Harry's got a posh new machine in the caff, though.'

Fran turned and looked at her. 'You could have said you'd prefer tea.'

Libby grinned. 'Why? I'm giving you the chance to play with your new toy.'

Fran scowled and turned back to her cupboards.

'OK, you said exactly what you saw –'

'I didn't see anything,' interrupted Fran. 'I said I expected to see tyre tracks. That's all.'

'But you also thought she'd been hidden until she was driven away.'

'That was pure speculation. She could have fallen, as Ian said – fainted even – then woken up and walked away before the other runners came looking for her.'

'But why would she walk away?'

'I don't know!' said Fran impatiently. 'I'm guessing! Look, it's nothing to do with us, so I don't know why we're discussing it.'

'OK,' said Libby meekly, and went to sit on the window seat. After a moment, Fran came in with the cafetière and mugs on a tray.

'Sorry, Lib. It just made me feel – oh, I don't know – uncomfortable.'

'That's all right. I do try to understand, you know.'

Fran smiled. 'I know you do. You all do. But Ian still seems to think I can turn it on like a tap.'

'He was right, though, wasn't he? You did feel something.'

'Yes, but it's unquantifiable. If that's the right word in the circumstances.'

'Or unexplainable. Yes. Never mind, as you say, it's nothing to do with us.'

Fran gave her friend a knowing look. 'And when has that ever stopped you before?'

They drank their coffee in companionable silence. Balzac came to join Libby in the window seat.

'Nobody's asked why she's disappeared,' said Fran, gazing past Libby to the sea beyond.

'Lisa? No. I suppose because we don't know what happened. Has she walked away, been kidnapped or murdered? Until we know …'

'But you always look at the victim first,' said Fran. 'Whatever's happened. The victim's the key to it all. Was

33

she depressed, for instance.'

'Well, we can't ask anyone,' said Libby. 'We've no reason to, and anyway, we've already agreed it's none of our business.'

'No.' Fran shifted in her chair. 'I think it's got under my skin a bit.'

'Up there, do you mean?'

Fran nodded. 'It made me so uncomfortable. And I just knew those tyre tracks would be there. They've got something to do with it, I know.'

Libby watched her uneasily.

'Let's go and see if Sophie's in the shop.' Fran stood up suddenly. 'I can't just sit still.'

'All right.' Libby scrambled off the window seat, giving Balzac a final pat on the head. 'Are we asking questions?'

'Oh, yes.' Fran opened the door. 'I want to know.'

Libby's eyebrows rose. 'It's usually me.'

Fran turned back to look at her friend.

'Come on, admit it. You want to know, too. Let's start with Sophie.'

Chapter Five

Sophie, it appeared, was upstairs in her flat, supposedly studying for her master's degree in the History and Philosophy of Art. Unlike her first degree, she had been able to find a part-time course at Canterbury, which meant she could stay at home, thus saving money – causing Guy, however, to spend it.

She looked up from her laptop as Fran followed her knock into the sitting room.

'Hello, Step-ma. And Libby. This is nice. I'm getting bored.'

'We're not interrupting, then?' Libby grinned at her.

'Not exactly. Can I get you anything?'

'No, we've just had coffee, thanks,' said Fran, sitting down. 'We wanted to ask you about Lisa.'

Sophie looked bewildered. 'I told you, I didn't really know her. Why?'

'Ian asked me to go up and look at the supposed spot of her disappearance. We've just got back.'

Sophie's eyes widened. 'Really? What happened?'

'There are tyre tracks,' said Fran.

'And?' prompted Sophie, after a pause.

'Your step-ma expected to see them, and there they were. It made her uncomfortable.' Libby sat beside Fran.

'Was it a "moment"?'

'Yes. Not much of one – I just knew the tyre tracks would be there. And Ian said there were signs that she had fallen. Not on the path though.'

'We're speculating that she had an underlying heart condition and that one of those energy drinks triggered a heart attack,' said Libby, 'but it doesn't explain the tyre tracks.'

'Perhaps they've got nothing to do with it?' suggested Sophie.

'In that case,' said Fran, 'where is she?'

Sophie looked at Libby. 'What do you think?'

Libby shrugged. 'I don't really know. But I trust Fran's moments. If her strange brain has connected the tyre tracks to Lisa's disappearance, I'm inclined to believe her.'

'Strange brain? Thanks!' Fran made a face.

'We-ell,' said Sophie, looking from one to the other, 'I don't know who you would talk to, or even how you could get to meet them. You can't go asking people questions like the police, can you?'

'Always a problem,' agreed Libby.

'Did she run with anyone regularly?' asked Fran. 'You know – a pacer, or whatever they call it.'

'Pacemaker,' corrected Sophie. 'We don't use them at this level. But I think Lisa ran on her own mostly. She was a bit obsessive. Posted her mileage every day on social media, you know?'

'Could we look that up?' asked Libby.

'You wouldn't be able to see it,' said Sophie. 'You aren't friends with her.'

'But you are,' said Fran.

'We're both in the Harriers' group,' said Sophie, 'so, yes. I could try.'

She pulled her laptop towards her. 'Don't stand over me,' she said as both older women stood up. They sat down again.

'Here you are. We're not actually friends on here, and

her profile is heavily protected, but I can see some of her friends.'

She read and scrolled for a moment. 'Yes – she seems to be friends with a couple of the Harriers – Davy Long and Kirsty Trent.' She looked up. 'Do you want to meet them?'

Libby looked at Fran. 'Do we?'

'If we can do it without triggering suspicion,' said Fran.

'I think that's going to happen however you do it,' said Sophie. 'I think the best thing you can do is to come to the pub with me this evening.'

'Which pub? Why?' asked Libby.

'The Sergeant At Arms. It's in one of the backstreets and it's the Harriers' regular meeting place. Steve called an extra meeting tonight about Lisa.'

'Who's Steve?'

'Our chair, Steve Reid. You know – the ogre.'

'Ogre? Oh, yes, the one who was having the Indian meal the other day.' Libby looked back at Fran. 'So, do we go?'

'I think so. I'm not going to rest until we've looked into this.'

Libby and Sophie looked at each other.

'That's a first,' said Libby. 'It's usually me saying that.'

'And then saying you want nothing to do with it,' said Fran with a smile. She stood up. 'Thanks for your help, Sophie. What time tonight?'

'Eight-ish. It won't be formal. Bring Dad and Ben, if you like.'

'What do you think?' asked Libby, when they were outside.

'It'll give us a chance to meet them,' said Fran,

pushing open the door of Guy's shop and gallery. 'Let's ask Guy.'

But Guy was wary. 'By all means bring Ben down and we can go for a pint at The Sloop, but I'm not going sleuthing with you in this – what did you say it was called?'

'The Sergeant At Arms. Funny name for a pub,' said Libby.

'No sillier than "I Am The Only Running Footman", or "The Case Is Altered",' said Fran. 'So do you think Libby and I should go, Guy?'

'Are you really asking my opinion?' Guy looked closely at his wife.

'Yes. I do take your advice, you know.'

'Sometimes,' he said and gave her a quick hug. 'What do you think, Libby?'

'I'm not sure. It'll feel like barging in. And they won't want to talk to us.'

Sophie appeared from the back stairs which led between the flat and the shop.

'I've just thought,' she said. 'What about GPS?'

The other three stared at her blankly.

'Eh?' said Libby.

'GPS,' repeated Sophie. 'We all use it. Well, most of us who are serious do. We have tracker watches, or the app on our phones. Some of us even have trackers in our trainers.'

Fran frowned. 'What for?'

'To see how far we've run, how fast we did a section – all sorts of things. Sometimes we post the map on social media. There are lots of apps, and we can find out our own stats. Like muscle use, speed –'

'Whoa!' said Libby. 'What on earth do you need all that for?'

It was Sophie's turn to frown. 'We have to keep on top of our bodies. Know what we can and can't do.'

Libby looked helplessly at Fran and shook her head. Guy merely looked amused.

'What use would it be in finding her?' asked Fran.

Sophie looked surprised. 'You could find out where she was, of course.'

'But – she'd have her tracking device – whatever it was – on her. How would anyone know how to access that?' asked Libby.

'It would be synced –' Sophie narrowed her eyes at her stepmother '– you do know what that means, don't you?' Fran nodded. 'Well, it's all synced up. And probably uploaded to the cloud as well.'

Guy, Fran and Libby all stared.

'I suppose,' said Libby, pulling herself together, 'the police probably know all this and will be looking at it.'

'It depends where it was uploaded,' said Sophie. 'If she only had it on her phone or her watch, no one would be able to get at it, as Libby just said.'

'Should we mention it to anyone?' asked Fran. 'And do we know Lisa definitely used one of these systems?'

'Oh, yes, she was fanatical about detailing her routes, calories burned – all that stuff.'

'Calories?' said Libby faintly.

Sophie grinned. 'You wouldn't believe it!'

'I don't,' said Libby. 'But I suppose it's like any obsession.'

'Except that this one is supposed to be for the sake of a healthy body,' said Guy. 'If I were you, I'd leave it unless Ian or someone else asks you. You've tried to tell him things before only to find he already knew them. And this is one of those things he's almost bound to know.'

'They'll have taken her computer away by now,' said

Libby, 'so if there was anything there, they'll have found it.'

'Exactly,' said Guy. 'And you can ask the club members tonight if they've been asked about their own systems, can't you.'

'I haven't yet,' said Sophie. 'I don't know about the others.'

'Why would they ask the other members?' asked Libby.

'To see if any of them had deviated from the route and made off with Lisa, of course,' said Guy.

Libby, Fran and Sophie gasped.

'Dad! You're so devious!' said Sophie.

'I never thought of that,' said Fran. 'But in that case, why did he take me up to the cliff path this morning?'

'He might see a strange route on paper – or screen – but you might be able to tell him why,' said Guy. 'Anyway, it looks as though he hasn't got round to that yet.'

'So we'll go,' said Libby to Fran. 'Shall I pick you up here?'

'We'll walk,' said Sophie firmly. 'You can leave the car here.

When Libby got home she called Ben at the Manor estate office to ask if he wanted a trip to Nethergate that night.

'I've only just come back!' he said. 'I'll give it a miss, if you don't mind. What is it you want to do?'

Libby explained, adding Sophie's explanations about GPS systems and Guy's surprising deductions.

'He's been rubbing shoulders with you two too much,' said Ben, laughing. 'Where's Adam at the moment? If he's got a system on his phone he could show you.'

'I'll call him,' said Libby. 'See you later.'

However, Adam was out on his other job, working with his friend Mog the garden designer at a minor stately home the other side of Ashford.

'No,' he said, in answer to his mother's query, 'I haven't got any kind of app. I only started doing this recently – I haven't really got into it yet. Good idea of Sophie's, though.'

'Oh, very,' said Libby dryly.

When Ben arrived late in the afternoon, they had an early supper and Libby was back on the road by seven. Harbour Street was full, so once again, Libby had to use the Blue Anchor's car park. Sophie and Fran were waiting for her at Coastguard Cottage.

'It's not far,' said Sophie. 'Just up the high street and turn left.'

'It would be up the high street,' said Libby gloomily. 'Your high street is far too steep for comfort.'

'Just think what it's like to run up it!' said Sophie with a grin.

'Ooh, don't.' Libby shuddered.

Sophie moderated her pace to Libby's amble and they set off towards the high street.

'Did you tell anyone we were coming?' asked Fran.

'I told Steve. And I asked him about the GPS apps. He seemed to think we should tell the DCI about them.'

'I can't believe the police haven't thought of it,' said Libby. 'I looked them up online this afternoon and they're all over the place. And the police themselves use tracking devices, so they're bound to know.'

'If he decides to do it, we're off the hook.' said Fran. 'Hurry up, Libby, it's nearly eight.'

The Sergeant At Arms was a narrow-fronted pub that listed slightly to one side and looked as if it belonged to a century before Nethergate had grown into a seaside resort.

'They'll be upstairs,' said Sophie, making for a worn staircase in the corner of the crowded bar.

Upstairs, a coat rack stood in the tiny hallway, which opened out into a reasonable sized room with a bar at the other end. A large table stood in the middle, around which sat about twenty people.

'This is my stepmother, Fran Wolfe,' began Sophie, 'and this is Libby Sarjeant. Steve said they could come along. They –'

'We know who they are,' said a large, unsmiling woman at the end of the table.

'I thought they might help find Lisa.' Sophie started again.

'And I agreed.' A balding, fit-looking man stood up. 'I'm Steve,' he said with a non-ogre-like smile. 'And this afternoon, I got in touch with that Detective – Connell, is his name? – and told him I thought they ought to look through all our GPS apps after Sophie mentioned it.' He laughed and sat down again. 'I think he thought I was being naive.'

'Why?' asked Fran.

'He said they'd already started.'

Chapter Six

'Told you so,' Libby muttered under her breath.

Various comments were being thrown about among the Harriers, some indignant, some approving.

'But how?' One voice rose above the others. 'We haven't given them our phones.'

'Social media, bet you, Davy.' A young woman with a fresh complexion and a pint glass spoke up.

'The Harriers' page,' said Steve. 'Quite right, Kirsty. You all post your runs on there, don't you?'

'I shall think twice about that in future,' said Davy, sounding grumpy.

'What do you want to drink?' asked Sophie, under cover of the burst of chatter this remark provoked.

'Tonic, please,' said Libby gloomily.

'Dry white, please,' said Fran, with a smug glance at her friend.

They found seats near Steve, who beamed at them.

'So you thought of checking the trackers?'

'No, it was Sophie,' said Fran. 'I'm afraid we knew nothing about them.'

'Oh.' Steve looked slightly bewildered, as if he couldn't believe there were people in the world who knew nothing about the running community.

'But you're involved in looking for her?' he continued after a moment.

'Only peripherally,' said Fran, standing on Libby's foot.

'But you've looked into things before, haven't you? That body on the island? And the people trafficking? And that body over at Creekmarsh?'

'Er – yes.' Libby cleared her throat and accepted her tonic water from Sophie.

'Have the police asked you to help?' The woman named Kirsty leant forward. 'They've asked you before, haven't they?'

'It isn't normally the police who ask,' began Libby.

'But you've got this special gift, haven't you?' Davy now butted in, looking somewhat belligerent.

Fran turned pink, shrugged and sipped her wine.

'Well, we'd like you to look into it, wouldn't we?' Steve looked round the table at his members, some of whom nodded, some said 'Hear, hear' and some looked blank.

'We don't really know much about Lisa,' Libby said hastily, before any arguments could break out. 'Kirsty and Davy, Sophie thought you were friends with her.'

Davy shook his head, looking wary.

'Only on social media, really,' said Kirsty. 'She didn't seem to socialise much. Obsessed with the sport, it seemed to me.'

'So no one knew if she had other friends?' asked Fran, now recovered.

Kirsty shook her head. 'Even on social media she had so many privacy settings you never saw anyone else. I only ever saw her interact with members here.' She turned to the rest of her table companions. 'Anyone else friends with Lisa outside of the Harriers?'

Everyone shook their heads.

'Anyone live near her? Share lifts?' Libby asked.

'I did, once.' A man of about fifty at the other end of the table lifted his hand. 'I live in Bishops Bottom and she lives in Shott. My car wouldn't start one evening and I had to ask her for a lift.' He grinned. 'You would have thought I was asking her to sell herself. But she didn't have much choice in front of everybody.'

'No one went to her house, then?' said Fran.

'I delivered something to her a few months ago,' said Kirsty. 'Newsletter, was it, Steve?'

'Race lanyards,' said Steve.

'You didn't go in?'

'No. I didn't even see her. I had to push them through the letterbox.'

'Nice house?' asked Libby.

'Charming, actually,' said Kirsty with a grin. 'I was really surprised. A detached cottage, with a really pretty front garden. At least, it looked as though it would be in the summer.'

'And she lives alone? What about the husband? Apparently there is one,' said Fran.

'Really?' Eyebrows were raised all around the table. This had obviously come as a surprise.

'How long has she been a member?' asked Libby.

The committee members looked at each other.

'A year?' said Steve.

'More like eighteen months,' said Sophie.

'And you knew nothing about her private life? Nobody ever came to watch her run?'

'The only thing we knew about was when she moved,' said Sophie. 'She had to give us her change of address.'

'When was that?' asked Fran.

'Where from?' asked Libby.

'She was in Canterbury. It must have been late last summer when she moved.'

'I wonder if she left the husband behind in Canterbury,' Libby said to Fran.

Steve was frowning. 'I must say, I'm surprised,' he said. 'She seemed to run every day. I don't know how she had time for a husband. She worked, as well.'

'What at?' asked Libby.

Steve looked vague. 'Office, somewhere?'

'I think she worked from home,' said Davy. 'We had a rare chat one day about broadband connection in the villages, and she was saying how difficult it was for work.'

'Did she only run with the Harriers?' asked Fran.

'No.' Kirsty shook her head. 'She ran every weekend with us, and sometimes during the week, but she ran her own routes nearer to home. I suppose I assumed that was why she'd moved, because there are more places to run in the country than on city pavements.'

'She told you that, did she?' said Libby.

'Not that that was why she'd moved, she just said it was much better running round the villages than in Canterbury.'

'So, a woman of mystery,' said Libby. 'Funny, isn't it, in this day and age when all our details are available for practically everyone to find out.'

'It looks deliberate,' said Fran.

'Well, of course it's deliberate – you don't hide yourself away by accident, do you?'

'I meant there must be a reason, not just a dislike of other people. If it was that, she would hardly have joined a running club, would she? It's a sport you can most definitely do on your own.'

'Although it's more fun with someone,' said Sophie. 'That's why Ad's been running with me for the last few months.'

Steve leant forward and looked round the table again. 'Anyone else got anything to tell these ladies about Lisa?

Something you haven't told the police?'

'They haven't spoken to all of us,' said someone.

'They will,' said Libby. 'Give them time.'

The talk turned to the merits of various tracking systems, and Sophie sat back in her chair.

'That wasn't much help, was it?'

'Oh, I don't know,' said Libby. 'We know where she lives, now. Ian wouldn't have told us.'

'You can hardly go poking around there,' said Fran, 'and there wouldn't be anything to see anyway.'

'Such a pity no one really became friends with her,' said Libby.

'I thought so, too,' said a voice behind her.

Everyone turned to look at the young man hovering diffidently beside the bar.

'Did you know her better than the others, then?' asked Libby.

He went faintly pink. 'No, not really. We occasionally ran together. She was always nice to me.'

Out of the corner of her eye Libby saw Sophie's eyebrows shoot up.

'Well, it's nice to hear someone saying something good about her,' said Fran. 'I'm Fran.' She held out a hand.

'Roly,' said the young man, turning pinker and taking the proffered hand.

'Hello, Roly, I'm Libby.' Libby in turn held out her hand. 'Did you live near her like Davy?'

'Itching,' said Roly, 'the other side of Shott. We used to do a circuit of the two villages.'

'I wonder why she didn't do it with Davy?' said Sophie.

'I don't know.' Roly shrugged. 'We just happened to meet one morning on the road between our two villages and fell into the habit. She never seemed stand-offish to me, like she did to the others.'

'Did you ever go to her house?' asked Libby.

'Oh, no!' Roly looked shocked. 'We always ran in the morning, you see, and never at weekends because we came here, then. So we always had to go to work.'

Libby opened her mouth to say "But she worked from home," and thought better of it.

'Thanks, Roly,' said Fran, smiling kindly. He nodded and wandered away, looking miserable.

'At least somebody's upset,' said Libby, looking after him.

'He's a bit weird,' whispered Sophie.

'Weird?'

'Well, a bit of a loner.'

'Just like Lisa, then,' said Libby.

'Suppose so.' Sophie drained her glass. 'Ready for another?'

They sat through a long and rather boring discussion on race times before turning to security measures.

'I suggest,' said Steve, calling for silence with a raised hand, 'that we all start to post our routes to a central hub. Then we can track where everybody should be. It's no use if no one can see them except ourselves.'

'I always post to Facebook,' said someone.

'Yes, but only your friends can see that,' said Davy.

'I post to the Harriers' page,' said someone else.

'That's helpful,' said Libby, 'but only members can see that. What you need is an access point that other people can see – like the police, in this case.'

They all turned to her in surprise, but Sophie nodded.

'Dropbox,' she said. 'That's the answer.'

'Is it?' muttered Libby, but the other Harriers were all agreeing enthusiastically.

'You know what,' said Fran quietly, 'although this is helpful, it's a little worrying.'

'Why? Because it's too late for Lisa?' said Libby.

'No, because of the Big Brother aspect.' Fran shook her head. 'Just think, we could all be tracked everywhere we went. Everything we do. Nowhere to hide.'

Libby turned to look properly at her friend. 'I hadn't thought of that.'

'Two sides to every story,' said Fran wryly. 'And yes, it's too late for Lisa.'

'I think the meeting's breaking up,' said Sophie. 'Do you want to stay for another drink, or go home?'

'Go home,' said Libby. 'I don't think we've learnt much except where she lives.'

'They have said they'd be pleased if we looked into it,' said Fran.

'Well, Steve did. But I don't see how we can. We have no access to her life. And no reason for Ian to tell us anything.'

'No.' Fran sighed and stood up. 'Home then.'

Libby retrieved her car from Harbour Street and drove slowly home. For once, she was glad to be out of an investigation, despite wanting to know why Lisa had disappeared. Life had a habit of getting complicated when she and Fran started investigating, and neither Ben nor Guy were entirely happy when their best beloveds got themselves into potentially dangerous situations. No chance of that this time, though.

'Somebody rang for you,' said Ben as she walked through the door. 'A man.'

'Who was it?' Libby dumped her bag onto the table.

'I don't know.' Ben narrowed his eyes at her. 'When I asked who was calling, he said it didn't matter and he'd try again.'

Libby frowned. 'How odd. What did he sound like?'

'Ordinary. No special accent or anything.'

'Do you think it could be one of the people at the Harriers' meeting? With something they didn't want to share in public?'

'How do I know? You were there, I wasn't.'

'Hmm.' Libby went through to the kitchen to pour herself a whisky. 'Did he ask for me by name?'

'Yes. Well, actually, he said Mrs Sarjeant.'

'Cold caller?' suggested Libby, coming back into the room.

'Didn't sound like it.' Ben shifted along the sofa to allow her to sit beside him. 'Haven't got a secret admirer, have you?'

'I don't think so!' Libby tucked her feet underneath her. 'I'm not that sort, am I?'

Ben twirled an imaginary moustache. 'Oh, I don't know!'

The following morning Libby realised she hadn't anything to do. There were no shows on at the theatre until two comedy one-nighters at the end of the week, she had delivered three paintings to Guy last week for sale in his gallery and she hadn't even any washing to do. She was quite relieved when the phone rang.

'Hello?'

'Mrs Sarjeant?'

Libby's mind sprang to full alert. Was this the mystery caller?

'Yes,' she said cautiously. 'Who's calling?'

'Never mind who's calling,' said the voice. 'Just stop looking for Lisa Harwood. And tell your friend to stop looking too.'

Chapter Seven

Libby stared blankly at the phone in her hand for a moment, then punched in 1471 and got the expected message that the number was withheld.

'Ian,' she said out loud, and, with fingers that weren't quite steady, found his number in her mobile.

'Libby.' Ian sounded irritated.

'I'm sorry to interrupt you, but I've just had a funny phone call.'

'Funny? What do you mean?'

Libby took a deep breath and repeated the caller's words.

Ian sighed. 'What have you been doing?'

'Nothing, I promise you. Well, except that Sophie took Fran and I to meet the Harriers last night –'

'Can't you keep your nose out for once?' Now Ian sounded more than irritated.

'We are!' Libby wailed. 'We walked away from it. Nothing to do with us.'

'Well, somebody thinks it is.' Ian sighed. 'Did you check the number?'

'Withheld.'

'Of course it was.' There was a short silence. 'Look. Think back over the last couple of days and work out if there's anything that struck you as odd. I'll call you back in a little while. In the meantime, you'd better call Fran.'

'I will.' Libby switched off the phone and sat down on the bottom stair. It was a good few minutes before she felt strong enough to call her friend.

'That's worrying,' said Fran.

'Worrying?' screeched Libby. 'It's bloody scary!'

'Have you told Ben?'

'No, and I'm dreading telling him.'

'Well, this time, it really isn't our fault,' said Fran. 'We went with Ian at *his* request yesterday morning, remember.'

'I didn't,' said Libby. 'I butted in.'

'Oh, look, Lib, we come as a pair, don't we? And who was it this joker rang? You, not me.'

'What I'd like to know,' said Libby, indignation overcoming fear, 'is how the hell he got my landline number.'

'You're in the book, stupid.'

'Oh. How did he know who I was then? And you?'

'Come on, Libby! We've been in the local papers several times, and even on *Kent and Coast*. And if someone saw us with Ian yesterday it would be easy to put two and two together.'

'You say someone who saw us with Ian. What about someone who saw us at The Sergeant At Arms last night?'

'It could be,' said Fran, sounding doubtful, 'but we could have been there for perfectly rational reasons. Parents of runners, say.'

'Actually one of the Harriers, then?' suggested Libby.

'I wouldn't have thought so. How old did the voice sound?'

'No idea. Not a young voice and certainly not an old one.'

'So we've got no clues to give Ian, then,' said Fran. 'We didn't see or hear anything odd.'

'No, we didn't.' Libby shivered. 'That means we were being watched.'

They both fell silent.

'Do you think it was accidental?' said Fran at last.

'What, Lisa's disappearance?'

'No – us being watched. Do you think someone was watching the place Ian took us to yesterday, and that's how they saw us?'

'But they wouldn't know who we were, despite you saying people know who we are.'

'DCI Connell appears with two middle-aged women, poking around a crime scene. If it's someone local, as I said, they could put two and two together.'

Libby's eyebrows drew together. 'I don't know.'

'Look,' Fran sounded exasperated, 'someone called you and warned us off. So they must know. Unless it was someone at the pub last night, as you suggested.'

'But you think that's unlikely.'

'Nobody looked suspicious.'

'Fran! We both know that isn't any sort of guide.'

'I know.' Fran sighed. 'What happens now?'

'I wait for Ian to phone, I suppose,' said Libby. 'Meanwhile, I'll work out the best and most sensitive way to break it to Ben.'

After ten minutes of dithering, she finally called Ben. There was no reply from the estate office, so she tried his mobile.

'Hello, Lib? Anything wrong?' He sounded breathless.

'What are you doing?'

'I'm in the timber yard. Why?'

Libby told him. Sound exploded in her ear.

'Call Ian.'

'I have. I'm waiting for him to ring back.'

'Then get off this phone. I'm coming back now.'

In fact, Ian and Ben arrived on the doorstep together, both looking as though they'd like to beat her to a pulp.

She swallowed.

'Shall I put the kettle on?' she asked weakly.

'I'll do it,' said Ben.

'Now, Libby. You've had time to think about this, so tell me what you know.' Ian sat on one of the upright chairs at the table in the window.

'Nothing.' She shook her head. 'I called Fran and we talked about it. She said if someone saw you taking us to the cliff path yesterday they might have put two and two together, as local people know who we are.'

Ian scowled. 'So now it's my fault?'

'I didn't say that,' said Libby hastily, 'but it's the only thing we could think of.'

'Except your visit to the Harriers last night.'

'Fran doesn't think it's very likely that it's one of them.'

'How unlikely? Does she know that?'

'Not like that, no. She just didn't think ...'

'Actually, Ian,' said Ben, from the kitchen doorway, 'I don't think it is their fault this time.'

'So you think it's my fault, too?'

'No,' said Ben, 'but it's the only thing that would link Libby and Fran to the disappearance, isn't it? After all, they're parents – or step-parents – of two of the Harriers. That isn't enough to link them to an investigation, is it?'

'Hmm.' Ian frowned at the carpet. Ben went back into the kitchen to pour the tea.

'So what does that mean?' asked Libby. 'Somebody was watching us? And why did they phone me and not Fran?'

'They don't know her married name?' suggested Ian.

'What's that got to do with anything?' said Ben, bringing in three mugs.

'The landline number,' said Ian. 'Were they looking

for Fran Castle or Fran Wolfe?'

'Oh, I see. Well, I think Coastguard Cottage's landline is still registered under Castle, so perhaps they didn't know Fran's former name. If they bothered at all.'

'It would have seemed more likely, as the disappearance happened in Nethergate, than to call you,' said Ian.

'Aren't we overthinking this?' asked Ben, sitting down beside Libby. 'The caller knew them both, from what he said, and warned them off. That should be enough.'

'It should.' Ian nodded. 'What I'm wondering is, though, what we do next. I can hardly move Fran out of Nethergate, even if she agreed to it, and I can't really stop you going there, either.'

'If we go nowhere near the – er – crime scene, we should be all right, though?' said Libby.

Ian shook his head, but didn't answer. Ben and Libby exchanged worried looks. Eventually Ian lifted his head.

'I think I'm going to have to take advice on this.' He stood up. 'You might get a call from the Superintendent.'

'Really?' Libby looked worried. 'Why?'

'I think I'll probably get a rocket for taking you out there yesterday morning, and I have no idea how to protect you.'

'Oh, hell. Don't tell me we've got you into trouble.'

'I got myself into trouble.' Ian's mouth twitched into a familiar wry smile. 'I'll be in touch when I can.'

'Heavens,' said Libby, as the door closed behind him. 'Now what?'

'We stay well clear of Nethergate,' said Ben. 'That's all we can do.'

'What about Fran? What about Ad come to that? He spends half his life with Sophie.'

'Tell him and warn him to be on his guard. And I

expect Ian will tell Fran.'

'I'll call her now.'

But Libby couldn't get through. Instead, she rang Adam, who was working with his friend Mog out at Creekmarsh, the renovated mansion whose garden featured regularly on television. Mog had landscaped the gardens and restored many of the original features, and was now charged with maintenance and experiments when the owner, Lewis Osbourne-Walker, wanted to showcase something on his television programme.

'I knew you'd get into trouble one of these days,' was her son's comforting reaction to the news.

'I like that!' Libby was indignant. 'It's not me, this time – even Ben agrees. You could even say it's your fault for getting me to come and see you run.'

Silence greeted this, as Adam obviously thought this over.

'Can I still go and see Soph?' he asked eventually.

Surprised, Libby laughed. 'Of course. I don't mind what you do, but just be aware of what's happened. Don't talk about me and Fran to anyone whatsoever.'

'OK. Sorry, Ma. I wasn't thinking.'

'That's OK. It's a bit disconcerting, that's what it is.'

'Like that fire someone started in the back garden,' Adam reminded her.

'Gosh, yes, I'd forgotten that. I wonder how many people hate me?'

'Loads!' said Adam cheerfully. 'I'll pop in before I go down to Sophie's tonight – see if you're still standing.'

As Libby switched off her mobile, the landline began ringing. Ben cautiously picked it up, then smiled.

'It's Fran,' he said.

'Hello, Lib,' said Fran. 'You've been trying to ring me.'

'Yes, to tell you what Ian said.'

'It's all right, it was him I was on the phone to. A very subdued Ian.'

'Isn't he? What shall we do?'

'About Ian? Nothing we can do.'

'No,' said Libby, 'I meant us. What do we do.'

'Absolutely nothing. Go about our normal daily business. Don't talk to strangers.'

'That's what I just said to Adam. I said he mustn't talk about you and me to anyone.'

'That's sensible,' said Fran. 'We just stay away from Nethergate, runners – anything connected.'

'You can hardly stay away from Nethergate – you live there.'

'Well, yes, but I needn't go out much. Or if I do, I'll go somewhere else to shop.'

'Will you come up for the Steeple Martin run next weekend?' Libby asked. 'Or do you think that might be cancelled?'

'I don't see why it should be,' said Fran, surprised. 'Lisa wasn't one of the organisers, was she? And she isn't dead – she's only disappeared.'

'We hope,' said Libby.

Libby had just finished loading the dishwasher after supper when there was a knock on the door.

Ben put his head round the kitchen doorway. 'It's Amy from Maltby Close.'

Libby raised her eyebrows and he shook his head.

'Hello, Amy.' Libby came out of the kitchen wiping her hands on a tea towel. Amy, old fashioned crossover apron under her raincoat, stood awkwardly in the sitting room.

'Miss Libby.' She ducked her head, and Libby marvelled at how this anachronism of a woman had managed to survive into the twenty-first century.

'How can I help you?'

'It's the Steeple Martin Fun Run, see.' Amy thrust out a hand holding printed tickets. 'We're doing a raffle, see? Mrs C said we can serve teas an' that in Carpenter's Hall.'

'During the run? That's a good idea,' said Libby, taking the tickets. 'How much are they?'

'Well, see, m'duck, it do start and end at the church, so we thought – good idea to serve teas.'

'Excellent,' said Libby. 'And the tickets?'

'Mrs C said as how you'd sell some for us?' Amy ended on an upward, hopeful note. 'There's some good prizes.'

'Ah.' Libby looked down at the tickets and handed one to Ben. There certainly were some good prizes. A large television, a meal for four at The Pink Geranium, a Sunday lunch at the pub, a huge box of mixed fruit and vegetables from Cattlegreen Nurseries and a fifty-pound voucher from Farthing's Plants.

'OK,' said Libby. 'How much are they?'

'A pound.' Amy beamed. 'Will you sell some, then?'

'Yes, I'm sure we can.' Libby looked at Ben. 'Can't we?'

'We can try,' said Ben, looking puzzled, 'but I can't see how we can find anyone who hasn't already got one.'

'Oh, I'm sure we will.' Libby looked confident. 'We'll take them, Amy. Not much time, though.'

'What did you do that for?' asked Ben, when the door closed behind their visitor. 'Who will we sell them to?'

'Fran and Guy for a start,' said Libby with a grin, 'and the Nethergate Harriers, of course.'

Chapter Eight

'So will the Harriers be meeting before next Sunday?' asked Libby.

'I doubt it,' said Sophie. 'Why?'

'I've got raffle tickets to sell before the Fun Run.'

'Oh?' A suspicious note crept into Sophie's voice.

Libby explained about the Carpenter's Hall teas and raffle.

'Oh. Well, that sounds all right. What's the money going to?'

Libby looked quickly at the raffle ticket she held. 'Help the Aged and a local hospice. I thought I might sell them to your members.'

'I don't know that they'll be very receptive on Sunday morning.'

'No. Well, I thought if you gave me their addresses I could actually go and harass them on their doorsteps.'

'Ah! An excuse to investigate! Now I see.'

'Well ...'

'But my step-ma said you've been warned off.'

'We were. But do you know, I've had a thought about that.'

'Oh? What thought?'

'I'm surprised Ian took it so seriously. After all, it was the surest way to get people to take notice of Lisa's disappearance. If the phone call hadn't been made, it might have faded into the woodwork.'

Libby was sure Sophie was frowning at the other end

of the connection.

'I don't get it. Look, you come down and talk to Stepma and I'll see if I can give you any addresses. Which, actually, I doubt.'

Libby cut the call. She had expressed the same thought to Ben at breakfast this morning, who, surprised, had actually agreed with her, but was not in favour of her hunting out the Harriers in their dens.

The phone in her hand rang.

'Hello, Fran. Has Sophie been talking to you? That was quick!'

'She has. It was a bit garbled. Are you going to brave Nethergate and come and tell me all about it, or shall I come to you?'

'Oh, I'll come to Nethergate. All right if I come now? Then we can have lunch.'

'OK. See you in half an hour.'

'So,' said Fran, when they were settled in the sitting room of Coastguard Cottage with tea, 'what exactly is this theory of yours? I don't think Sophie had it quite right.'

'If that phone call hadn't been made, I think Lisa's disappearance would have – well, not been ignored, exactly, but wouldn't have been looked into so thoroughly.'

'Could be, but I don't think a disappearance would be shelved as quickly as that,' said Fran.

'If they don't know anything about it, it could just be that they feel the police weren't doing enough and wanted to draw attention to things.'

Libby stared thoughtfully into her tea. 'I thought the phone call would make sure the police looked into the case properly, but what I was surprised about was Ian taking the threat to us seriously.'

'I think what he was *actually* worried about was

getting in trouble with his boss for involving us. I'm sure he doesn't really think there's a threat to us.'

'Really?' Libby wasn't sure whether to be insulted or pleased. 'So he's only concerned with himself?'

Fran was amused. 'Come on, don't be silly. This isn't about us, is it? Somebody's vanished. Whether it's suspicious or not, it's about Lisa, no one else.'

'Oh, OK. So I ought to tell Ad to forget what I said?'

'What did you say to him?'

'Told him not to talk about us. He wouldn't have stayed away from Nethergate anyway, because of Sophie.'

'She also said,' Fran fixed her friend with a stern stare, 'that you wanted the addresses of the Harriers to go and sell them raffle tickets.'

'I thought better of that,' said Libby, sheepishly. 'I know that was a bit daft. I'll try and sell them in the village.'

'Leave some here and we'll see if we can sell any in the shop,' said Fran. 'And now I'm going to put the soup on, so you can come and talk to me in the kitchen. About anything other than running.'

After a bowl of Fran's famous lentil and tomato soup and a large chunk of fresh bread, Libby got back into her car and drove away from Nethergate feeling rather foolish. She'd over-reacted to both the phone call and the effect on Ian, and in fact, to Lisa's disappearance altogether. Yes, it was odd, and someone had to get to the bottom of it, but the more she thought about it, the more she was convinced that the answer probably lay with Lisa herself. They knew next to nothing about her, except that she had moved from Canterbury to Shott, ran most mornings and had a husband tucked away somewhere. Nobody even knew what she did for a living.

'I suppose,' she said to Harry, who had popped round for a chat that afternoon, 'I've got so used to things being mysteries and murders I turn everything into one.'

'Anyone could have told you that.' Harry stretched out his long legs and clasped his hands behind his head. 'But to be fair, people do *ask* you to look into things, so you can't be entirely blamed.'

'Anyway, no more looking into the disappearance of the long-distance runner,' said Libby. 'I daresay she's gone off on her own.'

'I daresay she has. Or it's white slavers.'

Libby giggled. 'Oh, God, yes! Why didn't I think of that?'

Harry sat forward. 'Actually, it isn't that funny any more, is it? With illegal traffickers forcing people into slavery and prostitution.'

Libby sobered immediately, remembering a recent adventure which had centred around that very branch of criminality. 'No, that's true. But this isn't that.'

Harry quirked an eyebrow. 'No? But you aren't going to find out, are you?'

'No,' said Libby impatiently. 'And why did you come round, anyway? Are you interrogating me?'

Harry laughed. 'No, dear heart! I've been coming round for chats with you for years, haven't I? Actually, I was going to tell you Max and Owen are coming down for the weekend.'

'Are they?' Libby cheered up. Max Tobin and his partner Owen Talbot ran an all-male dance company which had used the Oast Theatre for a preview of a new ballet some months earlier. 'Aren't they on tour or something?'

'No – they're preparing for their West End debut.

They've got a theatre for *Pendle*.'

'Oh, wow!' The new ballet's transfer to a London theatre had been delayed last year due to unfortunate circumstances. 'That's fantastic. So they're coming here for a bit of R and R, are they?'

'Yes, Friday to Monday – or possibly Tuesday morning. They're staying with us, as the pub's full of people to do with this blasted Fun Run.'

'Mad, isn't it? I still don't get the appeal. I mean, you can't even take in the countryside and surroundings when you're pounding along like that, can you?'

Harry shook his head. 'Waste of energy, if you ask me. If you're going to work out, why not go to a gym?'

'Isn't that more expensive?' asked Libby doubtfully.

Harry shrugged. 'I suppose so, but they all have to have special clothing and gadgets, don't they?'

'Yes – those calculator things that we thought might track the missing runner.'

'Her phone would do that anyway, wouldn't it?' said Harry.

'It would have to have the right – um – app?'

Harry laughed. 'How old is this woman?'

'I don't know. Thirties? Forty?'

'Then she'll have a smartphone, so yes, it will have all the bells and whistles.'

'Oh.' Libby looked up into the cherry tree. 'I still get caught out by modern technology.'

'Never mind, petal.' Harry patted her hand. 'We keep you on the straight and narrow.'

Over the next few days, the matter of the missing runner was allowed to lie fallow. Posters about the Steeple Martin Fun Run appeared all over the village, in Ali and Ahmed's eight-til-late store, the pub, even in the window of the Pink Geranium. Libby, having volunteered to sell raffle tickets, was coerced by Amy to help put posters up in the surrounding villages, and spent the whole of Thursday driving around the countryside in the Land Rover. She went to The Red Lion in Heronsbourne and The Poacher in Shott, where she knew the landlords, and The Ashton Arms in Cherry Ashton and The George and Dragon at Steeple Cross, where she didn't. The Reverend Patti Pearson put a poster up in the St Aldeberge community shop, and the bakery in Steeple Mount actually took some raffle tickets as well.

Pleased with her efforts, and having not had the traditional Wednesday evening meeting in their own pub with Ian Connell, she called Fran.

'Heard anything?'

'About what?'

'Lisa Harwood, of course.'

'No, of course not. It's nothing to do with me.'

Libby sighed. 'I know. I just wondered if Sophie ...'

'She won't have heard either. She's been out running on her own and with Adam, and as far as I know, hasn't seen anyone from the Harriers or anywhere else.'

'Oh.' Libby stared thoughtfully at the empty fireplace. 'I went out postering today.'

'Posturing?'

'Postering! Sticking up posters in the villages. George at The Red Lion and Sid from The Poacher said to say hello.'

'Posters for what?'

'The Fun Run! You're coming up for it, aren't you? We were going to go to the caff on Saturday night. Oh – and I forgot to tell you – Max and Owen are coming down for the weekend.'

'For the Fun Run?' Fran sounded totally confused.

Libby sighed. 'No, for a weekend off before *Pendle* goes in.'

'Oh, they've got a theatre at last!'

'They have. They're staying with Pete and Harry as the village is full up with runners.'

'Oh, well, that'll be lovely. We're staying with you, are we?'

'That was the idea, if you remember,' said Libby. 'And Sophie will stay with Adam. Shall I see if we can book a meal at the pub on Sunday evening? Hal will be closed.'

'Good idea. I hadn't really forgotten ...'

'Of course you hadn't,' said Libby, with a grin. 'See you Saturday evening, if not before.'

On Friday, Ben appeared at lunchtime with a scowl on his face.

'You'll never guess what.'

Libby placed a bowl of soup in front of him.

'No, I won't. What?'

'The idiots who are organising this bloody Fun Run had forgotten to make provision for parking.'

'Oh.' Libby sat down at the kitchen table and took a paintbrush from behind her ear. 'And that means – what?'

'They've asked me.'

'You? What can you do?'

'Apparently, as the largest landowner in the village I'm bound to have the odd field to spare.'

Libby looked at him seriously. 'Well, you have.'

Ben looked up sharply. 'I have? Where? If you're thinking of the field at the top of our lane –' he gestured wildly with his spoon 'think of the chaos it would cause getting up there.'

'No,' said Libby calmly, 'I was thinking of the field

between the theatre and the back of the high street.'

Ben stared at her, his mouth open.

The Manor drive ran up from the high street to the Manor itself and the Oast Theatre. On the right of the drive was an open space from the theatre to the backs of all the premises in the high street, including The Pink Geranium and the pub.

'And there's access at the top of the drive,' Libby continued, 'and it's wide enough to allow traffic both ways.'

Ben closed his mouth. 'You're right.' He squinted at her. 'It'll need stewarding, though.'

'That's up to the organisers,' said Libby. 'Who are they?'

'The Nethergate Harriers.'

66

Chapter Nine

'Really?' Libby gaped at him.

'Yes, really.' Ben grinned. 'I was surprised, too. But I didn't ask and they didn't explain. No doubt you can find out more.'

'Well, I expect I will, but why didn't they tell me last week?'

'Why should they have?'

'When Fran and I were asking questions.'

'Did you tell them where you were from?'

'Er – no.' Libby frowned. 'I don't suppose it's relevant.'

'I don't suppose it is.' Ben began to drink his soup. 'Anyway, now you've given me the idea, I shall go back to the office and put wheels in motion.'

Libby stuck the paintbrush back behind her ear and started on her own soup.

'But why,' she said after a moment, 'didn't Sophie tell us? We've actually talked about the Fun Run. And you said did the Harriers know where we came from. Sophie bloody well does!'

'I don't suppose she thought it was in the least important,' said Ben.

'What about that Steve? The chair of the Harriers. He asked us to look into Lisa's disappearance.'

Ben sighed. 'That was just over-reaction at the time. It's all gone quiet now, hasn't it? I expect the police have discovered she's just gone off somewhere on her own.'

'Ian hasn't told us that.'

'Why should he?' asked Ben reasonably.

'Well, for a start, he dragged Fran up to the cliff path to see if she could sense anything, and then he got bothered about that phone call. He could at least have called to tell us we were safe.'

'I suppose so.' Ben stared thoughtfully into his bowl. 'We'll see if he appears tomorrow. Or Sunday morning.'

In fact, Detective Chief Inspector Connell did appear on Saturday, while Ben and Libby were attempting to set up the car parking area behind the Pink Geranium and the pub.

'Have the police been informed?' he asked, as Libby paused and wiped her forehead.

'That's the Harriers' job, surely?' she said, tying the tape she was holding to a post.

'Yes, it is. I just haven't heard anything about it.'

'Oh, come on, everyone knows about the Fun Run, Ian.' Ben stomped across the slightly muddy ground looking weary. 'I just wish they'd thought about this earlier.'

Ian looked amused. 'When did they tell you?'

'Yesterday.' Ben snorted. 'Why they hadn't sorted something out before, I really don't know.'

'They do seem a little disorganised,' said Ian.

'Any more news about Lisa Harwood?' asked Libby.

Ian looked round sharply. 'None. Have you heard anything?'

'No. But after that phone call ...'

Ian smiled. 'I think that was an attempt by someone to get us to take notice.'

'Yes, we came to that conclusion.' Libby scowled at him. 'But you could have let us know.'

'I'm sorry, Lib. I have been rather busy.'

'You must have been – we didn't even see you at the pub on Wednesday.'

'I do have crimes to work on other than those you've involved yourself in.'

'Ooh, cutting.' Libby grinned at him. 'Nothing you can tell us about, I suppose?'

'You know better than that, Libby.' Ian turned to Ben. 'What's this field usually used for? I've only ever seen it when we've had to search it for something – or someone.'

'Not used for anything,' said Ben. 'There's no access for farm machinery except from the theatre car park, and it backs on to the pub, Hal's caff, Bob's butcher shop and the eight-til-late.'

'Surely it would be good for village events, then?' said Ian. 'You haven't got a green here in Steeple Martin. You don't ever have Morris dancers or a Maypole ...' He broke off to find Libby and Ben staring at him in surprise. 'What?'

'Since when have you been interested in that sort of thing?' asked Libby. 'You've always seemed rather disdainful of good old English folklore when we've come up against it in the past.'

'Just thinking.' Ian grinned rather sheepishly. 'I happened to be at a small music festival yesterday, so ...'

'Really?' Ben's eyebrows rose even higher. 'You?'

Ian sighed. 'I do have a life outside the force, you know.'

'Sorry, Ian.' Libby went over and patted his arm. 'We don't see much of you outside working hours, except on Wednesdays.'

'And even that tends to be work-related. And, as it happens, so was the music festival.'

'Oh?' said Libby hopefully.

'Oh, no, Lib, you're not getting it out of me like that.'

Ian shook his head at her. 'But it struck me that this would be an ideal space for a small festival, especially as it backs on to the pub at one end and the theatre the other.'

Ben looked startled, then turned to survey the space behind him.

'It would, Ben,' said Libby.

Ben shook his head. 'No. What about car parking? We've had to let the Harriers use this for car parking. There isn't anywhere else in the village.'

'What about the field at the top of Allhallow's Lane? The one that goes past the Hoppers' Huts?' Ian suggested.

Ben stood with an arrested expression on his face.

'It's a possibility,' said Libby, watching him, 'even if you did say it wouldn't work yesterday.'

'I'll give it some thought.' Ben gave Ian a reluctant grin. 'Serve you right if I do it and someone murders one of the musicians.'

'Hmm,' said Ian.

'Anyway, why are you here?' Libby shoved her handkerchief back in her pocket.

'I was passing.'

Libby raised her eyebrows again. 'On the way to where?'

Ian burst out laughing. 'Actually, to Canterbury and back to the office. No clues there. As it was round about lunchtime, I wondered if anyone wanted a drink. I've been working what seems like non-stop for two days, so I'm off duty.'

'Great idea!' Ben beamed. 'Can I just pop into the Manor for a wash?'

'I'll come with you,' said Ian. 'I haven't seen Hetty for months.'

When Libby and Ben had washed the grime from their faces and hands, they followed Ian down the Manor drive to the pub. They waved as they passed The Pink Geranium, and Harry waved back.

As usual, Ian ordered coffee, while Libby and Ben both had beer.

'Are you going to watch the Fun Run tomorrow?' asked Ian when they were settled with their drinks.

'Yes. Fran and Guy are coming over this evening and staying the night. Sophie and Adam are running.' Libby leant back in her chair. 'I can't think why they want to put themselves through it. I'm exhausted just setting up the car park.'

'We aren't very fit.' Ben rubbed his slightly expanded waistline. 'I suppose we ought to do something about it.'

'But not running miles in sweaty clothes,' said Libby. 'Not my style.'

Ian laughed. 'Sorry – but I can just picture it!'

Libby smiled reluctantly. 'I bet you can.'

Ben was regarding Ian thoughtfully. 'Where was this music festival?' he asked suddenly.

'What?' Ian looked puzzled. 'Why?'

'I just wondered. I hadn't heard of any round here.'

'The other side of Canterbury actually. Between Canterbury and Ashford.'

'Then why are you on your way back to Canterbury from this direction?'

Ian stared back at him.

'Well?' said Libby, having finally worked this out. 'He's right. You should have hit Canterbury before you got to us.'

'I really don't have to answer that,' said Ian, in his most apologetic tone. 'Do I?'

'Legally, no,' said Libby. 'Personally, yes. There must be a reason. And it isn't for the sake of my blue eyes.'

Ian's mouth quirked. 'As if I'd do anything for the

sake of your blue eyes,' he said. 'Even if they aren't blue.'

'Stop stalling,' said Libby. 'Come on, tell us.'

Ian sighed. 'Actually, it was to do with Lisa Harwood.'

'I knew it.'

'I reported your phone call to my boss, and we had a meeting about it. The general consensus was that it was a hoax to get us interested. Probably to make fools of us. We reviewed all the evidence we had so far, which, after all, wasn't much, and came to the conclusion that she must have gone off on her own accord.'

'I don't believe that,' said Libby. 'Nothing was gone from her house, was it?'

'We don't know. Nobody knew her.'

'The husband. What about him?' asked Ben.

Ian shook his head. 'A devoted father to their two sons. He'd never even been to her house. She used to come to his place to pick the boys up and take them out, that was all.'

'So even the boys had never been to her house?' Libby was aghast. 'Those poor children.'

'It was a very odd set-up altogether,' said Ian, twirling his coffee cup in his hands. 'The husband said she'd never really wanted the children, and when she started running, she became obsessed. Eventually, he told her to go, because she was never there anyway.'

'Did she look after the children?' asked Ben.

'She was supposed to, but she farmed them out.' Ian shook his head again. 'At least now the arrangement is on a proper footing and the husband isn't having to support her.'

'That sounds a bit hard,' said Libby.

'According to Don Harwood, she didn't work and made no contribution to the household. He offered to make her some kind of allowance when she left, but she refused.' Ian drained his coffee cup. 'That's why I said it was odd. If she didn't work, how was she supporting herself? The rent on her cottage can't have been cheap.'

'How far have you looked into it?' asked Libby. 'Shouldn't there have been more of an investigation?'

'We followed the missing persons guidelines. There is a risk assessment process, and the risk seemed minimal.'

'Really?' Libby seemed doubtful.

'Think about it,' said Ian. 'A woman who lives alone, who has virtually shunned her family, who invites no one to her house, who doesn't socialise and whose only hobby is running. She doesn't have much of an online presence, merely a profile, such as it is, on the Harriers' social media pages.'

'You took her computer, didn't you?' said Ben. 'And tracked her status?'

'Yes. She used a popular app, but it only appeared on the Harriers' page. It's been silent ever since. Her computer was virtually empty, if you can imagine such a thing. Virtually no emails, no banking information.'

'Isn't that suspicious?' asked Libby. 'Doesn't it look as though she's hiding? Or hiding something?'

'If so,' said Ian, 'then she had another life. And how she could have done that when she was still living with her husband and children ...'

'But you said she was hardly ever there. Couldn't she have begun her other life then?'

'Don Harwood gave us all the details of where he and she met and married. We even got in touch with her father.'

Libby looked at him solemnly. 'And this wasn't enough of a risk?'

'No. It's a deliberate situation. I know it's suspicious, but we traced her as far as we could. Then – whoosh!

Gone in a flash.'

'There must be a footprint somewhere,' said Ben. 'Virtual, I mean.'

'You would think so.' Ian shrugged. 'We tried to find the agents who rented her the house, but couldn't. There was no documentation about it anywhere. The account only ever received deposits by cash and was only used to pay household bills and as far as we could see, no rent payments – no online trail at all.'

'You wouldn't think that was possible, would you?' said Libby.

'Except that an awful lot of people over eighty are the same,' said Ian.

'You're right,' said Ben. 'My mum and her friends are quite happy with modern technology, although they only use it sparingly. They prefer to do things face to face. But all of them would have a limited online footprint.'

'And Lisa Harwood doesn't.' Ian shook his head again. 'And the reason I'm here today, to be truthful –'

'I knew it,' muttered Libby.

Ian shot her an amused look. 'The reason I'm here is to check out this route, for one thing, and because I'm going to be here tomorrow to talk to some of the runners.'

Chapter Ten

Ben and Libby stared at Ian suspiciously.

'Why?' said Libby eventually. 'Is one of them a suspect?'

'They could all be suspects,' said Ian. 'You're quite capable of believing everyone is a suspect, aren't you?'

'Yes, but particularly.'

Ian sighed. 'I have to investigate the stewards. And the cup that was found.'

'Oh, I'd almost forgotten about that,' muttered Libby.

Ian fixed her with a warning eye. 'You are not to go round talking about it. And I shall be here tomorrow on my own time, so it will be very unofficial.'

'In that case, do you want to come to the pub with us tomorrow evening? We're going there for dinner,' said Ben.

'As long as I'm not compromising myself, thanks, I'd love to.' Ian grinned at Libby. 'Although I'd prefer to be able to stay overnight. Drinking is usually involved with the Steeple Martin contingent.'

'I daresay you could use one of the guest rooms at the Manor,' said Ben. 'We haven't opened it up for the runners as we didn't really know anything about this Fun Run until this week.'

'Won't Hetty mind?' asked Ian.

'Of course not. I'll give her a ring now.' Ben fished out his phone.

'We've got other visitors arriving,' Libby said while

Ben talked to his mother. 'Max and Owen are coming for the weekend, too.'

'For the run?' Ian raised his eyebrows.

'No, of course not. They're here for a spot of R&R before *Pendle* goes in.'

'Goes in where?'

'They've got a London theatre. Isn't that terrific? That's what it's called if a piece that's been in the provinces manages to get a theatre. "Going in." See?'

Ian nodded. 'So it'll be quite a gathering of the clans.'

'You could come with us to the caff tonight, too, if you wanted to.'

Ian shook his head. 'No, I'd better get off home. Besides I'm already going out tonight.'

Libby opened her mouth, but Ben interrupted.

'Hetty will be pleased to see you whenever you want.' He cast Libby a minatory glare. 'And we'll see you sometime during the day. The run finishes at the end of Maltby Close and there will be refreshments in Carpenter's Hall.'

Ian stood up. 'Thanks, Ben. And shall I park at the Manor or in your brand new car park?'

Ben grimaced. 'The Manor. You might never get out of the field.'

'You must not ask him where he goes,' Ben said after Ian had left.

'I didn't,' said Libby, huffily.

'You were going to.'

'But I didn't.' Libby looked at him sideways. 'And why not?'

'He keeps his private life to himself. If he wanted us to know, he'd tell us.'

'I know. But we've known him for years, now, and all we know about him is that he has family still in Scotland

and he went up there for a wedding. We don't even know where he lives. And he knows *everything* about all of us.'

'Because we've been part of his official investigations. We don't need to know about him.'

'Hmm,' said Libby.

Ben grinned at her. 'Just because you fancy him!'

Libby went bright red. 'I don't!'

'Yes, you do.' Ben reached across and patted her hand. 'It's all right, I know it's not serious and I'm not jealous. But he's a very attractive man, in a saturnine sort of way. If ever we wanted to do a version of *Jane Eyre* or *Pride and Prejudice* at the theatre –'

'He'd be a brilliant Rochester or Darcy,' Libby finished for him. 'I just can't understand why he's single.'

'He might not be,' said Ben. 'For all we know he's got a wife and seven children tucked away somewhere.'

Libby gave him a disgusted look.

That evening, having showered away the effects of setting up the car park, Ben and Libby, Fran and Guy joined Peter, Max Tobin and Owen Talbot at the Pink Geranium. After affectionate greetings had been exchanged and drinks provided, Max asked Libby what she was investigating at the moment. Fran's lips tightened.

'Nothing,' said Libby brightly, concentrating on her wine.

'What about this missing runner?' said Max, leaning forward.

Libby looked up at Peter reproachfully. He held up his hands in surrender.

'I just happened to mention it. And we know you've been warned off.'

'We just don't think there's anything to investigate,' said Fran, with an air of shutting down the conversation.

'Then why is Ian coming over tomorrow?' Harry appeared at the table with menus.

'How ...?' Libby, Ben and Fran all stared. Guy, amused, took a menu.

'He popped in after the pub. Of course, that could have been because I was on the watch for him, having seen you all go in.' Harry beamed round at his guests. 'Now, come on, order up before I run out of everything.'

When dishes had been chosen and orders given, despite Libby trying to turn the conversation towards tomorrow's Fun Run, Owen returned to the attack. In the end Libby capitulated.

'Ian's visit is strictly unofficial. He doesn't want us talking about it, but as far as I can see, he thinks there's something more to it.'

'More than what?' asked Max.

'Than a simple missing person,' said Ben.

'She was such a solitary, hidden sort of person.' Fran frowned down at her napkin. 'As if she didn't want anyone to know anything about her.'

'And yet she had a perfectly legitimate husband, children and father. But the police couldn't find any online traces of her after she left them in Canterbury.' Libby made a face. 'Weird.'

'We had a couple of those,' said Owen. 'Remember?'

Max nodded. 'That was weird, too.'

'Weirder than that boy Paul from last year?' said Libby.

'Oh, he was par for the course,' laughed Max. 'No, these were a couple of boys who auditioned about a year ago, was it, Owen?'

'One of them in March and another in May,' said Owen. 'They both gave minimal information, and we took them both on – they were good, but neither of them really talked to any of the others.'

'What about each other?' asked Guy.

'I didn't make myself clear – they didn't come together. The first one, in March, when we began to research his background – you know, where he'd trained, what he'd actually done – he disappeared. Then exactly the same thing happened with the other one.'

'How odd,' said Fran. 'Presumably they both gave details of where they'd trained?'

'Both at the same place, oddly,' said Max, 'which couldn't supply a current address for either of them. After they'd graduated the school didn't keep in touch.'

'Really?' Libby leant forward. 'But they were proper dancers?'

'Oh, yes,' said Owen. 'They were both good.'

'Oh, God.' Ben put his head in his hands.

'What?' Libby looked worried.

'Now you'll want to investigate that.'

Everyone laughed. Except Fran.

'Shouldn't it have been investigated at the time?' she asked.

Owen and Max looked surprised. 'Investigate what?'

'The two boys disappearing.'

'They just didn't turn up,' said Max. 'Happens all the time. And when we tried to get in touch, their phones were off and they weren't at the addresses they'd given. But you know what youngsters are – especially in the business, whichever end of it they're in.'

Fran nodded, but didn't look convinced.

'Don't worry about it,' said Libby. 'It's nothing to do with us.'

'No.' Fran looked down at the table. Libby exchanged glances with Guy, who shook his head slightly.

The food arrived and with it a new conversational

topic, when Max asked where Adam was.

'Resting before tomorrow, I should think,' said Libby. 'He's doing the Fun Run with Sophie, Guy's daughter.'

'Did we meet Sophie last year?' asked Owen.

'I don't think so,' said Guy, 'but to be honest, I can't remember. The last few days of your visit were a bit hectic, weren't they?'

Owen laughed. 'The whole visit was! I'm surprised you've let us back into the village.'

'Oh, we're like Jessica Fletcher's Cabot Cove,' said Peter. 'More dodgy characters than you can shake a stick at.'

At the end of the meal, when Harry had brought out the brandy he kept for special customers, Adam appeared via the kitchen.

'I thought he wasn't here?' said Owen.

'He lives upstairs,' said Libby. 'He's come down the back stairs.'

'Hey, Ma.' Adam looked round the table and acknowledged everyone. 'I just wondered if you knew that there are people in the back field.'

'Already?' Ben stood up.

'There are tents there,' said Adam.

'Oh, Lord.' Ben moved round the table, taking his mobile out of his pocket as he went. 'Will you excuse me a moment, everyone? I'll have to get them to move, or there won't be room for cars there tomorrow. Who told them they could camp there?' Still talking, he left the restaurant.

'Well!' Libby looked round the table, as Adam left in pursuit of Ben.

'Explain,' said Peter. Libby explained.

'And the organisers are the Nethergate Harriers?' said Guy.

'Yes, amazingly.'

'They're remarkably disorganised, then, aren't they?' Guy shook his head. 'Why didn't Sophie say anything about that?'

'It probably didn't occur to her. Perhaps she thought we already knew, what with Ad running with her.' Libby shook her head. 'I don't know – first they lose a runner, then they fail to organise themselves for a fun run.'

'I don't think they did either on purpose,' said Peter.

Ben and Adam came back into the restaurant.

'Well?' asked Libby.

Ben looked ruffled. 'I've had to let them stay, but told them they have to strike camp before eight o'clock. We also blocked the entrance.'

'How?' said Libby.

Adam grinned. 'We asked the campers to park their cars across it. They were only too pleased!'

'And did you find out who told them they could get in?' asked Max.

'Steve, apparently,' said Adam. 'Do you mind if I go back upstairs, now?'

They waved him off, and Libby turned to Max and Owen. 'Sorry about that.'

'Oh, don't be,' said Owen. 'It's so different from life in London – it's fascinating.'

'And who's Steve?' asked Max.

'The chairman of the running group,' said Fran. 'I suspect somebody reminded him yesterday that there was no provision for parking and then checked up today to see if he'd done anything about it.'

'And he gaily said he'd organised Ben,' said Libby. 'But how did they know where?'

'Ah.' Fran looked puzzled. 'Hadn't Ben told Steve where to go?'

'Well, yes, he had to. I expect he put it on their Facebook page or something.'

'There you are then.' Fran smiled. 'All mysteries solved.'

Libby grinned. 'All right, all right.' She turned to Max and Owen. 'So, tell us more about *Pendle*. Terribly exciting, going in, isn't it?'

Eventually Ben stood up. 'We've got to be up early tomorrow to check on this blasted car park, so we'd better get going.'

Fran, Guy and Libby also stood up.

'Can you put it on the tab, Hal?' asked Libby. Harry had joined them after his last guests had gone. He now smiled smugly.

'Already taken care of, petal.'

'Our treat,' said Max, holding up a hand. 'And don't argue.'

After many profuse expressions of gratitude, the Allhallow's Lane party left.

'Funny about those dancers disappearing,' Fran said as she and Libby strolled along the high street behind Guy and Ben.

'I don't suppose it's that unusual in London,' said Libby. 'I can remember a lot of itinerant actors in my day. Some I never saw again after working with them for a season.'

Fran nodded. 'I suppose so. It was just the similarity to Lisa's disappearance.'

'Not that similar,' said Libby. 'Let's forget it for now.'

The following morning Libby was cooking a full English breakfast when Ben appeared, back from opening up the car park.

'OK?'

'Fine.' Ben washed his hands at the kitchen sink.

'They said someone else tried to get in earlier on this morning, though.'

'Really? Cheeky.'

'Whoever it was managed to turn round and drive away, though. But they were all queuing up to get in by the time I got there this morning.'

'What time do they start?' asked Guy, wandering in from the garden.

'Ten o'clock,' said Ben. 'It'll be all over by the time the pub opens.'

Libby, Ben, Fran and Guy watched the field go past from the corner of Allhallow's Lane, and when the last stragglers had passed into New Barton Lane, they crossed over and went to wait on the corner of Maltby Close for the winners.

After a few people had run in to an enthusiastic welcome and refreshments from the ladies in Carpenter's Hall, the runners trickled to a stop.

'Where are they?' murmured Fran, as onlookers began to frown and mutter to each other.

And that was when they heard the sirens.

Chapter Eleven

'Text,' said Libby, fumbling to get her phone out of a pocket.

'Ad,' she relayed to the others. 'Oh, God!'

'What?' Ben took the phone from her hand. 'Body found,' he read out and looked up. 'You don't suppose …?'

Fran, who had gone white, shook her head. 'Can't see …'

Guy put his arm round her.

'What shall we do?' asked Libby. 'Will they let the runners carry on?'

She was answered by the appearance of a police car driving very slowly, lights flashing, from New Barton Lane, where it led a crocodile of dispirited walkers. The onlookers watched in silence as the little convoy approached, until the police car pulled up across the high street and the erstwhile runners funnelled into Maltby Close. Friends and relations joined them, asking questions in agitated whispers. Adam and Sophie were not among them.

'Where are they?' Fran grabbed Libby's arm, as near to panic as Libby had ever seen her.

'I don't know – perhaps they were the ones that found the – er – body.' Libby covered Fran's hand with her own. 'Nothing will have happened to them. The police are there. Look – Ben's gone over to ask the officer.'

Ben returned.

'The group of people who found the body were kept at the scene to wait for the SIO,' he reported.

'Will it be Ian?' asked Libby.

'If he sees it's Steeple Martin, I expect so. We'll know soon enough.'

'What shall we do?' asked Fran suddenly. 'We can't just stand here doing nothing.'

'Well,' said Libby doubtfully, 'we could go into Carpenter's Hall for refreshments.'

'No, we'd get bombarded by questions,' said Ben. 'Let's go and wait in the pub. I'll pop into the caff on the way to tell Pete and Harry.'

Libby sent an unanswered text to Adam to tell him where they were, while Guy did the same to Sophie. Fran sat silent and pale while Ben, joined by Peter, fetched drinks.

'What is it?' Libby asked her quietly. 'What did you see? Or not see?' she added, remembering Fran's first words on hearing Adam's text.

'It was like –' Fran took a deep breath. 'Do you remember me telling you about when I felt Aunt Eleanor's death? It was like that.'

'Suffocation?' said Libby, feeling a shiver of horror.

'I couldn't see.' Fran dropped her eyes to her lap. 'It was horrible. Thank God I don't get many of these any more. I never want another one. And it isn't going to help, anyway.'

'You don't know that.' Libby tried to be bracing. Fran looked up with a wry smile.

'Rubbish. We're old hands now. It isn't.'

The door of the pub opened and Sophie and Adam, both as pale as Fran, came in and more or less collapsed on the benches round the table.

Fran held up a hand as the others began to speak.

'Let them tell us what they can without us asking questions,' she said and Adam smiled at her gratefully.

'Ian's the SIO and said he'd talk to us later. The first officers on the scene asked a lot of questions, but weren't really up to speed on the – er – the – well, Lisa's disappearance.' He swallowed hard.

'Was it Lisa?' Fran asked quietly.

Sophie and Adam nodded.

'How –' began Libby, but Ben silenced her with a hand on her arm.

'Who found her first?' asked Guy.

'A guy I didn't know,' said Adam. 'He was just in front of us – there was a bunch of us more or less running together. He just stopped and we all ran into him.'

'I think that's enough questions,' said Fran. 'They'll only have to go over it all again with Ian. What do you both want to drink?'

In fact, it was only about fifteen minutes later that Ian, accompanied by a young officer in plain clothes, came into the bar.

'Could we perhaps go somewhere a little more private?' he asked.

'My flat?' suggested Adam, standing up.

'Good idea,' said Ian. 'And I suggest your support team comes with us.' He smiled round at the others. 'You know you're dying to hear.'

'Good choice of words,' said Peter dryly. 'I won't come up. I'll stay downstairs with Hal and keep a nice bottle of red warm for when you've finished.'

Ian followed Adam up the stairs and stood at the top looking round as the others filed in after him.

'It's a long time since I was up here,' he said, and Libby saw Fran's face go from pale to pink. Guy, luckily, didn't seem to notice, but went to sit beside Sophie.

'Now,' Ian went on, taking an upright chair and turning it to face them all. He indicated another chair and motioned for the officer to sit. 'This is DC Tomlinson. He'll be doing all the note-taking.' He turned to his colleague. 'You're probably wondering about the informality of all this, but these people are my friends, and I was actually here in Steeple Martin with Mrs Sarjeant and Mr Wilde yesterday.'

Libby and Ben nodded in confirmation.

'You'll also know that a week ago, we were involved in a missing persons case over in Nethergate.' Ian raised an eyebrow.

'Yes, guv,' said Tomlinson. Ian winced.

'So now we come to how her body turned up in Steeple Martin, the very next destination for a run organised by the Nethergate Harriers, and how she was recognised.'

Libby watched Sophie's horror struck face.

'You think it's something to do with the Harriers?' said Adam.

'I have no idea,' said Ian. 'What I want to know is who recognised her and how?'

Sophie looked sick and Adam covered her hand with his own.

'It was Soph,' he said. 'The – er – bag was split, and she could see ...' He swallowed and looked down.

'Her clothes, yes,' said Ian. 'Pink and grey? Did she always wear those colours?'

Sophie nodded. 'To run in, yes.'

'All right, Sophie, thank you,' said Ian gently. 'Adam – what happened next?'

'I dialled 999. I couldn't think what else to do. And the other runners began to pile up behind us. I just stopped them, I'm afraid.'

'You did exactly the right thing,' said Ian. 'What did you tell them?'

'I had to tell them we'd found a body. I didn't say we thought it was Lisa.'

'I think you behaved admirably under the circumstances,' said Ian. 'We'll leave you in peace now. You can sign your statements another time.'

'I didn't say much,' said Sophie in a small voice.

Ian smiled. 'Enough. Do you want to go back and finish your drinks now?'

'I think I'd like to stay here,' said Sophie.

'We'll go,' said Libby. 'I suppose I'd better go and see how the ladies in Carpenter's Hall are coping.'

'Will they draw the raffle now?' asked Fran, as they followed Ian and DC Tomlinson down the stairs.

'I don't know. There isn't really an etiquette for this sort of situation,' said Libby. 'Are you coming to see the other runners, Ian?'

'The other officers will have taken the names and addresses and I should think told everyone to go home.' He smiled at her. 'You could, too.'

'Oh, those poor women!' said Fran. 'All that food they prepared.'

'Maybe people stayed to eat it after all,' said Ben. 'Come on, let's go and see. That all right, Ian?'

'Of course. I expect I'll see you soon.'

There were, in fact, quite a lot of runners still in Carpenter's Hall, making inroads into the buffet. Flo, the benefactress of the hall, sat at the side with Amy hovering over her.

'Now whatcher got yerself into?' said Flo, as soon as Libby came in sight.

'Nothing!' said Libby in surprise. 'Nothing to do with me at all.'

'Young Adam, then.' She turned to Guy. 'And your gal. That means these two'll be at it again.'

Fran and Libby looked at each other.

'It's nothing to do with us,' repeated Libby.

Flo gave a disbelieving snort.

'We just came to see if everything was all right,' said Fran. 'What about the raffle?'

'We said we'd draw it later on and let everyone know,' said Amy. 'People's names are on the ticket stubs, so we can do that.' She looked worried. 'It'll take a long time, though.'

'I'll help,' said Libby.

'So will I,' said Fran. 'Just let Libby know what you want us to do and when.'

Amy's face brightened. 'Oh, would you? That would be such a help, see. I really can't ask the residents to do it.'

'Too old and loopy, eh?' said Flo.

Amy's face went nearly as red as her cardigan. 'No, Mrs Carpenter – not at all!'

'Flo, don't tease,' said Ben. 'What have you done with Lenny?'

'Gone up to Het's. Why aren't you there?'

'Because we're here,' said Libby patiently. 'We were supporting the runners.'

'Stupid business runnin' when you don't have to,' said Flo.

Privately agreeing, Libby smiled placatingly and turned to Fran. 'I think we ought to go and speak to Steve if he's here, don't you?'

'Do you think they know it was Lisa by now?'

'I've no idea. We'll go and find out, shall we?' She turned to Ben and Guy. 'Do you two want to go back to the pub? We won't be long.'

Guy shrugged. 'We'll expect you when we see you. Come on, Ben.'

'I don't think they're too happy,' murmured Libby as she watched the two men leave the hall.

'Who can blame them? Yet another murder, dumped almost on their doorstep, with their children involved. And don't say Adam isn't Ben's, you know what I mean.'

Libby nodded. 'Look there's Steve. And that Roly. Shall we go over?'

Steve was holding court to a small group of runners who Libby thought she'd probably seen the previous week. Roly stood to one side looking as pale as Fran had earlier.

'Oh, it's you!' Steve turned to them gratefully. 'You'll look into this now, won't you?'

Startled, Libby stepped back onto Fran's foot.

'Ow!' Fran hopped sideways. 'I don't know about looking into it. It isn't anything to do with us. And it's murder. The police –'

'Invited you to help last week,' Steve interrupted. 'And you've already been talking to them today, haven't you?'

'How –?' began Libby.

'Only because our children were the ones who found – or recognised – the body,' said Fran.

'So you already know more than we do,' said Steve.

'No, not at all,' said Libby. 'And we know nothing about Lisa. You all still know more about her than we do.'

'Do they think she would have still been alive if we'd found her last week?' A middle-aged man Libby didn't remember spoke from the back of the group.

'No idea,' she said. 'I don't suppose they know anything at all yet. They'll be having to do post-mortems and forensic analysis and all that stuff.'

'Only I think she would have been,' the man went on, sounding faintly aggressive. 'If she's been held somewhere, she could have been found and saved if the police had done their job properly.'

There was a muttered reaction to this statement, but Fran shook her head.

'Oh, no,' she said. 'She's been dead since last week.'

Chapter Twelve

There was a short silence, then a flood of questions. Libby watched, knowing that Fran had not been told by the police, as the members of the Harriers assumed. Eventually, she intervened.

'Come on, Fran, Ben and Guy will be waiting.' She smiled round at the agitated runners. 'I hope they find out who did this.'

'They think it was one of us, don't they?' The aggressive man now appeared between Libby and the door.

She stopped in surprise. 'Do they? How do you know?'

For a moment he looked puzzled. 'Well, it's obvious.'

'Is it?' Fran shook her head. 'I hope it all gets sorted out quickly.'

'All right, gal?' Flo materialised beside the aggressive man, who she nudged in the side with a sharp elbow. 'This is my hall, young man, so you behave yourself. See you later.' She winked at Libby and Fran and went back to her chair, leaving an open-mouthed runner and his amused companions behind.

'Pub,' said Libby firmly, and they left smartly.

'Do you think he was right? The police think it was one of them?' she said, as they crossed the high street.

'Probably.' Fran was focusing on the ground in front of her.

'And – pardon me for asking – but do you know

positively that she'd been dead since last week?'

'I've told you so many times –'

'I know, I know. Things just appear in your head. Is that what happened?'

'I suppose so. I shouldn't have said anything.'

'No,' agreed Libby. 'But you ought to tell Ian.'

'Why? Their pathologist will find out soon enough.'

During the next hour at the pub, Fran was preoccupied. Eventually, at her suggestion, they cancelled their booking for that evening and she and Guy decided to go back to Nethergate.

As Libby and Ben waved them off, the landline began to ring.

'Libby? Ian. Is Fran still with you? She isn't answering her mobile.'

'No, we cancelled the rest of today's plans and she and Guy have gone home. They've only just left and she was driving, so that's why she isn't answering.'

'I've been ringing for over half an hour,' said Ian, faintly accusing.

'Ah. We were in the pub. She may have turned it off.'

'I wonder why?'

Libby was silent.

'Look, Libby, what has she said?'

'What do you mean?' Libby was wary.

'You know what I mean!' Now Ian was exasperated. 'One of the officers on duty in Steeple Martin has had a group of those people from Nethergate asking questions. Apparently they think Lisa Harwood has been dead for a week.'

Libby made a face at Ben, who was sitting on the sofa looking enquiring.

'She just mentioned it in passing …'

Ian made an explosive sound. 'Did she say any more?'

'No. She wouldn't talk about it. Look, Ian, don't blame me. It's got nothing – absolutely nothing – to do with me, or Fran, come to that. She couldn't help having that whatever it was moment, and she knows she shouldn't have said anything. She wasn't going to say anything to you because she said your pathologist would tell you.'

'Yes, but it happens to be one of the facts we would have preferred to keep to ourselves for now.'

'Sorry,' said Libby inadequately.

Ian's voice softened. 'I know it isn't your fault. Just try not to talk to any of those people again if you can help it.'

'Except Adam and Sophie.'

'Well, yes. If you speak to Fran, ask her to call me.'

Libby relayed the conversation to Ben as she searched the kitchen for something to eat now that their dinner plans had been cancelled.

'Look, we can always go to the pub, just the two of us. There was no need to cancel our booking.' Ben perched on the kitchen table. 'So what are you going to do about Fran?'

Libby turned and looked at him. 'Do? How do you mean?'

'Are you going to tell her about Ian?'

'Only if she gets in touch. It was fairly clear she wanted to be left alone, wasn't it?'

'It was, rather. So come on – shall I ring the pub?'

'Oh, go on, then. And see if Pete and Harry want to come.'

'They're still entertaining Max and Owen.'

'Ask them anyway,' said Libby.

At seven thirty Peter and Harry joined them in the dining room of the pub, Max and Owen having gone off to visit other friends in Canterbury. Peter picked up the menu and frowned.

'I wonder if the menu will get any better with the new owner.'

'New owner?' echoed Ben and Libby.

'Didn't you know?' Harry's eyebrows rose in surprise. 'Sale's going through now.'

'Why didn't we know?' Libby was indignant. 'Locals should be told these things.'

'Do you ever read the local paper?' said Peter. 'No, I thought not. It's been in there once or twice. We knew about it from the trade press.'

'I don't think I even know who owned it before,' said Ben. 'It's a free house, isn't it?'

'Owned by the same family since our mothers' time,' said Peter. 'Run entirely by the staff. The old boy didn't want to sell it, but his children don't want it, they've got lives of their own, so it's had to go.'

'I'm surprised they didn't just shut it down,' said Ben. 'That's what seems to be happening all the time these days.'

'As pubs go, this place is thriving,' said Harry. 'Its rooms are full a lot of the time, people come out here to eat and there's a sizeable chunk of local custom within walking distance. And no competition.'

'So who *is* the new owner?' asked Libby. 'Don't tell us it's a consortium or something.'

'It's a couple who have just finished turning round a village pub in Sussex that they rescued from the developers.'

'Then why do they want to come here?' asked Ben.

'I only know what was in a news release,' said Harry. 'I haven't actually met the man!'

Libby looked down at the menu. 'I don't think the food here's bad. It's always served us well. And Max and Owen seemed perfectly happy with it.'

Max and Owen had stayed at the pub the previous autumn.

'By the way, did you check your improvised car park?' asked Peter. 'In case anyone's decided to stay?'

'I didn't have to,' said Ben. 'The police got rid of everybody. It looks like even more of a wasteland than it did before.'

Libby was looking thoughtful. 'Do you remember what Ian was talking about yesterday lunchtime?'

'Eh? Oh, the festival thing.' Ben looked up.

'Well, maybe the new pub owner would be interested.'

'In a music festival?' said Ben.

'Is that what Ian suggested?' said Harry. 'Blimey!'

'He'd just been to one,' said Libby, 'and he thought the field would make a good venue.'

'He's right – but I'd suggest a beer festival. You can still have music, but that would bring in the punters more.' Harry gazed at the ceiling, a faraway look on his face. 'Great possibilities.'

'Right,' said Ben warily. 'I'll go and get the drinks.'

The manager himself came to take their order.

'It was good of you to fit us back in after we'd cancelled,' said Libby.

He sighed. 'Only too pleased. We lost most of our bookings for tonight.'

'Oh, of course. Not good for anybody.'

'How was lunchtime?' asked Harry. 'We were all right – fully booked and they all came, but the whole – er – thing had happened much before, so ...'

The manager brightened. 'Lunchtime was fine. There were a lot of people in the village who had nothing to do, so they came in here. You did yourselves,' he said to Libby.

'I'll have the soup and the lamb shank,' said Ben,

putting an end to the conversation. 'Anyone else?'

'I wanted to ask him about the new owner,' complained Libby, when the manager had left with their orders.

'I know you did. We'd have never got our food,' said Ben with a grin. 'You can ask him later.'

Libby got her chance when Harry asked the manager to join them for a drink at the end of their meal.

'New owner?' he said. 'Seems very nice.' He shrugged. 'Don't know if I'll be out of a job or not yet, but he's said nothing.'

'Hal said he came from a pub in Sussex?' prompted Peter.

'In a village near Lewes. The brewery shut it – or were going to – and there was the usual flurry of interest from the villagers who wanted to keep it, but they couldn't quite raise enough capital. So our new owner stepped in. He's handing the running of it to the locals now and coming here.'

'Is his background in the trade?' asked Ben, frowning. 'Seems an odd thing to suddenly turn to in his – I don't know. How old is he?'

'Fifties? No idea where he came from. I'm sure we'll find out.'

The talk turned naturally to the discovery of Lisa Harwood's body. As Libby and Ben knew far more about it than most people in the village, they soon had a small crowd round them asking questions. Libby was very glad of Ben's foot landing sharply on her own every time a question threatened to take her into forbidden territory.

Eventually taking leave of the manager and the locals, the friends left to go home.

'Nightcap?' offered Peter, as they stood outside the pub.

'I think I'd rather just go home to bed, thanks all the same,' said Libby. 'It's been an odd day.'

'Let us know if there's any progress,' said Harry. 'Night, old trout.'

'Do you think there will be?' Libby asked, as she and Ben walked along the silent high street towards Allhallow's Lane.

'Will be what?'

'Progress. In Lisa's murder.'

'I expect so. They'll pull out all the stops now.'

'I wonder who called me.' Libby scowled at her feet. 'I wonder if that's part of it all?'

'Ian agreed with us that it was probably someone trying to get the police to take it seriously, so I doubt if it was the murderer,' said Ben, fishing keys out of his pocket.

'No, but someone who knew, or guessed, that it was more than simply a missing person.'

'So someone who knew a lot more about her life than they've let on?'

Arriving at the door of number 17, Ben let them in and Sidney shot out.

'I do wish he wouldn't do that,' said Libby, exasperated. 'Now I'll have to stand out here in the cold to get him in again.'

'He'll come and tell you when he wants to come in. Don't be so daft.' Ben pulled her inside and shut the door. 'Now, are you sure you don't want a nightcap?'

The following morning Libby received a phone call from Max.

'We've hardly seen you this weekend, so we wondered if you'd like to have lunch with us. Pete's got some restaurant he wants to visit, so we thought we'd have a trip out.'

'Sounds wonderful,' said Libby, only too glad to be torn away from the accusing gaze of the painting on the easel in the conservatory.

'Will Ben be able to come?'

'Give him a ring and ask him,' said Libby. 'He's less likely to turn you down than me!'

As it happened, Ben was unexpectedly busy with a tenant farmer.

'Milk quotas,' Libby explained gloomily, when she was picked up. 'Dairy farming's a horrendous business these days.'

Everyone in the car nodded glumly.

'So where are we going?' asked Libby, after a decent pause to mourn the decline of the dairy industry.

'That pub you went to that did the Middle Eastern night, The Dragon, remember? You and Ben said how good it was,' said Peter.

'Yes, but it was a special. I don't think they do it as a regular thing. And it's Monday.'

Harry, sitting next to her, dug her in the ribs. 'Do you think he didn't check, petal? And I have an appointment with the chef to learn about his tagines. He'd heard of me,' he added proudly.

'And we were thinking about your mystery woman who was murdered,' said Owen.

'You were?' Libby was surprised. 'Why?'

'Well,' he looked at her in the driver's mirror. You remember we told you about our two boys?'

'Who went missing? Yes.'

'We think,' said Max, turning round to face her, 'that there are similarities. And that's not good.'

Chapter Thirteen

'How do you know it's not good?' asked Libby. 'You said there was nothing to investigate.'

'We reported them missing,' continued Owen. 'The police weren't very interested. We weren't parents, merely employers.'

'But then there was a lot of talk amongst the rest of the boys,' said Max. He looked at Harry. 'You know about the sex party circuit, don't you?'

Harry and Peter both nodded, Peter having adopted his most fastidious expression.

'Is that what it sounds like?' asked Libby.

'Yes, petal.' Harry patted her leg. 'Not very nice.'

'So what about it?' asked Libby. 'Did your boys go to them?'

'It's not quite like that, Lib.' Peter leant forward to face her. 'It's a bit more than that.'

'Nasty goings on?' said Libby. 'So what was the connection?'

'A couple of the boys said they'd been approached by people. Apparently because they were fit – as in athletically fit. Specialist tastes, that sort of thing.' Owen looked uncomfortable and fixed his eyes on the road. 'Where do I go now?'

Libby began giving directions, and a little later, they were pulling into the car park of The Dragon.

'Last time I was here at lunchtime it was practically empty.' Libby got out of the car and stretched.

'That was in November or December, wasn't it?' said Peter. 'This is the beginning of the season.'

'This is hardly a tourist destination,' said Libby. 'Back of beyond.'

'It's recommended in all the guides,' said Harry. 'And its grading has improved over the last couple of years. Chef was telling me.'

'Oh, you've spoken to him?'

'Told you – he's going to give me the secret of his tagines.' Harry flung an arm around her shoulders. 'Come on, inside.'

Installed at a large round table overlooking the garden, which Libby hadn't been aware of the last time, after the chef himself had been out to greet them and taken their orders, Max and Owen bought drinks and returned to the subject of their missing dancers.

'When we talked it over,' said Max, 'we thought that perhaps it was similar, because your missing runner apparently had become obsessed with running and everything else seemed to have been cut out of her life. Our boys were the same.'

'They haven't turned up dead, have they?' said Harry.

'Not as far as we know, but suppose they'd given us false names?' said Owen. 'We couldn't find any trace of them online or at the school they'd attended.'

'Doesn't make any sense.' Libby frowned.

'Do you think they joined you because for some reason they knew they'd be approached by these people?' asked Peter.

Owen and Max looked horrified.

'I bloody well hope not!' said Max.

'If your other boys had been approached –' began Harry.

'And they told us.' Owen's mouth was a grim line.

'Not until after the other boys had gone, though, didn't you say?' said Libby.

Silence fell around the table, broken eventually by Max's sigh.

'Can't have been just us, though. Think of all the ballet companies in London,' he said.

'You perhaps should ask around,' said Libby. 'Don't you all talk to each other?'

'Of course we do, but this is a bit – well – under the counter, isn't it?' said Owen.

'Oh, come on! Surely you'd know?' said Harry.

'Anyway,' said Libby, 'I can't see that there are any similarities other than obsession. And if your boys were danseurs then obsession was a good thing.'

Owen sighed. 'Maybe. I think perhaps your detective instincts are catching.'

'Well, she isn't doing any detecting at the moment,' said Peter, 'are you, dear trout?'

'Trout?' said Max and Owen together.

'That's her,' said Harry. 'Our dear old trout.'

'Do you really let them talk to you like that?' asked Max.

'It's become a bit of a habit,' said Libby apologetically.

'I have to tell you,' said Harry, banging the table with a spoon, 'that we saved this woman's life. Languishing, she was, all the way over there the other side of Canterbury. So Pete and I started the Search For Bide-a-Wee, found her the cottage and here she is. With a theatre to run, a man to look after and a pillar of the community.'

'Golly, am I?' Libby was impressed.

'Did you actually ask them to find you a cottage in their village?' Max asked.

'No, I was just complaining. They told me I had to move.'

'And how right we were,' said Harry. 'Ah – food!'

The food was exceptional, and as the only customers for lunch, the chef was able to come and join them, while Harry ruthlessly pumped him for culinary secrets. Owen, Max, Peter and Libby left him to it and strolled out into the garden.

'Very focussed on his food, isn't he?' said Owen.

'Very.' Peter looked amused. 'People take him for a bit of a clown until they know him really well.'

'Andrew said he knew an old friend of his?' Max sent a quizzical look in Peter's direction.

'Yes. Quite a coincidence,' said Peter firmly.

Sir Andrew McColl was the actor who had introduced Max and his company to Libby and Ben.

'How is he? Have you seen him lately?' asked Libby, as determined as Peter that the conversation shouldn't be led into the realms of Harry's background, which was still a little painful to him.

'I saw him at a charity thing at the Coliseum a couple of months ago,' said Max. 'Opera, though, not ballet. I'm never sure about opera.'

'Me neither,' said Libby. 'Although I'm a huge fan of Gilbert and Sullivan.' She assumed a beatific expression. 'I did Pitti-Sing and Lady Angela in a G&S tour when I was young.'

'I didn't know you sang.' Peter looked surprised.

'I sing every year in The End Of The Pier Show,' said Libby rather huffily.

'But that's not proper singing, is it?' Peter said innocently, and Max and Owen roared with laughter. Peter winked at Libby.

'Subject closed,' he whispered, coming up and taking

her arm.

After refusing complimentary liqueurs, the little party left The Dragon with many promises to return, and the chef waved them off with a promise to come to The Pink Geranium on his next day off.

'That was lovely,' said Libby. 'You wouldn't believe how gloomy the whole area was when we saw it before.'

'Amazing what a drop of sunshine will do,' said Harry.

'Your young dancers,' said Peter suddenly. 'Couldn't it have been the ballet school where they trained which was the link to the sex parties?'

'That occurred to me when the boys – my boys, I mean – told me about the approaches that had been made,' said Max.

Owen frowned at the road ahead. 'But the approaches were made – hang on, where *were* they made?'

Max looked at Owen, Libby looked at Peter and Harry looked at Max.

'Yes, where were they made?' said Libby and Harry together.

'I have no idea.' Max shook his head. 'I'll ask when we get back, but it doesn't really help your poor young woman, does it?'

'No,' admitted Peter. 'I was just curious.'

'It's the Steeple Martin disease,' said Harry.

As Max and Owen were returning to London on Tuesday morning, Libby and Ben joined them and Harry and Peter in the pub that evening for a farewell drink.

'Have you managed to keep Stan's lovely set?' Libby asked, referring to the original set of *Pendle* used in the Oast Theatre last autumn.

'Amazingly, yes. Scaled up of course,' said Max. 'Young Seb's turned out to be a godsend. I think Stan rather kept him under his thumb.'

Sebastian Long had been the assistant stage manager, now promoted.

'He told me he wanted to do "real" theatre,' said Libby. 'He's got his wish, now, hasn't he?'

'Some good came out of it all, then,' said Ben. 'Shame that can't be said for all Libby's adventures.'

'Oi!' said Libby. 'They aren't *my* adventures! I don't start them.'

'You just get involved by accident,' said Harry. 'Fall down the rabbit hole, like.'

'It isn't my fault,' insisted Libby.

'Well, I think you should get involved with this lady's disappearance,' said Owen.

'It's not a disappearance any more,' said Libby gloomily.

'No, but no one knows where she was between last weekend's run and this one,' said Peter.

'Look, I can't just go barging in and asking a lot of questions,' said Libby.

'That doesn't usually stop you,' said Ben. Libby sent him a fulminating glare.

'Anyway, I wouldn't know where to start, it's not as if I know anything about the woman – or the Harriers, come to that. The whole thing's a closed book to me.'

'Didn't you tell us you had a phone call telling you to back off last week though?' said Owen.

'Yes, why?'

'I would have thought that would have piqued your interest.'

'It scared me,' said Libby. 'And Fran and I and the police all decided it must be someone who wanted the police to take notice of Lisa's disappearance, not actually a direct threat to me or Fran.'

'And it was someone who knew your phone number –

or where you lived in order to find it. So it does make you directly involved,' said Owen triumphantly.

'Oh, Gawd, don't tell her that,' groaned Harry.

'I suppose we could try to find out who that was,' said Libby, casting a wary look at Ben, who rolled his eyes.

'I shall blame you two if she gets mixed up in this,' he said, wagging a finger at Owen and Max. 'Now, who's ready for another drink?'

Libby called Fran on Tuesday morning.

'Owen and Max suggested we try and find out who made the threatening phone calls last week,' she said bluntly. 'What do you think?'

There was silence for a moment.

'Fran? Did you hear me?'

'Ye-es,' replied Fran slowly.

'Well?'

'I'm a bit worried about it.'

'In what way?'

'Um …' There was another silence.

'Look, Fran, if you just don't want to do anything about it, just say so. We aren't involved, other than being parents of two of the runners, so we can just walk away. Everyone else will.'

'The two runners who found the body.'

'Well, yes, but that was an accident.'

'Was it?'

Libby's solar plexus contracted involuntarily. 'What?'

Fran heaved a long, irritated sigh. 'Oh, I don't know. I suppose I ought to talk about it.'

'OK. Would you like to come here? I can do lunch. Soup or something.'

'I'll be there about twelve. Is that all right?'

'Fine,' said Libby. She ended the call, puzzled.

Fran had been slightly off-kilter ever since the visit to

the cliff path, and particularly since the discovery of Lisa Harwood's body on Sunday. Libby thought back. First there was the car she expected to have been parked by the supposed spot where Lisa had disappeared. Then there was her definite statement that Lisa had been dead since last week, and her withdrawal after the preliminary questioning of Sophie and Adam. It was beginning to look increasingly as though Fran's oddly wired brain had started working in the background again, and Libby wondered exactly what it had thrown up this time.

Chapter Fourteen

Libby made red pepper soup. By the time Fran arrived, a little after twelve, it was simmering on the Rayburn and a large round loaf sat on the table.

'Do you want anything to drink?' Libby asked. 'Soup's ready, but it can keep hot.'

'Have you got any of that fizzy elderflower stuff?' said Fran.

Libby took a bottle out of the fridge. 'Shall we take it into the garden?'

Settled under the cherry tree with tall glasses of elderflower cordial, Libby waited for Fran to start explanations.

'It's all a bit difficult,' she began.

'Start with our visit to the cliff path with Ian,' said Libby.

Fran nodded. 'I'd already started feeling a bit odd about the whole thing,' she said, 'and I didn't really want to go.'

'No, I remember.'

'And I was certain a car had been at the side of the track – where the tyre marks were. A big black car – four-wheel-drive. After that, I felt very uncomfortable when we went to see the Harriers in the evening.'

'You didn't tell me that!'

'No, I know. I wasn't sure what I was uncomfortable about. Then there was the phone call ...'

'Which we decided was someone trying to make the

police take notice,' said Libby, as robustly as she could.

'In that case, who? Someone who knew us and knew that there really was something wrong. Someone who knew she was murdered.'

Libby shivered.

'After that, it was – the body. And I just somehow know she was taken there in that big black car. I kept thinking it was imagination, but it wasn't, I'm sure. And there's something very nasty swirling round among the Harriers.' Fran looked up at Libby. 'And I'm scared for Sophie. And Adam.'

Libby stared back at her, then took a healthy swig of elderflower cordial.

'Have you told Ian any of this?'

Fran shook her head. 'There's not one scrap of evidence for any of it. It's all in my head. My bloody head!' she finished viciously.

'Let's go and have the soup,' said Libby, 'and we can think about what to do.'

'And we both know,' said Fran, standing up, 'what we will decide.'

'Well,' said Libby ten minutes later, a half-empty bowl of soup in front of her, 'we have to try and find out, we know we do. And you said you wanted to find out right at the beginning, didn't you?'

Fran toyed with her spoon. 'I think I was hooked then. Why, I have no idea, especially as my – instincts, or whatever you like to call them – have been almost non-existent for ages.'

'Do you think you saw a threat to Sophie? I don't mean did you actually *see* it –'

'I know what you mean. Yes, it could be, which makes it all the more imperative that I try and at least find some proof of what I know.'

'That *we* try,' corrected Libby.

Fran smiled. 'Of course.'

'Do we tell Ben and Guy?' asked Libby. 'More soup?'

'No more thank you. And I suppose we shall have to. Guy's Sophie's father after all.'

'I haven't told you about Max and Owen's disappearing danseurs, have I?' Libby put the soup pot back on the Rayburn.

'They were talking about them the other night, weren't they?'

'Yes, but they enlarged a bit on them yesterday.' She repeated all that Max and Owen had told her.

'Even I know about those sort of goings-on,' said Fran. 'You're not really that innocent, are you?'

'Well, no, and we did hear a bit about it last year, didn't we, but that was all in the past.'

'It still goes on. There are some very exclusive "parties" catering for very specific tastes. That's obviously what the dancers were approached for.'

Libby wrinkled her nose. 'The other dancers assumed that was what had happened. I don't see why Max and Owen saw a connection between that and Lisa Harwood.'

'Neither do I, except the lack of a footprint.'

'Eh?'

'Web presence,' said Fran. 'Keep up, Lib. The only social media presence she has is on the Harriers' group page, and there's no mention of her anywhere else. If it wasn't for the fact that she has a husband and sons alive and well, I would have said she was a made-up persona.'

Libby thought this over. 'I suppose she *is* her?'

'You mean is someone pretending to be her? In that case, her husband would have unmasked them by now.'

'Oh, yes.' Libby pushed away her soup bowl. 'So what do we do? We can't start questioning the Harriers individually. And when you said there was something nasty about them ...'

'Not all of them,' said Fran. 'It's just that I feel there's something there. It could be just one person.'

'Has Sophie told you everything she knows about them, do you think?'

Fran looked surprised. 'I think so. She certainly doesn't have any reason not to.'

'Not something she may have thought unimportant?'

'You saw how concerned she was when Lisa disappeared, and how shocked she was yesterday. She'd never keep anything back.'

'How was she this morning?'

Fran shrugged. 'I don't know. She doesn't live with us, after all. She may have stayed here with Adam.'

'I suppose she might.'

'What are you thinking?' asked Fran after a moment's silence.

'If we could ask Sophie ourselves if there's anything she knows.' Libby looked warily across at her friend.

But Fran nodded slowly. 'We could. It's also the only way we're likely to find out anything about the others in the group. After all, she did more-or-less involve us at the start.'

'As long as she doesn't blame us for the escalation from missing to murder,' said Libby darkly.

A phone call to Guy established that Sophie was home, and had covered him in the shop for his lunch hour.

'Do you think she'd answer some questions?' Fran asked him. She listened, then gave Libby a thumbs up. 'OK, darling. Will you tell her we'll be over in about half an hour?'

She ended the call and took her soup bowl to the sink. 'Just time to wash up.'

'Dishwasher,' said Libby promptly. 'I'll pop up to the loo, you get started and I'll follow you.'

'Oh, yes, I forgot you'll have to get home. OK, see you in a bit.'

Five minutes later Libby was climbing into her 'little silver bullet', as her small Fiat was known, and then turning to follow Fran to Nethergate. Once again, she had to park at the end of Harbour Street in the car park behind The Sloop, and by the time she'd walked back to Guy's gallery and shop, Fran had already joined Sophie in the flat upstairs.

Libby panted a little at the top of the stairs.

'Steep, aren't they?' Fran grinned over at her. 'Sophie says it's what keeps her fit.'

'I thought that was the running,' said Libby, as she went to join them round the table in Sophie's bay window that jutted out over Harbour Street.

'Well, yes.' Sophie turned to look out of the window. Libby glanced at Fran, who shrugged.

'When did you start running, Soph?' asked Libby. 'Was it recently?'

'I started at uni.' Sophie turned back from the window. 'Then it sort of lapsed. But a couple of years ago everybody started doing it.' She shrugged. 'So I joined in. And then someone told me about the Harriers, and ...'

'Who told you?' asked Fran.

'I can't remember.' Sophie frowned. 'I was doing a run over towards Creekmarsh with an old school friend and we met some of her mates, and well, you know.'

'So it wasn't a present member of the group?' said Libby.

Sophie shook her head. 'Oh, no. I looked them up online when I got home that day and sent an email, then I got an email back from Steve and that was it.'

'You said you were on the committee. That was quick, wasn't it?'

'I suppose so. But I was keen.' Sophie smiled ruefully.

'Who are the others?' asked Fran. 'Apart from Steve.'

'Kirsty Trent and Davy Long – you met them at the pub – a guy called Nick Heap, he's the one who does the social media and runs our website, and Jean Michaels who's the treasurer. Kirsty's the membership secretary and Davy and I are just ordinary committee members.'

'Are there lots of rows?' asked Libby. 'There always are on committees in my experience.'

'No, not really. We have very informal meetings, and there's very little to discuss really. Our biggest problem is getting volunteers to steward the external runs.'

'External runs?' echoed Fran.

'Like the Nethergate 5K and the Whitstable Fun Run,' explained Sophie. 'Our regular meetings are at the sports centre at the Sir Philip Stewart School.'

'Oh, I see.' Libby nodded. 'So you could start there and build up, so to speak, if you were a beginner?'

Sophie grinned at her. 'Thinking of starting, Libby?'

Libby looked at her in horror. 'Good Lord, no!'

'Does everyone go all the time?' asked Fran.

'No – but there are always committee members there. Usually Steve and me, and mostly Kirsty and Dave. Roly's always there, but then as you gathered he had a bit of a crush on Lisa.'

'Poor Roly,' said Libby. 'Have you seen him since Sunday?'

'No, but we shall be at the sports centre tonight as usual, so I'll see him then.'

'No new members recently?' asked Fran.

'A few. Running's getting more and more popular and it's Marathon season at the moment which always inspires a few people. Mind you, they drop out again fairly quickly.' Sophie looked down at her hands clasped in her lap. 'It wouldn't surprise me if we don't lose a few now, too.'

Libby and Fran nodded in agreement.

'Anyway, why did you want to ask questions? I mean, I don't mind, but now we know she's ... she's dead, the police will look into it, won't they?'

'And when did that stop us?' asked Libby. 'No, there's more to it than that.'

Sophie cocked an eyebrow at her stepmother. 'Is this because of one of your moments?'

Fran looked uncomfortable. 'In a way.'

'You know about the phone call last week warning us off?' said Libby. 'Well, we want to know who that was and why they did it. And Fran was certain she died last week.'

'Oh.' Sophie looked uncertainly at Fran. 'Is that all?'

'More or less,' said Fran. 'But it worries me.'

Sophie looked from one to the other solemnly. 'And you think one of the Harriers is involved.'

Libby looked at Fran.

'Who else would know about the 5K last week? And the energy drink? Lisa's heart problem?' Fran sighed. 'And the fact that Libby and I were there. It has to be someone involved.'

'But we were all running. No one had the time to pop out and drive a car up to the cliff path, or impersonate a steward.' Sophie began to look truculent.

'That's true, Fran,' said Libby.

'Were you all running? The whole membership?' asked Fran.

'Everyone who knew Lisa was.'

'So some people weren't?'

Sophie frowned. 'We've got a lot of members. I suppose someone could have known Lisa and I wouldn't have known.'

'It's got to be someone who's close enough to her to have a motive,' said Libby. 'This was a planned murder.'

'So you're going to look into it?'

Fran reached out and took her stepdaughter's hand. 'Don't you want us to?'

Sophie sighed. 'It doesn't matter what I want, does it? Just don't get into trouble this time.'

Libby opened her mouth but shut it on encountering a warning glare from Fran.

'We'll try not to involve you as far as we can,' went on Fran, 'but we might want you to introduce us to people.'

'All right. Do you want to come up to the sports centre this evening? Or you could come to the pub again – we usually go there afterwards.'

'What do you think?' Fran asked Libby. 'We didn't actually learn much last week, did we?'

'I think,' said Libby, 'that we'd be better thinking about the whole situation and working on a plan of action before we dive in. I can't see a way forward at the moment, and it isn't as if we have the resources the police do.'

Fran and Sophie were both looking at her in surprise.

'All right, I know, it isn't like me, but as Sophie says, we don't want to get into trouble, and although I don't think I believe in Max and Owen's sex party theory, I want to know what we're up against.'

Chapter Fifteen

'What did Fran actually say?' asked Ben when he came back from the Manor later that afternoon.

'Not much, when I think about it.' Libby poured tea into two mugs. 'She was positive there had been a big black car at the cliff path, that Lisa had been taken away in it, and dumped from it here on Sunday. And that there's something odd going on in the Harriers.'

'What, with the club itself?'

'I don't think so. She's quite vague about it. But she's worried about Sophie.'

Ben frowned. 'She thinks Sophie's in danger?'

'I don't think she knows exactly.' Libby sat down on the sofa. 'As she said, her "moments" have been very few and far between over the last couple of years, and she may be either misinterpreting something or pushing too hard. I mean, it would be hard not to be worried about the murder of a young woman on your doorstep, as it were, under any circumstances.'

'And you've discounted the sex party theory?'

'I can't see how on earth Max and Owen ever thought there could be a link. I think perhaps they were hoping there would be more to the story. People do seem to enjoy getting involved.'

'Don't they just?' Ben grinned at her.

'So what do you think? I'm not sure there's anything we can do. We can hardly go and interview every member of the Harriers, and there's no way we can find out anything about Lisa's private life.'

'No way you can trace a "big, black car", either,' said Ben. 'Although I suppose you could hide in the car park at the sports centre and see if one came in.'

'Ha ha.' Libby cradled her mug in both hands and looked thoughtful. 'I think I must be becoming sensible in my old age.'

'That'll be the day,' said Ben. 'What are you going to tell Fran?'

'I'll wait until she gets in touch. It was her idea to get involved, after all.'

'I'll just be waiting for the other shoe to drop,' said Ben, and took his mug into the kitchen.

Things returned to normal in Steeple Martin. Ben spent a lot of time on Wednesday quartering the field between the theatre and high street, which looked rather the worse for wear after its short role as a car park, and in discussion with the manager of the pub.

'He thinks we should be able to launch a small beer festival next year. He'll get on to the owner and find out,' Ben told Libby over supper. 'As it's a freehold pub we don't have a brewery to worry about.'

'Or to put money into it,' said Libby.

'Oh, I expect we'll be able to drum up sponsorship from some of the indie breweries,' said Ben. 'Anyway, if we're going to meet Patti and Anne tonight you can ask him what he thinks then.'

The Reverend Patti had her day off on Wednesday and came over to spend the evening with her friend Anne Douglas. Their regular routine was dinner at The Pink Geranium and then a drink in the pub with Libby, Ben and whoever else happened to be around. Quite often, DCI Connell would drop in on his way home.

'Actually, you know,' said Libby later, 'we don't know that Ian is on his way home from work when he comes for a drink, do we? Does he always finish that late?'

'He does when he's working on a big case,' said Ben. 'You know he does.'

'We still don't know where he lives. He could just pop out to meet us, couldn't he?'

'Oh, Libby! If he wanted us to know where he lives, he'd have told us by now. He's so often involved with you for work, I expect he wants to keep his private life to himself.'

'Hmm.' Libby made a face. 'Well, come on. Let's go and see if he's going to grace us with his presence tonight.'

When they arrived at the pub, Patti and Peter sat at their usual table with Anne's wheelchair between them. Ben and Peter went to the bar to fetch drinks and Libby sat down beside Patti.

'So tell us all,' said Anne.

'What about?' said Libby warily.

'The murder!' said Anne. 'I honestly don't know how you do it.'

'It's nothing to do with us,' said Libby.

'The woman went missing in Nethergate and was found in Steeple Martin,' said Patti. 'It looked a bit suspicious to us.'

'It was just that Guy's daughter Sophie and Adam were running in both races – runs, or whatever they're called. That's all.'

'And happened to fall over a body,' said Anne.

Libby sighed. 'Actually, it was Sophie who found her. Poor girl's still in shock.'

'So what are you doing about it?' asked Patti.

Libby widened her eyes. 'Nothing! Why should we be?'

'There's a mystery and you're not ferreting about in it?' said Anne. 'Pull the other one!'

Ben and Peter came back with glasses.

'They aren't looking into it,' said Ben. 'At least, that's the theory. They didn't know the victim, or anything about running, come to that, and there's no personal connection, so they're having to sit on their hands and let the police do their work.'

'And speaking of that,' said Peter, 'here come the police now. Probably with handcuffs.'

Ian Connell came over to their table.

'Harry's just on his way,' he said. 'I popped in there first.'

'Really?' Peter lifted an eyebrow.

'More dodgy brandy in the system,' said Ian. 'Nothing too serious.'

They made room for him at the table, and Ben ordered coffee. He looked round at the expectant faces and laughed.

'Am I the entertainment?'

'We were just wondering –' began Anne.

'If you were coming tonight,' Libby interrupted hastily.

Ian looked amused. 'And you weren't hoping I'd tell you just how far our investigation into Lisa Harwood's death had got?'

'We can't really, can we?' said Libby, a little gloomily. 'We're not connected to it at all.'

'As it happens, there is something I can tell you, and I rather expected you to know already.' Ian took a sip of coffee.

'Eh? How?'

Ian looked at Patti and Anne. 'Not a word, now.'

They shook their heads.

'We're having to question the Harriers' committee. Lisa appears to have been connected in some way to the sale of Class A drugs.'

There were gasps from everyone.

'But – why the committee?' asked Libby eventually. 'Why has it got anything to do with the runners?'

'I can't tell you that, Libby, you know I can't, I only told you as much as I did because Fran will be on the phone telling you about Sophie being questioned, so there was no point in me keeping it to myself.'

'Oh, Lord. Poor Sophie. Fran's been terribly anxious about her.'

'Has she?' Ian looked interested. 'How anxious?'

'Well – I don't know.' Libby wriggled in her seat. 'You know – anxious.'

'And should I be – anxious?' He raised his eyebrows.

Libby looked at Ben for support and received none.

'I don't know, honestly. She seems worried about the whole Lisa Harwood thing and says she thinks there's something – well, nasty was her word – somewhere in the Harriers. I don't know if she means the members, the committee or what. We talked to Sophie this afternoon, but she didn't really tell us anything.'

'Poking your nose in again?' Ian's expression hardened.

'No,' said Ben. 'Fran's concerned about her stepdaughter, and incidentally, Adam. She apparently feels uneasy. That's all. There was no question of any sort of investigation, or poking noses in.'

'Sorry.' Ian held up a placating hand. 'Do you think I ought to speak to Fran?'

'Up to you.' Libby was wary. 'But why did you have

to question Sophie? Surely you couldn't possibly believe she had anything to do with drugs?'

Ian sighed. 'We questioned all the committee members. We'll probably have to question all the members of the club, as well. And as for Sophie, she did go to university, didn't she, not known for being a drug-free paradise.'

'They don't all take drugs, Ian,' said Patti gently. 'I don't mean to butt in, but I wouldn't have thought you were the sort to tar everyone with the same brush.'

'I'm not, Patti, but thank you for reminding me. No, as it happens, I can't see Sophie being mixed up in anything illegal, if only because she knows her parents have a copper as a friend.'

'A fact she was only too aware of when Lisa went missing,' said Libby. 'She and Adam came to ask Fran and I if we could tell you about it before it was reported to the police.'

'I wish it had been reported straight away,' said Ian with a frown.

'Do you think there might have been a chance of finding her, then?' asked Peter.

'The trail wouldn't have been so cold.'

'But surely,' said Anne, 'if someone doesn't turn up for an hour or so when expected, you don't automatically report them to the police? We had a friend, didn't we, Patti, whose son went missing and the police said he'd probably gone of his own volition and they couldn't do anything until – what was it? Forty-eight hours?'

'It depends entirely on circumstances,' said Ian. 'There is no one size fits all – have a look at the Missing Persons charities and see. All I'm saying is, if we'd known the day she vanished, it might have helped.'

'That will really make us all feel better,' said Libby,

'when we realise we could have helped. Sophie's going to feel so guilty.'

'I'm sorry, Lib. I wish I hadn't said anything, now, but I was so sure Fran would have told you.'

'It's OK.' Libby sighed. 'I'm just glad I didn't know Lisa personally. I'm sorry if that's selfish, but I can't help it.' She looked across at Patti. 'I don't know how you do it, you know.'

Anne grinned affectionately. 'It's because she's a very good person. Very much better than most of us.'

'I think you're embarrassing her,' said Ian. 'Can we change the subject?'

'Beer festival,' said Ben promptly. 'I was speaking to the manager here about it.'

'Really?' Peter's eyebrows shot up.

'Ian's suggestion,' said Ben, 'so I thought I'd see how the pub felt about it. He's going to speak to the owner.'

Everyone was interested in the project, and when Harry came in he offered to source a few street food vendors who would come along. They had reached the knotty problem of car and tent parking by closing time, and Libby was trying to persuade Ben to schedule it for later in the summer.

'It'll take longer than that to organise,' he said as they walked home, 'and as Ian reminded us, we have to get all sorts of permits and things. And if we want music, as I suppose we do, all the local bands will be booked up by now.'

'I bet we could do it if we tried hard,' said Libby. 'Perhaps we could do just a one-day festival and then expand it next year?'

Ben looked thoughtful. 'That's not a bad idea, actually. Let me have a think about it.'

'Good. I really want to have something to get involved

with this summer.'

Ben gave her a sideways look. 'Just not Lisa Harwood's death, please.'

Libby looked up at the dark sky. 'Of course not,' she said.

Chapter Sixteen

Libby, restrained for once, waited for Fran to call her on Thursday morning. She didn't have long to wait.

'The police have questioned Sophie.'

'I know,' said Libby gently. 'Ian told us last night because he thought you would have already done so.'

'Did he say why?'

'Because Lisa was somehow involved with drugs. He didn't say any more.'

'Yes.' Fran sighed. 'Ian didn't come himself, but the officers who came were very nice and polite. They didn't really tell us anything, though.'

'What did they ask?'

'Had Sophie been offered drugs by any member of the Harriers, did she know of anyone who had, was there a drug culture among the runners ... Eventually, Sophie asked what they meant by drugs – did they mean performance-enhancing, in which case it was ridiculous because they were a tiny club who simply ran for pleasure, not in any way competitive in the same way that the big clubs are.'

'And what did they say?'

'They seemed amused, and said they were thinking more of recreational drugs. Sophie simply looked disgusted.'

'It would never have occurred to me to think of performance-enhancing drugs,' said Libby. 'But obviously it wasn't, anyway. I wonder what Ian meant when he said Lisa was involved.'

'Distributing?' suggested Fran. 'If she was, I don't think it was to the Harriers. They really don't seem the type, do they?'

'Could he have simply meant she was taking drugs? Perhaps the post-mortem turned that up. Although he said she was connected to the sale of Class A drugs. That's heroin and cocaine, isn't it?'

'I think there are quite a lot of others, but yes, those seem to be the most common.'

'He said,' said Libby, 'that they may have to question all the members, not just the committee.'

'I suppose they'll have to question all her contacts. But she hardly had any, did she?'

'She must have had some. I just wish I knew how she was connected to the sale. What does that *mean*?' Libby blew out a frustrated breath.

'I don't know.' Fran sounded troubled. 'I told you I was worried about this.'

'Ian said – or rather, he asked – if he should talk to you. Do you want him to?'

'What about?'

'I told him you were worried about Sophie and he thought you might have had, well, *thoughts* about it. You know.'

'There's nothing to tell, is there?'

'The black car. You were sure about that.'

'I don't know, Lib. I doubt everything these days.'

'Well, I don't think Soph or Ad are in any danger. Based on nothing at all, granted, but I can't see there's any connection to them, and why on earth should they – or any other member of the Harriers – be at risk?'

'We don't know the other members,' said Fran.

'No,' said Libby. 'Bother.'

'Hang on – Lib, I've got to go. My mobile's ringing. I'll call you later.'

Deprived of her conversation, Libby reluctantly decided she ought to tackle long-neglected housework. Or, at least, the much hated bed changing. She remembered her mother and grandmother having strict routines about this – stripping the beds on Sunday and washing the bedlinen on Monday, but somehow she'd never managed to achieve the almost automated regime of her predecessors.

She was almost halfway through manhandling the duvet into its clean cover when the phone rang. Thankful for the extension to the landline in the bedroom, she sank down on the half-made bed.

'It's me,' said Fran. 'That was Ian.'

'What did he ask?'

'The usual. I told him about the black car. He said he'll look into the cars owned by the Harriers.'

'It might not be a Harrier. And how would he do that, anyway?'

'Through the DVLA, I think.'

'Anything else?'

'He asked why I was worried about Sophie and Adam. I said I didn't know. I think he was a bit frustrated, to be honest.'

Libby thought for a moment. 'They must have found something in her cottage to do with drugs, mustn't they?'

'I suppose so,' said Fran, 'But I thought they'd searched her cottage before she was found. Why didn't they find it then?'

'Perhaps they didn't search that thoroughly. Perhaps they aren't supposed to while there's a chance the person is still alive.'

'Mmm ... but there's a mystery about that cottage, too,

isn't there?'

'Is there?'

'Yes,' said Fran. 'You told me Ian was telling you about it.'

'Did I?' Libby frowned at the phone. 'Do you mean when he came over on Saturday?'

'Didn't you say the police couldn't find the agents who'd rented her the house? And she made no rental payments?'

'Oh – yes. I suppose that is a mystery. Still they'll have gone into everything much more thoroughly now, won't they. And gone to the Land Registry or whoever it is to find out who owns it.'

'Don't you think it looks as if Lisa knew the owner, who let her have it on an informal basis?'

'I suppose so, but the police will have found that out by now,' said Libby. 'Why are you interested, anyway?'

'Aren't you?'

That stopped Libby short. 'Yes,' she admitted at length.

'Ian will tell us to leave it alone,' said Fran.

'And so we should. We've got no possible connection to this. It's none of our business.'

'The police have questioned Sophie.'

'And they'll probably question Adam and every other member of the Harriers,' said Libby. 'It would be pretty bad if relatives of all of them starting poking their noses into the case.'

Fran laughed. 'What's got into you, Libby?'

'Well, what's got into you? You're not seriously suggesting we start investigating? And investigating what?'

'There's something I don't like about the whole thing,' said Fran.

'So you've said.'

'I thought the cottage might be a start.'

'The cottage?'

'Find out who owns it – that sort of thing.'

Libby made an exasperated sound. 'What good will that do? And Ian – or someone – has already done that, you can bet. He's probably swearing out an arrest warrant or whatever it is as we speak.'

'It didn't sound as though he was that close when he was speaking to me just now.' Fran sighed. 'All right, I get your point. I'm just being nosy.'

Libby was quiet for a moment. 'I suppose,' she said at last, 'we could go out for lunch today. We haven't seen Sid Best for some time now.'

'Sid …? Oh!'

'Well, I did take him some Fun Run leaflets last week, but apart from that …'

'You're just as nosy as I am,' said Fran.

'With even less reason,' said Libby with a sigh. 'Well, shall we? I'll meet you there.'

The Poacher was the village pub in Shott. Libby and Fran had first visited when they got mixed up in a previous murder case. It stood at the corner of a village green, a long, low building. On the other side of the green, between two cottages, stood a Norman church, one of Patti's, in her huge parish of St Aldeberge, Shott and Bishop's Bottom.

Libby parked the silver bullet behind Fran's Smart car and went into the pub.

'Well, well, if it isn't that Libby Sarjeant!' Sid Best, his bright blue eyes as sharp as ever, held out his hand. 'Fran here says you want some lunch.'

'Well – er – if you're doing lunch?' Libby shook the proffered hand.

'Sausage and mash or shepherd's pie,' said Sid. 'That do you?'

'Shepherd's pie would be lovely,' said Libby. 'Have you ordered, Fran?'

'She has,' said Sid. 'I'll go and tell the missus.'

'Have you said anything yet?' Libby whispered to Fran, who shook her head. Sid came back behind the bar.

'Now what do you want to drink?'

'Tonic water, please,' said Libby.

'How did your run go last weekend?' asked Sid, passing over her change. 'Wasn't that where they found that body? Can't stay away from them, can you, you two?'

'She lived here,' said Fran. 'Haven't you seen any police cars around?'

'Yeah, down-along here.' Sid pointed along the lane on which the pub stood. 'Didn't know what it was for. No one did.'

'In a village pub? And no one knew?' Libby's eyebrows shot up in disbelief.

'Funny, innit? No, nobody. Empty for years, it was. Then someone moves in, but no one knows who. As I said, funny.'

'Why was it funny?' asked Fran.

'Well, see, as far as the village knew, it was part of the old Notbourne Estate. Had been, anyways, until the estate was broke up.'

'When was that?' asked Libby, antennae twitching.

'Oh, back before the First World War,' said Sid, and Libby's antennae drooped.

'Who bought it?' asked Fran.

'Dunno. Changed hands a few times – though I don't know if they bought it or was renting. So who was this body, then?'

'A woman called Lisa Harwood,' said Libby. 'It's been on the local news.'

'Yeah, but I don't take much notice. They talked about it in the pub, but I don't reckon anyone connected her to Chestnut Cottage.'

Fran obviously decided that it was time to change the subject. 'Have you seen anything of Mike and Cassandra?'

Mike Farthing, the owner of Farthing's Plants just up Rogues' Lane from The Poacher, was the part-time partner of Libby's cousin Cassandra.

'In here for the quiz every week, now that the ukulele group's broken up. Can't say I'm upset about that.' Sid gave a cackle and disappeared back into the kitchen.

'Chestnut Cottage,' said Libby. 'Are we going to take a look at it?'

'Might as well,' said Fran. 'Have you ever heard of this – what was it? Nutwood Estate?'

'Notbourne, yes, vaguely. There's part of the main house left standing, but I didn't realise it was broken up so long ago. I wonder if there's anything left?'

Fran took out her phone. 'I'll look it up.'

Libby was impressed. 'I can't get to grips with smartphones.'

'You've only just caught up with computers,' said Fran, amused.

'That's not fair. I can even use your tablet and Ben's. I just don't want to be uber-connected all the time.'

'Here,' said Fran, holding the phone so that Libby could see the screen. 'It's a wiki article, so probably not entirely accurate.'

'It's too small,' said Libby, squinting. 'What does that say? Lord Cheveley of Notbourne?'

'Yes. The estate was broken up in 1908. Not really

relevant, is it?'

'No, but quite interesting. I might have a look when I get home.'

Sid arrived bearing two steaming plates.

'Sorry it took a bit of time, missus was making the mash.' He beamed and set the plates before them.

'Thank her very much,' said Fran.

'We're the only people in here again,' said Libby, looking round the bar for the first time.

'Must be an evening crowd,' said Fran, making a tentative hole in her shepherd's pie to let the steam out.

'And a lot of the residents are commuters, aren't they, so not around during the day.'

'Lot of retired, though.'

They ate their meals in appreciative silence, then Libby sat back and sighed.

'We could pop up to see Mike while we're here. He might know something about Lisa.'

'Mike? I doubt it. Unless she was a customer. He's not exactly the curious sort is he?'

'Worth a try,' said Libby.

They bade Sid goodbye and asked if they could leave one of the cars in his car park, then Fran drove the Smart car along Rogues' Lane to the little track which led to Mike's nurseries.

He emerged from his office wiping his hands on a rag.

'Hello, Libby, Fran.' His smile was diffident. 'Cass isn't here, I'm afraid.'

'No, it was you we came to see,' said Libby. 'We've just had lunch at The Poacher.'

'Oh?' Mike put his head on one side.

'You know they've had another murder in Steeple Martin?' said Fran.

Libby murmured a protest, but Mike nodded.

'Well,' continued Fran, 'she lived here, and I know it's a long shot, but we wondered if you knew her. Nobody else seems to. Lisa Harwood, she lived in Chestnut Cottage.'

Mike raised his eyebrows. 'Her, was it? Poor Lisa.'

Libby and Fran both gasped.

'You knew her?'

Mike nodded. 'Yes. She was a customer.'

Chapter Seventeen

Libby and Fran looked at each other.

'Well,' said Libby. 'There's a turn up.'

'You say a customer,' said Fran. 'For plants?'

'Of course for plants,' said Libby. 'Somehow I didn't take her for a gardener, though.'

'I'm not sure she was,' said Mike with a small smile. 'She used to buy large tub arrangements.'

'Oh?'

'Come in here, and I'll show you.'

They followed Mike's rather shambling figure into the nearest greenhouse, where he took them towards a corner in which huge decorative pots filled artistically with a variety of exotic-looking plants were ranged beside a water feature.

'Not your sort of thing, I would have thought,' said Libby, eyeing the water nymph thoughtfully.

'No, they aren't. Cass helps me plant them up and we grow a specific range of plants for them.' He shook his head. 'Lisa used to come up every couple of months and choose one, we'd deliver it and that would be that. We supply a couple of local hotels with these.'

'So she had loads of these?' Libby frowned. 'Was the garden at Chestnut Cottage that big?'

'I don't know. I only ever saw the front when we delivered the pots. There's fence either side of the house, so you can't see the back garden.' Mike shook his grey head. 'It did strike me as strange, though. We left the pots by the house, yet we never saw any of the ones we'd delivered before. And I don't think she was strong enough to have carried them on her own.'

Both Libby and Fran were frowning now.

'Perhaps she had one of those things on wheels you can move them around on,' said Libby.

'I don't think they make them that big,' said Mike. 'We have industrial ones and mini fork lifts. Perhaps she had one of those hidden away.'

'And she lived alone apparently,' said Fran.

'Did she?' Mike looked surprised. 'I always got the impression that there was someone else around.'

'Really? Did you see someone?' asked Libby.

'No.' Mike frowned. 'Actually, I don't know why I thought that. Perhaps it was just that she was an attractive young woman and I assumed she wouldn't be alone. You say she was on her own?'

'Well, she was married, but not living with her husband and children.' Fran's voice was at its most disapproving.

'Oh.' Mike looked nonplussed.

'Do you know anything about the Notbourne Estate?' asked Libby. 'Sid at the pub thought Lisa's cottage would have been part of it once.'

'I don't know about that. I know Notbourne Court, though.'

'You do?'

'Well, what's left of it. It was demolished in nineteen something. Very early, anyway.'

'Sid told us the estate was broken up in 1908, but not that it was demolished,' said Fran.

'Some of it was kept by the family, but a lot was sold off. Much of the stuff in the old Court itself – you know, paintings and so on.'

'Oh, how awful,' said Libby. 'Was it debt?'

Mike shrugged. 'I don't know. I know lots were sold off after the Second World War because they were too expensive to keep up, but I didn't know it was happening as early as that.'

'Where are the remains of the Court?' asked Fran.

'Just over there.' Mike pointed in the opposite direction to Rogues' Lane. 'There's a lane leading to it just off Rogues' Lane a bit further along.'

'Parallel to the road the pub's on?' said Libby.

'And Chestnut Cottage, yes. It leads eventually back to the Canterbury Road.' Mike gave them a quizzical smile. 'Are you two investigating again?'

Libby felt herself going red. Fran, however, wasn't fazed.

'No. Just interested. My stepdaughter found Lisa's body and used to run with her.'

'Oh.' Mike was taken aback. 'That's awful. I'm so sorry.'

'You knew she ran?' said Libby.

Mike nodded. 'She ran round here in the early mornings. Well, along the lane, I mean.'

'Did you ever see anyone with her?'

'A young bloke sometimes,' said Mike.

'Roly,' said Libby and Fran together.

'Anyone else?' asked Fran.

'Not that I saw,' said Mike. 'You *are* investigating, aren't you?'

'Not really.' Libby sighed. 'We just got involved by accident and it's become second nature to ask questions, I suppose.'

'But if you don't mind, Mike,' said Fran, 'we will tell DCI Connell you knew her. He's having trouble tracing her friends.'

'Oh, we weren't friends. She was just a regular customer,' said Mike.

'By the way, how did she pay for the tubs?' asked Libby.

'Credit card,' said Mike, looking surprised.

'Ah, right. Well, we'll be going then. Say hello to Cass when you see her.'

They left Mike looking rather puzzled and went back to the Smart car.

'That was interesting,' said Libby.

'It certainly was.' Fran started the engine. 'Shall we go and look at Chestnut Cottage first or Notbourne Court?'

'Oh, we're going to both, are we?'

Fran turned to her and grinned. 'Of course we are. And in between I shall call Ian and leave him a message about Lisa and her pots.'

Chestnut Cottage stood on its own about a quarter of a mile beyond The Poacher. Whitewashed, with a tiled roof, it looked to Libby to be a perfect example of a converted longhouse. Either side were fences with gates leading to the back of the property, but no pots or tubs.

'Nothing to see,' said Fran, pulling up opposite. 'Not even any police tape.'

'No.' Libby swivelled in her seat. 'And no neighbours. Do you know, if she'd been killed here she wouldn't have been found for ages – unless she had visitors no one knows about.'

'And that's probably why she wasn't,' said Fran. 'Let's go and look at Notbourne Court.'

They turned round and went back to the green, back along Rogues' Lane, past Farthing's Plants until they came to a lane leading off to the left.

'This isn't used often,' said Libby, as Fran squeezed

the car between banks of hawthorn and burgeoning cow parsley.

'It was perhaps the drive to the Court once,' said Fran.

'Maybe.' Libby tried to peer through the vegetation. 'Look! That looks like something.'

The lane widened very slightly and Fran pulled as far into the side as she could.

'I'll have to get out your side,' said Libby.

The both scrambled out and, pushing through the branches, clambered to the top of a bank. They were looking down on a large, cleared area of grass, bordered by what looked like a range of gothic arches, which crumbled at both ends.

'Is this all that's left, do you suppose?' said Fran.

'Could be, but it's a bit suspicious, isn't it?' Libby was staring down at the grass.

'Eh?' Fran looked at her startled. 'What's suspicious?' She looked back at the grass. 'Oh, I see.'

'Someone's looking after it,' said Libby. 'Why?'

'Well, someone must own it, even if it isn't the original family. That's not suspicious.'

'Hmm,' said Libby. 'Look! Is that the back of Chestnut Cottage?'

They could just see a roof above a stand of trees some distance away.

'You know what this reminds me of?' Libby turned to Fran. 'White Lodge and the old barn.'

'Only because there's a house and another building that back on to one another,' said Fran. 'There's no other similarity.'

'I suppose not,' said Libby. 'I'm seeing problems where there are none.'

Fran nodded slowly. 'I wonder what the story here is?'

'We can look it up when we get home. I can't read

anything on your phone.' Libby shivered. 'Let's go. This place gives me the creeps.'

Fran looked surprised. 'Really?'

'Doesn't it you?'

'No.' Fran shook her head slowly. 'That's odd, isn't it?'

They returned to the car, and Fran was forced to drive right to the end of the lane which turned back on itself until it came out on the Canterbury Road, as Mike had said, and then back through Itching to reach The Poacher and Libby's car.

'Speak to you later,' said Libby, as she climbed out of the Smart car. Fran waved and turned round to leave the car park.

Libby sat in the car for a few minutes thinking. Were she and Fran making mountains out of molehills and poking their noses into something which didn't concern them? She sighed. Possibly, but at least Mike had come up with some rather odd information about Lisa. She fished out her old, basic mobile and sent Fran a text.

Don't forget to tell Ian about Lisa and the tubs.

Then, she switched on the ignition and pulled out of the car park.

At home, she put on the kettle and opened her laptop, typing "Notbourne Court Chestnut Cottage" into the search engine. There were various links, mainly to Notbourne Court itself, but scrolling though, Chestnut Cottage was actually mentioned in one of them, which turned out to be a document detailing all the properties held on the estate at the time it broke up. Libby went to fetch her tea, then settled herself down to read.

Notbourne Court, she read, had been given to Lord Cheveley's ancestor in the late sixteen hundreds. It had been rebuilt in 1790 – here was a painting of the Court in its heyday – but by the end of the nineteenth century it was falling into disrepair and the family's money had all but disappeared. When the late Lord Cheveley offered it to the young National Trust, it was turned down, the Trust having insufficient funds for its upkeep. It was put up for auction, including buildings on the estate and the contents of the house – here there was a facsimile of the auction catalogue, which included several cottages. The article went on to list some of the properties to be sold at auction, including 'one now known as Chestnut Cottage' for five shillings.

'Blimey!' said Libby to herself.

The further history of the estate was a sad one. Lord Cheveley, unable to sell the Court, had it demolished, though it appeared he had retained ownership of the land. The last member of the family, Stephanie Hays, died unmarried and childless and left the estate to her old friend Christobel Harris in 1985.

Libby tried a new search for Stephanie Hays and Christobel Harris and found a newspaper article entitled "Suburban housewife becomes Lady of the Manor". Christobel and Stephanie had apparently met during the Second World War as nurses and remained friends ever since. Christobel, interviewed by the paper, said that there wasn't much of the estate left, but that she and her husband would maintain it as Stephanie would have wished. Frustratingly, there was no mention of where Stephanie had been living, or whether Christobel now lived there.

Libby sat back in her chair and stared at the screen. Nowhere could she find any reference to who owned the estate now, what there was of it, or if Chestnut Cottage *had* actually been sold for five shillings, or remained part of the estate. Had Christobel Harris and her husband,

Robert, lived there? Had they left the estate to their own children? She assumed they were dead now, having been reported as 71 and 76 respectively in 1985.

Her mobile rang.

'It's me,' said Fran. 'I've just been talking to Ian.'

'Oh? Actually talking to him?'

'Yes. I wasn't dismissed out of hand, which I rather thought I would have been. He was really interested in Mike and the tubs. And he said they're expecting news from the Land Registry about who owns the property.'

Libby repeated what she'd just found out from the internet.

'So it could be someone called Harris?' said Fran.

'Or anything if it came down through the female line,' said Libby.

'And whoever it is, let it to Lisa.'

'For reasons which appear dubious,' said Libby.

'Well, they do to us. Could just be someone kind doing a favour to a friend.'

'Under such secrecy? And I still want to know about the tubs!'

142

Chapter Eighteen

'I had a look,' said Libby the following morning, 'on the Land Registry site. All you have to do is fill in a form and pay a fee to get details of a property. How come Ian was waiting for the information? It should have been there immediately.'

She and Fran were backstage at the theatre sorting costumes for The End Of The Pier Show. Music had been sourced and sent to Susannah and rehearsals would start next week. Luckily, it was a well-worn format and needed very little rehearsal. Individual acts were expected to rehearse on their own, but every year there were a few set pieces which need more thorough preparation, especially if choreography was incorporated.

'I expect he said that to put me off,' said Fran. 'Anyway, I suppose we could pay the fee ourselves and have a look, couldn't we?'

'I don't see why we should,' said Libby, sneezing as a stray boa feather wafted across her nose. 'We'd then find ourselves paying to search births, marriages and deaths to find out if the person was related to the Harrises.'

'And why do we need to know that?' asked Fran, shaking out a Victorian bathing costume.

Libby paused. 'Actually, I don't know. All we – or rather, the police – need to know is who loaned or let the cottage to Lisa and did they have any connection to her murder.'

'And we don't need to know at all.' Fran frowned

down at the pile of clothes. 'I don't honestly know why I've got this niggle about it.'

'Because it concerns Sophie?' suggested Libby.

'But it doesn't really, does it? She was simply part of the same running club, the same as several others. I don't know.'

'Could it be because of that phone call? He did try twice to reach me, after all.'

Fran looked up. 'Yes. And nobody's taken that very seriously, have they?'

'We all decided it was just to make the police take the disappearance seriously,' said Libby. 'We've heard nothing since.'

'No.' Fran sighed. 'I suppose I shall just have to hope Ian tells us what he can when he can.'

'Which won't be much as we've no connection to the case,' said Libby. 'Come on, I've had enough of this. I've got some soup on for lunch.'

Back at number 17, Fran made a fuss of Sidney while Libby stirred the soup and cut bread to go with it.

'Did you know you'd got a message on your answerphone?' said Fran, coming into the kitchen.

'Oh, bother. Now it doesn't beep at me I forget to look at the display. Don't get much anyway because of the mobile.'

'Hardly anyone has your mobile number,' said Fran.

'That's true,' said Libby with a grin. 'So I can't get bothered all the time.' She put the bread knife down and went out to the hall, where the landline stood on the third stair up. She pressed the button.

'Stop poking about Chestnut Cottage and Notbourne Court.'

Behind her Fran gasped.

'Is that the same voice as before?'

144

'Yes.' Libby swallowed. 'Someone's following us.' She lifted a finger to erase the message, but Fran stopped her.

'Ian will want to hear that.' She was already finding his number on her own mobile. She left a message on both his personal and work numbers and looked pensively at Libby's landline.

'If we unplug it, will it stop people ringing up?'

'I don't know. We can try 1471, I suppose.'

'It won't have the number,' said Fran.

They went back to the kitchen where Libby ladled soup into bowls. They'd barely sat down when Fran's mobile chirruped.

'I'm sorry, Ian,' said Fran when she could. 'But Libby's had another phone call. No – a message. Whoever it is has been following us. No – we haven't. We just went to The Poacher for lunch and to see Mike – no, we weren't!' She made an exasperated sound. 'Do you want to hear this message or not?'

She stood up and went back to the hall with Libby following. She held the mobile as close to the speaker as she could and pressed play.

'There. All right?' She shook her head at Libby and rolled her eyes to the ceiling. 'Yes, I'll tell her. Thank you.' She ended the call.

'Not happy, I gather?' said Libby.

'Anything but,' said Fran, as they resumed their places at the kitchen table. 'He's sending someone over to record the message as soon as he can, and whatever you do, don't erase it.'

'Not coming himself, then?' said Libby.

'I don't think he'd trust himself not to have a shouting match,' said Fran with a grin. 'He only just stopped himself from calling us interfering females. I could hear it shivering on the tip of his tongue.'

'Do you think,' said Libby, after a few mouthfuls of soup, 'that this was for the same reason?'

'What, to get the police to take it seriously?' said Fran. 'But why? They are taking it seriously. Lisa's dead – they have to.'

'Yes, but they aren't looking – or weren't – seriously at the cottage.'

'But they are after we told Ian about the tubs.'

'But my caller didn't know that, did he? By the way, did *you* think it was a he?'

'It was disguised, but yes, I think so. And no, you're right. He wouldn't know we'd told Ian about the tubs.' Fran looked thoughtful. 'And does he know about the tubs himself?'

'When you told Ian about Mike and the tubs, didn't you mention that we'd been over there?' said Libby, putting down her spoon. 'It sounded to me as if Ian didn't know.'

Fran looked guilty. 'No I didn't tell him. I just said you'd heard about it. I sort of let him think it was via Cass. I thought he'd be annoyed if we were poking about a potential crime scene.'

'And he was annoyed, but it isn't a crime scene, is it? She didn't die there.'

'No, but something tells me it has great significance.'

'Well, they'll go back and search it more thoroughly now, won't they? Although I would have thought they'd've already done that.' Libby stood up and picked up the bowls. 'There's more in the pot. Want some?'

'No, I'm fine.' Fran stretched. 'Do you want me to hang around and wait for whoever comes to pick up the phone?'

'Pick it up?' Libby was shocked.

'Whatever they're going to do. They might have to take it away, don't you think?'

'I don't know.' Libby frowned. 'Anyway, you don't need to stay unless you want to. I'd better sit down and work out some kind of rehearsal schedule.'

'I could help you with that.'

'You could.' Libby smiled gratefully. 'I sent out a group email and a Facebook post last week asking for availability, so I'll have to check through all the replies.'

Lunch cleared away, Libby opened her laptop and Fran her tablet.

'You check the Facebook posts and I'll check the emails,' said Libby. 'And I suppose I ought to do a chart thing.'

Fran looked amused. 'Do you know how?'

'No.' Libby shook her head. 'I'm hopeless.'

'Just open a second document and put names and dates in there. Then we'll sort out a proper schedule afterwards.'

They'd barely started when there was a tentative knock at the door.

'Detective Constable Turner,' announced the twelve-year-old standing outside the door. He held up his ID insultingly close to Libby's face.

'Yes?' she said, backing up a little.

DC Turner looked confused for a moment. 'I – er – DCI Connell said you'd be expecting me ...'

'Oh, yes,' said Libby. 'The phone message. Come in.' She pointed to the phone on the third stair. 'There it is.'

'Ah.' DC Turner squatted on his heels in a way that made Libby's knees ache in sympathy. 'Have you tried 1471?'

'We didn't think it was worth it,' said Libby. 'It was number withheld the last time.'

DC Turner tried, but got the expected reply. 'This is the charger unit isn't it?'

'Yes. Do you need to take it away? There's a second charger upstairs I can use for this one.'

'I'm afraid I will.' Turner stood up. 'We'll return it as soon as possible. I'll give you a receipt.'

He wrote out an official receipt and handed it over while Libby disconnected the charger unit.

'Thank you,' said Libby.

'Can I point out that the charger unit is not only connected to the mains but to the incoming telephone point?' said Fran appearing from the kitchen.

'Does that make a difference?'

'I'm afraid so,' said Turner apologetically. 'As I said, we'll get it back as soon as we can. Haven't you got a phone – I mean a mobile?'

'Yes, but not everyone has the number.' Now it was Libby sounding apologetic. 'Don't worry. I shall badger DCI Connell until I get this back.'

DCI Turner's expression changed from apologetic to horrified. 'Er – right.'

'Nice to meet you, DC Turner.' Libby held the door open and the young officer scuttled through. Libby and Fran returned to the kitchen.

'The landline isn't working,' said Ben as he came in through the back door later in the afternoon. 'Hello, Fran.'

'No, I know.' Libby stood up to put the kettle on. 'The police took it away.' She explained about the second threatening phone call.

'When do we get it back?' asked Ben. 'I know everyone's got mobiles these days, but that number is the one used for everything from the default number for the Manor to the theatre. I'm going to ring Ian. Even if I have to go to Canterbury to pick the bloody thing up.'

'I didn't think of that,' said Libby, 'although I doubt if I could have stopped them from taking it.'

'I suppose not.' Ben was finding Ian's numbers on his phone. 'I'll try his office phone first.'

Much to everyone's surprise, Ian answered straight away.

Libby made tea in the big brown teapot, listening to Ben's half of the conversation.

'He says yes, if we want it before tomorrow we can go and pick it up.' Ben put his phone back in his pocket.

Fran stood up. 'I ought to go.'

'I've just made tea!' said Libby, and Fran sat down again.

'We've been doing a preliminary rehearsal schedule for the show,' Fran told Ben. 'Libby's going to email me what she's worked out and I'll do a spreadsheet.'

'That's for accounts.' Libby frowned.

Ben and Fran laughed.

'Drink your tea,' said Ben, 'then I'm going to cart Mrs Sarjeant off to Canterbury to pick up a phone and treat her to dinner somewhere other than The Pink Geranium.'

Fran grinned. 'I won't tell Harry.'

When Ben and Libby arrived at Canterbury Police Station they were told DCI Connell would like to see them.

'Oh, I hate seeing him in his office,' muttered Libby, as they were ushered along a corridor. 'I wonder what he wants?'

Ian rose to his feet when they came in.

'Sorry to drag you up here,' he said, 'but it spares an officer the job of bringing it back to you tomorrow.'

'Thank you,' said Libby. 'What did you want to see us for?'

Ian smiled. 'The pleasure of your company?'

'Come off it,' snorted Libby.

'Sit down, for goodness sake,' said Ian. 'Ben, drag that chair over to the desk. Can I offer you anything? Tea, coffee?'

'No, we're going out to dinner,' said Ben. 'So what is it?'

'I wanted to tell you we'd found the owner of Chestnut Cottage.'

Chapter Nineteen

'Really?'

'Who is it?'

'It's actually the owners of the Notbourne Estate, which, of course, you were warned off.' Ian smirked. 'And it's a trust.'

Libby blinked. 'A trust?'

'Administered by a London law practice.'

'Have you asked them about why there was no documentation?' said Libby.

'Of course they have, Lib,' said Ben.

'They were completely unaware that anyone was staying in the cottage apparently. They see their job as purely management. They employ a company to keep the grounds tidy and place discreet advertisements in what they called the "quality magazines". They have two properties on the estate, and haven't had enquiries for either of them in a long time. They are only rented out as holiday lets.'

'If they have a company doing outside maintenance for them, why haven't they got someone looking after the two properties?' asked Ben.

'No idea. I asked them that, and they said if they rented them out they asked a local cleaning firm to go in.'

'So they've got keys?' said Libby. 'Is that how Lisa got in, do you think?'

'We have no idea about that either. By the time I got this information late this afternoon, both the outside

151

maintenance firm and the cleaning company were closed. I've left messages on their phones, emails and social media pages, but tomorrow's Saturday, so whether they'll be picked up is another matter.'

'How frustrating.' Libby bit her lip. 'And no joy with my message, either?'

'Not yet. You can have your unit back, but the message has got to be taken apart by our backroom boys. I doubt if we'll pick anything up.'

'You said a trust,' said Ben. 'Administered on behalf of who?'

'They were very cagey about that. I expect we could lean on them, but I can't see that it's relevant.'

'I found out that what was left of the estate was left to a Christobel Harris in 1985, but I couldn't find anything after that,' said Libby. 'Do you think she formed the trust? For her children, perhaps?'

'It's possible,' said Ian. 'If we come across evidence that it could be relevant, we'll dig into it, don't worry.'

'And what about my phone calls?'

'Apart from endorsing what they said,' said Ian with a grin, 'I'm of the opinion that it's the same person as before, for the same reason.'

'Wanting you to take it seriously?' said Ben. 'But whoever is making the calls knows exactly what Libby and Fran have been doing. They're being stalked.'

'If they don't do anything else that could be connected to the Lisa Harwood case they won't be stalked,' said Ian. 'There's no danger to either of them in my opinion.'

'The first time it was your fault,' said Libby. 'You took us up to the cliff path.'

'I took *Fran* up to the cliff path,' said Ian pointedly.

Libby, feeling heat creep up her neck, merely grunted.

'Well, thanks for filling us in, Ian,' said Ben, standing up.

'Yes, thanks,' muttered Libby.

Ian came round the desk to shake hands with Ben.

'Look, Libby, I know how difficult this is for you, but it really has nothing to do with you personally. If it'll keep you happy we've certainly no objection to you researching the Cheveley family, or even the Harrises, as long as you don't go poking around on the ground.'

Ian patted her shoulder and held the door open for them.

Libby managed to keep her temper under control until they got outside.

'Patronising idiot!' she thundered.

'Calm down, Lib,' Ben soothed. 'I don't think he meant to be patronising.'

'Well, he was.' Libby climbed into the passenger seat of the Range Rover. 'I've a good mind to …'

'To what?' said Ben. 'Please tell me you won't do anything stupid.' He turned round to leave the car park.

'He can't tell me –' she began.

'Tell you what to do? Yes, he can,' said Ben. 'He's a policeman, and a very forbearing policeman. If it was anyone else, any other force, do you think you'd be treated this way?'

Libby was silent for a moment. 'No, I suppose not,' she muttered eventually.

Ben drove to another of the city centre car parks nearer to the restaurant they'd chosen.

'He didn't even tell us the name of the law firm,' said Libby as they got out of the car.

'You could try looking in the – what was it? – quality magazines,' suggested Ben. 'For the small ads. That might tell you.'

'It might, but how would I know it was the right cottage? There must be hundreds of holiday rental cottages advertised in those sort of magazines. The "Country" ones.'

'What about an internet search? Surely nobody advertises only in magazines? You could be very specific with your search terms.'

'Worth a try, I suppose,' said Libby after a moment, then tucked her hand through Ben's arm. 'You know I'm awfully glad you helped me buy that first computer. I can't believe what a dinosaur I was before I met you and Fran.'

'You still haven't got a smartphone, though,' said Ben. 'I'll grant you entry to the twenty-first century when that happens.'

When they arrived home and plugged the charger/answerphone back in, the phone began to ring immediately.

'Go away,' said Ben. 'I'll listen, just in case.'

Libby went into the kitchen half listening, half trying not to.

Ben followed her, smiling.

'No worries. That was the treasurer of the Harriers asking for an invoice for the car park.'

'Really?' Libby let out the breath she didn't know she'd been holding.

'Chap called Nick Heap. Have you met him?'

'I don't think so,' said Libby with a frown. 'There were a couple of people at that meeting in The Sergeant At Arms who weren't introduced. The only people I know by name are young Roly, Steve the chairman, Davy Long and Kirsty Trent. Hang on – I know the name.' She thought for a moment. 'Sophie told us. But he isn't the treasurer. It was a woman's name who was the treasurer.

Now what did he do?'

'I don't know, and does it matter? He's presumably doing an errand for the treasurer. And we get paid. Not a lot, but we get paid.'

'That's something, I suppose.'

'I'll email him an invoice tomorrow. What should we charge, do you think?'

'I don't know! What does one usually charge for a field? And I don't suppose they've got much money.'

'No you're right.' Ben fetched the whisky bottle. 'Time I'm allowed a drink now.'

The following morning, after a discussion with Hetty, Ben decided to let the Harriers off payment as a gesture of goodwill.

'After all, I didn't expect to be paid in the first place,' he told Libby. 'I'll send him an email from here if I can borrow your laptop. Saves me from going up to the office.'

'Lazy,' said Libby, flicking him with a tea towel. 'And what are we doing after that?'

'I don't know. Do we have to do anything?'

'It's Saturday. People do things at weekends. Hobbies and stuff.'

Ben groaned. 'We're working tonight, remember? Do we have to do something today?'

'Oh, so we are.' Libby sighed. 'You know, these one-nighters are a pain. They make so much work.'

'They make money. And it's only you and me and Pete who have to work.'

When the theatre was hired out for a "one-nighter", usually either a singer or a comedian, Ben helped them sort out their staging, Peter worked lights and sound and Libby staffed the bar. If they could persuade anybody else to come in, they would, but most people who worked for the Oast Theatre were only really happy to work on their own shows. Tonight was a popular comedian, whose entourage had taken rooms at the pub. He apparently had a local lady friend who was being, as his manager said, "accommodating".

'Might as well go shopping, then,' said Libby. 'I can have a mooch round Canterbury.'

Ben eyed her warily. 'Do you want me to come with you?'

Libby grinned. 'No, of course not. I'll have lunch out, and try and think of something quick for tonight.'

'I'll do that,' said Ben. 'Seeing as how I've been let off the hook for the day.'

'Good lad,' said Libby. 'I'll go and get myself organised then.'

Canterbury was crowded. Never the emptiest of cities, weekends increased the amount of tourists to an uncomfortable degree. Having bumped and cursed her way through hordes of people, Libby gave up and made for the little pub she and Ben used whenever they came to Canterbury. Her friend the barman wasn't on duty, but a whey-faced girl with lank fair hair served her with a perfectly acceptable sandwich and glass of iced tonic water.

'Libby – Mrs Sarjeant!' said a voice behind her.

'Roly!'

He was standing by a corner table, a half finished plate of shepherd's pie in front of him.

'Won't you join me? If you're on your own, that is …' He went a familiar pink.

'Thank you,' said Libby, taking a seat. 'I escaped the crowds out there. I forgot what a spring Saturday could be like in town.'

'I don't really know why I came in, either,' said Roly,

resuming his seat. 'I get enough of Canterbury during the week.'

'You work here?' said Libby.

'Yes, in financial services.' He pulled the corners of his mouth down. 'Not exactly glamorous and not what I really wanted to do.'

'What was that?' asked Libby.

The pink deepened. 'I wanted to be an athlete. A runner.'

'But you are a runner,' said Libby, surprised.

'No, a professional runner. I wanted it to be a career. I was lined up to study Sports Science at uni.'

'And you didn't?' said Libby, after a pause.

'I had a medical. You have to.'

There was another pause, while Roly poked moodily at his shepherd's pie.

'And did they find something?' asked Libby gently. He nodded.

'I have a slight heart defect.'

Libby frowned. 'But you're still running.'

'Not competitively. I don't have to push myself. Believe me there's a difference.'

Libby took a chance.

'Was it the same heart problem that Lisa had?'

Roly looked up quickly and dropped his forkful of food.

'How – how did you –'

'Her husband told the police about it. That was why they were analysing the cup they found by the track.'

'They were?' Roly's eyes were wide with surprise. 'I didn't know about that.'

'So how did you know about it? Lisa's heart condition? We were told it wasn't common knowledge.' Libby watched him carefully.

'It wasn't talked about, but I think most people knew. She never took energy drinks or anything like that. She was very careful. I don't either.'

Libby ate some of her sandwich.

'Are you – er – investigating it, then?' said Roly carefully. 'Like Steve said?'

'No. We have no reason to, and the police are on the case.'

Roly frowned. 'Are they?'

'Of course they are. They must have questioned you? They've questioned everyone else, including my son Adam, who didn't even know her.'

'I still think if they'd looked a bit harder when she first went missing …'

'No, Roly. She was dead soon after she went missing. It wouldn't have helped.'

'How do they know that?' Roly's face was a picture of misery. 'They weren't taking it seriously!'

'They know it because of forensic tests,' said Libby, crossing her fingers. It was probably true.

She looked at him consideringly.

'Roly,' she said, 'have you been making threatening phone calls to me?'

Chapter Twenty

The pink in Roly's cheeks turned practically magenta.

'I'll take that as a yes, then, shall I?' Libby swallowed some tonic. 'A ploy to get the police to take the whole thing more seriously?'

Roly gave a jerky nod.

'Why bother yesterday, though? Lisa's been murdered. How much more seriously do you think the police could take it?'

'Because they're looking in the wrong direction!' Roly burst out. 'They don't know anything about her!'

Libby's eyebrows rose. 'And you do?'

He subsided back onto his bench seat, pushing his plate away.

'If you know anything about her that isn't common knowledge, you should let the police know,' said Libby virtuously. 'It doesn't do any good to try and hide things. Believe me, I know.'

Roly stayed silent. Libby sighed.

'Look, if you want to get the police to look in what you think is the right direction, you've got to tell them what that is.'

'I did,' said Roly gruffly. 'Yesterday.'

'When you warned me about Chestnut Cottage and Notbourne Court?'

He nodded.

'Were you following us?'

He shook his head. 'I drove past The Poacher and I

saw you and the other woman in the car park. I didn't know if you would know anything about Lisa's cottage or the Court.'

'So you told us.' Libby thought for a moment. 'Well, I think you'd better tell me what it is you think you know. Or tell the police.'

A crowd of people suddenly burst through the door. Libby tutted.

'Come on, let's go and sit in the gardens for a bit.' she stood up. Roly stayed seated. Libby bent towards him. 'Roly, if you want Lisa's murderer found you've got to tell somebody what you know. That's what you wanted, isn't it?'

She stood back and Roly got slowly to his feet, as pale now as he'd been pink before. She let him precede her out of the pub, then walked him firmly to Dane John Gardens.

'First of all,' she said, when they'd found a seat, 'why can't you tell the police exactly what it is you know?'

'Because I'm not supposed to know it.'

'Who says you're not?'

He looked surprised. 'I – well, Lisa, I suppose.'

'And she's dead. So what difference is it going to make?' Libby was getting exasperated. 'Don't make life more complicated than it already is, Roly. Just tell me what you know, or tell the police, I don't mind. I shall tell them, anyway.'

'Tell them that I told you?'

'Yes! You wanted me to tell them to look into Chestnut Cottage, so I'll tell them that.'

He didn't answer, just sat looking confused.

'Right. Let's try it another way.' Libby took a deep breath. 'Was Lisa doing something illegal?'

Roly practically fell off the end of the bench.

'She was. What was it? And what did it have to do

with Chestnut Cottage and Notbourne Court?'

'The owner,' Roly whispered eventually.

'Of the Court? And the cottage?'

Roly nodded.

'What did he – they – do?'

'She was working for him.' Roly was now deep in the throes of embarrassment.

'Working for him?' Libby was beginning to see. 'Was she – um – working in the sense of –' she searched for the right way to put it, 'of a "working girl"?'

'Parties,' he eventually managed. 'She told me it was parties.'

So Owen and Max's random theory had hit the nail on the head.

'And who is the owner?'

'I don't know. She wouldn't tell me that. Said it was better that I didn't know.'

'Why do you think she told you all this?' Libby stared at the boy curiously. 'She didn't tell anyone anything, according to the other members of the Harriers, and the police have found nothing at the cottage or on her computer.'

'She was different with me.' He sat up straighter, a small smile on his face. 'When we started running together, and she told me about her heart problems, I told her about mine. And she knew I was lonely.' The pink was returning. 'She told me she was, too. Despite the – the parties.'

'Were the parties at the cottage?' asked Libby.

'No. Although I never went there, but it isn't big enough, is it. And these were special parties.'

I bet they were, thought Libby, thinking of the parties she and her friends had heard about in the past.

'So where did you go?' asked Libby.

The pink once more became magenta. 'What do you mean?'

'I'm sorry,' said Libby, surprised. 'I assumed ...'

'Look, I've told you all you need to know.' Roly stood up. 'You can do what you like about it. I'm not talking to you any more.'

He turned and practically ran out of the gardens. Libby sat watching him for a minute before standing up and following more slowly. She was only just over the road from the police station, she reflected. Would it make sense to drop in there and leave a message for Ian?

Twice in twenty-four hours, she said to herself as she tentatively approached the desk.

'I believe DCI Connell is in the building. Who shall I say is asking?' The desk sergeant picked up the phone.

'Libby Sarjeant,' said Libby. 'With a J.'

A look of recognition passed over the sergeant's face, and he spoke into the phone. 'Take a seat, miss,' he said, ending the call.

Libby sat, feeling very uncomfortable. After a few minutes, DC Tomlinson appeared.

'Would you come this way, Mrs Sarjeant?' he said, indicating that she precede him. Libby led the way to Ian's office, then stepped aside for Tomlinson to knock on the door and announce her.

'Well, Lib, this is a surprise! Twice in two days. No, Tomlinson, stay. I may need you to take notes.'

Libby, surprised, sat down in the same chair she had used yesterday. 'Why do you think you might need notes?'

'I doubt you would come here if you hadn't got something you wanted to tell me.' Ian leant back in his chair and watched her face.

'Well, I have, but it might not be important.' She looked down at her hands. 'I've just seen Roly from the Harriers.'

'Roly ...' Ian reached for a file on his desk.

'Johnson, sir,' said Tomlinson.

'Thank you,' said Ian. 'How did this come about, Libby? Taking matters into your own hands again?'

Libby's stomach rolled and she lifted her chin defiantly.

'I came into Canterbury to do some shopping –'

'On a Saturday?' Ian's tone was disbelieving.

'Yes, on a Saturday. Ben stayed at home. I went into the little pub we use for lunch and this Roly was in there.'

'And you didn't know he would be, of course?'

'Oh, Ian, give it up. I don't know the boy. I don't even know what he was doing in Canterbury.'

'All right, all right, I believe you. And then what?'

'He brought the subject round to Lisa. He was the only one who had seemed be really sorry when she went missing. Said she used to run with him. Well –' Libby went on to repeat the conversation she'd had with Roly, including her ill-advised question which had sent him running for cover.

'And why didn't he tell us all this?' Ian's face had darkened.

'He seemed scared – I think because it was illegal. If it was – is. Oh, I don't know. But I thought I ought to tell you, and as I was only over the road ...'

'Thank you.' Ian stared at his desk for a moment. 'Tomlinson, where does this Johnson live?'

'I'll look it up –' began Tomlinson.

'Itching,' said Libby. 'He told us when we met the Harriers. He and Lisa ran a route through their two villages together.'

Ian looked amused. 'You have your uses.'

'Thank you,' said Libby, standing up. 'I'll get out of your way, now.'

'I'm sending Tomlinson over to Itching to have a word with Roly Johnson – he could give you a lift.'

'I've got the car, thanks,' said Libby. 'And it's going to cost me a fortune. I've been a lot longer than I intended.'

'Thanks again for the information, Libby.' Ian shook her hand and Tomlinson held open the door. 'You'd better get off and report to Fran, now.'

Libby grinned. 'I had, hadn't I?'

Libby rang Fran as soon as she got into the car, but neither Fran's mobile or landline was answered. She left a message on both, realising that it was probably because her friend was helping Guy in his gallery/shop. The weather was warming up, it was mid-May, Nethergate would be busy.

Back in Steeple Martin, she found Ben in the back garden, dozing under the cherry tree with Sidney on his lap. She made tea and took his out to him, waking him up and startling Sidney into an aggrieved bolt.

'I have news,' she said, sitting down on the other seat. 'Do you want to hear it?'

'What sort of news?' Ben's tone was wary.

'About Lisa Harwood.'

Ben groaned.

'It wasn't my fault and I've already told Ian all about it.'

'Go on then.' Ben struggled into a more upright position and took his mug.

Libby repeated her story and sat back looking triumphant.

'What does it mean, then?' Ben was looking faintly bewildered.

'What do you mean, what does it mean? The police have got something to go on, now! And that silly theory of Max and Owen's wasn't silly at all.'

'I still don't know how they managed to connect a missing runner with two missing dancers,' said Ben.

'I think it was the lack of evidence left behind,' said Libby.

'You don't think she would have been romancing to impress Roly?'

'Goodness, Ben! Even Ian was less sceptical.'

'Well, why did he tell you, of all people?'

'I expect because he knew who Fran and I were – we'd been introduced to the Harriers, after all – and he knew about us going with Ian to the cliff path. He knew – or suspected – there was more to Lisa's disappearance and death than was thought at first and he wanted to get it noticed. Just as we thought, if he made threats the police might take it more seriously. So when I tackled him with having made the phone calls, he more or less crumpled. Well, not right away, but in the end ...'

'You badgered the poor bugger,' said Ben, amused.

'A bit. Anyway, Ian was actually pleased with me. So I've got some brownie points chalked up.'

'Where did you say Roly lived?'

'Itching, just before you go down the little hill into Shott. Where Sandra and Alan Farrow live. Remember? Perseverance Row?'

'Vaguely. It's only a tiny place, isn't it?'

'Very. All the villages round there are a bit like something out of *Cold Comfort Farm*, actually.'

'Wicker men and rituals?'

'Not exactly. And we've had quite enough of those

sorts of things, thank you.' Libby stood up. 'I'm going to ferret about and find something for dinner.'

'I told you I'd sort it out, remember?' Ben got to his feet. 'So we're going to the caff.' He beamed and Libby laughed.

Peter joined them for an early dinner in The Pink Geranium. Ben had been up to the theatre to let in the comedian and his entourage, and promised to be back as soon as possible.

'He'll want a sound check,' said Peter. 'I'd better come up with you.'

'In that case, I might as well come too,' said Libby, so at half past six, they all trooped up the drive to the theatre. The comedian was on stage giving orders while his entourage darted hither and yon trying – and obviously failing – to obey them. Ben calmed everybody down and Peter called for the sound check to begin. Libby, always amused at the self-importance of some of the acts whom they entertained, departed to set up the bar.

Her phone rang.

'I've been trying to get hold of you,' said Fran.

'I tried to get hold of you, too, but I understood why I couldn't.'

'Sorry, did I sound peevish? What was your news?'

Libby once again repeated her story. Fran was silent for a long moment.

'Fran? What's up? Are you still there?'

'It's Saturday, isn't it?'

'Yes, all day.'

'Then why wasn't Roly here? They always run on Saturdays.'

'I didn't see him until lunchtime,' said Libby. 'He could have gone to Nethergate earlier.'

166

'I suppose so,' said Fran doubtfully. 'I just think it's odd.'

'Well, don't worry about it,' said Libby. 'Ian's got all the facts now, so it's in his hands. Look, I'll have to go, I'm setting up the bar, and I'll have to let the punters in soon – like in five minutes!'

'Sorry, I forgot you were on duty,' said Fran. 'Can we talk about this tomorrow?'

'Sure,' said Libby. 'Speak tomorrow.'

And why, she wondered, as she began pour ice into the ice bucket, did Fran want to talk about Roly's story. *As if*, she said to herself, as she went to open the main doors, *you don't want to talk about it yourself.*

Chapter Twenty-one

Fran called shortly after breakfast on Sunday morning. Ben, conforming to his role as English Country Gentleman, was sprawling on the sofa with the Sunday papers, so Libby sat at the kitchen table. The weather had turned grey and chilly, as is often its wont in May, so today was not a day for sitting under the cherry tree.

'So what do we think about Roly's story?' Fran began. 'It doesn't feel right at all, does it?'

'Doesn't it?'

'Well, the owner business. Ian already told you that the owner is a trust administered by a law firm – in the city, was it?'

'There must be a beneficiary of the trust somewhere, though, mustn't there?'

'I suppose it could always be one of those tontine things. They're administered by trusts, aren't they?'

'Tontine? Oh, I know, like the Alec Guinness film. He murders all the people who are in line for the succession.'

'No,' said Fran, 'that wasn't a tontine. A tontine is a sort of insurance policy. People hold equal shares in something – say the estate – and as each person dies, their share is divided among the remainder.'

'Ah,' said Libby. 'Not very likely, though, is it? The estate only seems to be a couple of cottages and a broken-down bit of wall.'

'Exactly. And this business of the parties. It sounds more like something made up to impress Roly.'

'That's exactly what Ben said,' said Libby. 'Perhaps I was too gullible, although I think he really believed it.'

'But why was he so scared of talking about it? Do you think she told him who the owner was, and that scared him?'

'Yes, she might have done, so that he would keep quiet.' Libby sighed. 'But that still leaves the question of why she was murdered and why there's no online or paper trail.'

'County archives,' said Fran. 'We could look there.'

'We could?' Libby's heart sank. All those dusty files and documents.

'We could ask Andrew Wylie.'

Andrew Wylie, Professor Emeritus of History, lived in Nethergate and had helped Libby and Fran with historical research on several occasions.

'We haven't spoken to him for ages,' said Libby. 'It would be a bit of a cheek.'

'Not if we phoned him and asked if he knew anything about the Court. He might know something, and if not, he might volunteer to find out. He's done that before.'

'Hmm.' Libby thought about it. 'It might work. And we might have to go to tea at his flat.'

'Is that so terrible?' asked Fran. 'I seem to remember he has a good line in cake.'

'Are you going to do it, then? Tomorrow, perhaps?'

'Who knew him better? You or me?' asked Fran.

'Equal,' said Libby, 'except that it was you who introduced me to Rosie. She introduced us to Andrew, really, didn't she?'

Rosie was the real name of the novelist Amanda George. She'd had a brief relationship with the professor, who had subsequently adopted her cat Talbot.

'All right,' said Fran, 'I'll ring him. I don't know what

we're going to find out, but it just seems a bit odd to me. Off-kilter. The whole thing has, right from the start.'

'What, even when she'd just disappeared?'

'Except that she hadn't, had she? She was already dead. Oh – and that reminds me. The heart condition. You said Roly knew about it?'

'Yes, and he has it, too. Or something similar.'

'But no one else knew?'

Libby frowned. 'I can't remember now. It was her husband who told the police about it, wasn't it?'

'I find that odd, too. I mean – why all this confiding in Roly, when the rest of the Harriers knew next to nothing about her, and she kept herself to herself so much.'

'I expect we're over-thinking this now,' said Libby. 'Let's just forget it for today, then we can see if Prof Andrew knows anything about the Court tomorrow. I've got to go and get ready for lunch at Hetty's now.'

'Already?' said Fran. 'I thought you didn't have to be there until one?'

'Half past twelve today, as she wants us all to have a drink together first. It would have been Greg's birthday.'

'Ah.' The late Greg Wilde was sadly missed.

'So I'll hear from you tomorrow, shall I?'

'Yes, I'll call you after I've spoken to him. Give my love to Hetty.'

'Goodness, Fran's got the bit between her teeth on this one,' Libby said to Ben on her way through the sitting room.

'And of course, you aren't encouraging her, are you?' Ben didn't look up from his newspaper.

'No, I'm not.' Libby paused. 'Well, no more than I can help.'

As well as Ben and Libby, Peter and his brother James, sons of Hetty's sister Millie (now resident in a luxury home for the bewildered), and Lenny and Flo were also gathered in the large sitting room at the Manor. Hetty brought out champagne and they all toasted Greg, who, said Ben, was the whole reason most of them were here in Steeple Martin.

'Hetty came down here because of him, Flo followed and married Frank Carpenter, Millie grew up here and married Dr David, and Pete and I just gravitated back.'

'I'm not, though,' said Libby.

'You are in a way,' said Peter. 'Harry and I bought the cottage and the caff because it was my home village and then we brought you here.'

'The search for Bide-A-Wee,' said Ben with a grin. 'I've heard all about it.'

'What's that?' Lenny squinted at them all. 'Whatcher sayin?'

'When I had to move,' said Libby, 'I needed to find an affordable house, so Peter and Harry, who I'd met through the theatre company I was working with, said they would help me find something.'

'Did they actually find anything for you that wasn't in Steeple Martin?' asked James, amused.

'A couple,' said Libby. 'A ghastly sixties bungalow and a brand new terraced house on an estate. They knew perfectly well neither of them were suitable. Then they turned up with three gorgeous cottages in Steeple Martin. They said I needed to be near them as I got older.'

'In case she fell,' agreed Peter solemnly.

Hetty snorted.

'Well I'm glad you brought her here, anyway,' said Ben, patting Libby's arm.

Hetty lifted her glass to Libby. 'Cheers, gal.'

They finished dinner and Hetty demanded they stay for port or brandy, according to taste, back in the sitting room. Libby stretched out on one of the sofas just as Harry came through from the hall.

'Finished with my lot so I thought I'd come up and see you all,' he said, beaming at Hetty. 'By the way, Libby, your phone was singing away to itself in the kitchen, so I rescued it and brought it in.' He tossed her the phone.

'One missed call,' she said. 'Oh, and a text message.' She sighed. 'Remember what it was like when people couldn't get hold of you?'

'Who is it?' asked Ben suspiciously.

'Ian.' Libby's face fell.

'What does he say?'

'Did Roly tell me yesterday where he was going when he left me?'

'And did he?' said Ben.

Libby shook her head. 'Of course not.' She looked up. 'Oh, Lord. It sounds as though he's disappeared now, doesn't it?'

'What's this?' asked Harry. 'I thought you were staying out of this murder?'

Flo and Lenny woke up and James said 'What?'

'She is,' defended Ben. 'This really isn't her fault.'

'What isn't? Who's Roly?' asked James.

Ben gave them a potted version of events since Lisa Harwood's disappearance.

'You're not talking about Roly Johnson, are you?' said James when Ben had come to a stop.

'I don't know –' began Ben.

'Yes! That's him!' said Libby. 'They told me at the police station. Do you know him?'

'Not very well.' James was frowning. 'He lives in Itching, doesn't he? With his parents.'

'With his parents?' said Libby. 'Oh, poor people.'

'Look, we're jumping to conclusions, here,' said Ben.

'He may not have disappeared, and to be honest, if he's still at home with his parents, it makes sense that he would take off every now and then.'

'That's true, Lib,' said Peter. 'You haven't actually spoken to Ian. You don't know what's happened.'

'It's the investigative nose,' said Harry. 'Twitching like mad.' He gave Hetty a kiss and sat down next to Peter. 'Turn off the phone, love, and pretend to be normal.'

Libby smiled weakly and did as he suggested.

'Come on,' said Ben, 'let's load the dishwasher before we go.' He stood up and pulled Libby to her feet.

'Why did you do that?' she whispered as she followed him into the kitchen. 'Hetty obviously doesn't want us to go yet.'

'Well, we won't go, but the dishwasher's still got to be loaded, even if we leave her to do her pots as usual. But you want to return Ian's call, don't you?'

'Oh!' Libby's face cleared. 'You're clever. I'll send him a text.'

She switched her phone back on and replied to Ian's text.

Ian replied almost immediately. *Sorry – forgot you'd be at Hetty's!*

'Well, it obviously isn't that serious, then,' said Ben.

'How can you tell?' Libby began scraping leftovers into the bin.

'You wouldn't have got a light-hearted apologetic answer if it was.'

'Oh. Well, I hope so.' Libby concentrated on the plates.

'You're not convinced.'

'I don't know. I'll wait and see.'

Ben sighed and began collecting glasses.

174

It wasn't until they arrived home that Libby's curiosity could be assuaged. As well as the original message from Ian that duplicated the one on her mobile, there was another.

'Just to let you know, as you will be consumed with curiosity,' Ian said, 'young Roly Johnson didn't return home on Saturday, but his mother said he's frequently away at weekends. He runs with the Harriers and spends the rest of the weekend with some of them. We'll catch up with him on Monday.'

'But,' said Libby to Ben as she deleted the message, 'he wasn't running yesterday. Fran and I wondered why. And another thing – Sophie said he was a loner like Lisa.'

'He still might have had a couple of friends among the Harriers,' said Ben. 'Don't be suspicious of everything, Lib.'

'I'm sorry.' Libby sighed. 'It's a habit, I suppose.'

'As Hal said, the investigative nose. Go and sit down and I'll make us a cuppa.'

After Ben had gone to the estate office on Monday morning, Libby called Fran and told her about Ian's phone calls.

'Everyone thought I was over-reacting when I said it looked as though he'd disappeared too.'

'That was the conclusion I would have jumped to,' said Fran. 'And you say James knows him?'

'Not well, he said. He knew he lived in Itching with his parents.'

'Nothing else?'

'I didn't dare ask. They were all shutting me up.'

'Oh, well, I expect we'll hear eventually. Now, do you want to hear what Andrew said?'

'Oh! You've already called him?' said Libby in surprise.

'Yes. I remembered he gets up early. Anyway, he knew Notbourne Court.'

'Really? How well? Does he know who owns it?'

'Slow down, Lib.' Fran laughed. 'He knows it because – get this – it's a listed ancient monument!'

'No! But there was no mention of that online anywhere, I'm sure of it! And it isn't that old, surely?'

'The old Court was built on the site of an earlier burial place, or possibly a fort. Andrew said he would go off to Maidstone and start digging – if you'll pardon the pun. His, not mine.'

'What, today?'

'Yes, today. You know what he's like. I think he's bored again. He'll let us know as soon as he's got anything.'

'So the chase is on,' said Libby.

'Yes, I rather think it is,' said Fran.

Chapter Twenty-two

'Have you heard anything about Roly, Ma?'

'Oh, hello, darling. How nice to hear from you.' Libby regarded the phone with disfavour.

'Sorry, Ma, but one of Ian's minions has just been round to question Sophie.'

'What?' Libby sat down on the stair.

'He's gone missing, apparently. I thought you might know something about it.'

Libby's stomach performed a somersault.

'I might. But I didn't know he was officially missing.'

'What, then? Only it rather upset Sophie. I think the whole club's getting jittery.'

Libby sighed. 'I don't blame them. As far as Roly's concerned, I saw him by accident in Canterbury on Saturday and he told me a few things I then reported to Ian.'

'So it's your fault he's gone?'

Libby's stomach performed another loop. 'How can it be my fault?'

'He's run from the police.'

'No. He left me and never arrived home. He had no idea the police wanted to see him.'

This probably wasn't true, she realised. Roly would have guessed she would go straight to the police with his information.

'How do you know he never arrived home?' Adam sounded positively accusatory.

'Ian called me yesterday to ask if he'd said where he was going when he left me.'

Adam let out a gusty sigh. 'Oh, Ma! Why can't you leave things alone?'

Libby felt her cheeks heat up. 'Adam, that is totally unfair! I bumped into Roly by accident, and, as it happened, he confessed to being the person who'd made those threatening phone calls.'

'He – what? What phone calls?'

'Look, this is nothing to do with you.' Libby fought to keep her temper. 'I'm sorry Sophie's been questioned again, but it isn't my fault, or Fran's. I'm also sorry young Roly's disappeared, he seems a nice lad, if misguided, and I'm even sorrier that Lisa Harwood is dead. I did not ask to be mixed up in any of it, and next time you or Sophie consider asking Fran or I if we could approach the police for you, you'd better think again. You now know why we said no.'

There was silence at the other end of the line. Determined not to be the one who broke it, Libby concentrated ferociously on her feet.

'I'm sorry, Ma.' Adam spoke quietly. 'I didn't – well, realise, I suppose. Sorry.'

'That's all right. If I hear anything from Ian, I'll let you know, but I'm unlikely to.'

'OK, thanks. Sorry.'

'Oh, stop it. Shall I see you at the caff on Wednesday?'

'I think so. I'll let you know.'

Libby was still sitting on the stairs when Ben came in from the estate office.

'What's up?'

'I had a row with Adam.'

'You what?' Ben's eyebrows flew upwards. 'You never row with your children.'

'Well, I did.' Libby let out a shaky breath and stood up. 'Is the sun over the yard-arm? I could do with a drink.'

Over a comfortingly large gin and tonic, Libby regaled Ben with the telephone conversations of the day.

'And have you heard from Andrew Wylie yet?' he asked when she'd finished.

'No, but I'd hardly expect him to dash over to Maidstone, find everything they have on Notbourne Court and phone us back about it in one day.' Libby leant back against the cushions.

'Worrying about young Roly, though,' said Ben. 'Looks as though you were right yesterday.'

'Do you really think it's my fault he's gone missing?' Libby asked. 'I mean, although he didn't know the police were going to come after him, he would have guessed I'd tell them.'

'He told you about Lisa and the owner of Notbourne Court. It's his own fault, not yours. He should have told the police all this in the first place.'

'I know. But I can't help wondering if any of it was true. I mean, I'm sure she told him, as he said, but it sounds like romancing, to me. Why would she tell Roly?'

'Because he would be easily impressed?' Ben came and sat next to her on the sofa. 'Shall we watch the news?'

'I'd better start dinner,' said Libby. 'Call me if there's anything interesting.'

'Report on *Kent and Coast* about Lisa Harwood,' Ben called ten minutes later.

Libby looked round the doorway in time to see Campbell McLean doing a piece to camera in front of the Canterbury Police Station.

179

'... no news on the investigation so far,' he was saying. 'Police say they are pursuing various lines of enquiry. Back to you ...'

'What had he said before that?' Libby asked.

'Just a shot of the place her body was found, then it went to him – saying nothing, really.'

'Nothing about Roly, then?'

'No. Perhaps they've found him?'

'Perhaps. I hope so.' Libby went back to the kitchen.

Half way through the evening, Fran called.

'Andrew's back from Maidstone full of himself. He says would we like to go over tomorrow morning to see the results.'

'And you said yes?'

'Of course. I said, unless you said no, we'd see him at eleven in the morning.'

'Oh, good. Did he give you any clues?'

'Only that it had been very interesting. Let's hope it's interesting for us, too.'

Libby related the story of her phone call with Adam.

'It upset me, you know,' she concluded.

'The youngsters don't think,' said Fran gently. 'Sophie told Guy earlier, but she didn't blame anyone. She was a bit shaky about it, Guy said.'

'Adam said the whole group were jittery.'

'I expect they are,' said Fran with a sigh. 'Well, there's nothing we can do about it.'

'No.' Libby thought for a moment. 'Tell me, why are we investigating Notbourne Court?'

'To find the owner,' said Fran, sounding surprised.

'Hmm,' said Libby. 'Sure it's not just being nosy?'

'Perhaps it is, a bit,' said Fran after a pause. 'Do you want to stop?'

'No.' Libby sighed. 'We might as well see what

Andrew's found out.'

Andrew lived in a small block of apartments at one end of Canongate Drive in Nethergate. It had views over the roofs of the town to the sea, and, as usual, Andrew had opened the doors to the balcony when Libby and Fran arrived the following morning. On the big dining table in front of the open doors, the cat Talbot lay across a pile of papers in somnolent ecstasy.

As they came into the room, a slight woman with greying dark hair rose from a chair in the corner.

'Libby, Fran – I'd like you to meet Faith Conway,' said Andrew.

'Pleased to meet you,' said Libby, sticking out a hand.

'Hello,' said Fran, doing the same.

'Hello,' said Faith, in a soft Irish accent. 'I'm sure you're wondering why I'm here ...'

'I'll explain when we've all sat down with our coffee,' said a beaming Andrew. 'Now you sit at the table, Libby and Fran, and I'll bring the coffee. And cake, of course!'

Andrew brought in a tray containing the coffee pot, milk jug, cups and saucers and cake.

'Lemon drizzle this morning,' he said. 'Faith, come up here and join us.'

When they were all seated round the table and Talbot had been shooed off, Andrew drew his notebook towards him.

'This was absolutely fascinating,' he began. 'I already knew about the site, as I explained to Fran yesterday, as there have been one or two exploratory digs there. Late Roman and Romano-British finds have been made there, and although it's difficult to say, it is thought that a sixth or seventh-century hall stood on the site. What's remaining is part of the eighteenth-century house.'

He paused and pulled more papers towards him.

'I began searching the archives and managed to find out quite a lot about the Hays family. You know about them?'

'Lord Cheveley?' said Libby. 'Yes, I know about him, and the fact that Stephanie was the last of the direct line and died childless. She left the estate, such as it was, to Christobel and Robert Harris in 1985.'

'Ah!' Andrew held up a finger. 'But what she didn't know, and for some reason hadn't bothered to find out, was that there was another direct descendant, from a different line.'

'So she should have left it to them?' said Fran.

'Not exactly,' said Andrew, grinning at Faith. 'It should have gone straight to the other descendant.'

'Good Lord!' Libby looked from Andrew to Faith. '*You*?'

Faith smiled. 'My father, who knew nothing about it at the time. We lived in Ireland then, and I knew nothing about the family, or why I didn't seem to have any grandparents on my father's side. My children hadn't been born, either, so I didn't worry about it.' She picked up her coffee cup and looked at Andrew. He gave a quick nod, and carried on.

'I expect it seems odd that after having looked into it only yesterday, I should suddenly be able to produce the missing heir today, as it were.'

'It does, rather,' said Libby.

'I promise you, it's not as odd as it seems. When I was asking for access to all these old documents, my friend at the archive centre happened to remark that it was odd, but she'd had a request for the same material from someone else very recently.'

'And that was me,' said Faith. 'When my father died,

or rather, just before, he told me all about the row his father had had with the rest of his family. Apparently old Lord Cheveley had run through all the money – or his father had, anyway – and he couldn't afford the house.'

'We read about that,' said Fran.

'So he tried to give it away, sell what he could and pull the rest down. He had wanted my grandfather to stay there and try and put the family fortune back together, but my grandfather could see it was hopeless and left, eventually ending up in Ireland after the First World War. He never looked back, and never heard from the Cheveley family – or the Hays, as was their family name – again. My father had tried to find out a bit about them, but there was no internet back in the mid-eighties, so he gave up. But then ...' she paused and looked at Andrew '– this is the odd part – a few years ago, I received a letter from someone called Rowena Harris.'

'Related to Christobel and Robert Harris?' said Libby.

'How did she find you?' asked Fran.

Faith gave a soft laugh. 'She was doing genealogical research, she said, and she'd traced the line back from Stephanie – who was the daughter of my grandfather's brother – and discovered that the Notbourne Estate should have gone to our line as she died childless. Or that's what she thought.'

'Like a fairy story,' said Libby.

'Except that there's not exactly much value to the estate,' said Andrew.

'So what happened next? You said this was a few years ago,' said Fran.

'We kept in touch, and I couldn't see that there could be any gain for anybody by me trying to claim the estate. It would cost a fortune in legal fees, anyway. Then, quite suddenly, I stopped hearing from her. I tried to find her –

we'd got friendly enough to connect on social media, and we emailed regularly – but I couldn't.'

'In other words,' said Andrew, 'she'd disappeared.'

Chapter Twenty-three

'Not another one!' said Libby.

'Eh?' said Andrew, startled.

'This is the third disappearance we've heard about in the last two weeks,' said Fran. 'Although I must say this sounds rather different.'

'Who were the others?' asked Faith, leaning forward.

'We'll tell you all about it when you've finished your story,' said Libby. 'If there is more, of course.'

'Only a little,' said Faith. 'I was quite worried about her. She was a widow – Harris was her maiden name, of course – and I searched every letter and email I'd had from her for her married name, but she seemed to use Harris for everything. Her social media page has gone, and there's been no other activity, though her email address is still live. We had no mutual friends, so there was no one to ask. I knew where she lived, so in the end I decided to come over for a holiday. I'm a widow, too, you see, and the children are all flown, so ...' She looked down at her lap.

'And were you able to find out anything?' Fran asked gently, after a moment.

'I went to the address I had, but there was nobody there. She never mentioned any children, so I didn't know what to do. Which was why I'd been to the archive office, but I hadn't found out anything relevant, except that what Rowena said about the inheritance was true.'

'So I thought,' said Andrew, 'you would be bound to

know more than I do about what's going on in the present, if you bothered to ask me to do some research.' He sat back looking smug.

'So your obliging archives contact just handed over Faith's contact details?' said Fran doubtfully.

'No, she phoned Faith's hotel and then handed me the phone. All very proper.'

'And you came here? That was trusting of you,' said Libby.

'Oh, the lady at the museum said she knew him well,' said Faith, smiling at Andrew. 'So he came over to the hotel and we had a drink at the bar yesterday evening. And he told me all about his own research and,' she looked a bit confused, 'quite a lot about you two, I'm afraid.'

Libby let out a hoot of laughter. 'I bet he did! He did tell you how much he's been mixed up in our adventures, I hope?'

'I touched on it.' Andrew's cheeks were reddening. 'Now tell us what your interest in all this is.'

Libby looked at Fran, who nodded, and embarked on an explanation, starting with the disappearance of Lisa Harwood on the Nethergate 5K, and finishing with the disappearance of Roly Johnson on Saturday.

'And you aren't involved?' Andrew looked sceptical.

'No, we're really not. We're just collateral damage,' said Libby.

'It's because people expect us to be involved if anything like this happens. Hell, the Nethergate Harriers even asked us to investigate,' said Fran.

'You said that the police found out that a trust administered the estate,' said Faith with a frown. 'Rowena never mentioned that.'

'That is odd, isn't it?' said Andrew. 'And I found no

mention of it anywhere in the archives, either.'

'Do you think she set it up herself quite recently?' asked Libby.

'I've no idea. I would have thought, under the circumstances, she would have told me,' said Faith.

'What do we do now, then, ladies?' asked Andrew, leaning back in his chair.

'I think,' said Libby, after a moment, 'that with Faith's permission, the police ought to be told.'

Faith nodded. 'Rowena's missing. And we don't know how long she's been missing. I agree.'

'But it hasn't got anything to do with Lisa Harwood's death,' said Andrew, 'other than the fact that she lived in a cottage rented from Rowena.'

'Or the trust,' said Libby. 'I still think that's very odd. But perhaps with Faith's extra knowledge, the police can get through to the snotty lawyers.'

'What do I do next, then?' asked Faith. 'Could you do it for me?'

Fran and Libby looked at each other.

'In this case,' said Fran, 'even if we don't report it direct to Ian, I think it would carry more weight if one of us does it. If we say we've found out that the owner of Notbourne Court has gone missing, it'll be taken more seriously than if a member of the public does it.'

'Good.' Andrew beamed round at the three women. 'More cake, anyone?'

Fran stood up. 'I'm going to call the police now,' she said. 'Then, if they need to, they can set up a meeting with Faith on the spot.'

She went out on to the balcony, where Talbot joined her, rubbing round her ankles. Andrew watched him for a moment.

'I sometimes wonder if he misses Rosie, you know,' he said.

'I doubt it,' said Libby. 'She was always going off and leaving him, wasn't she?'

'That's true,' said Andrew. He turned to Faith. 'I adopted Talbot, you see, from a mutual friend of ours. He used to be an outdoor cat, but he seems to have adapted to living inside.'

Libby regarded the big cat with affection. 'He's too fat and lazy to rush about outside these days, Andrew. He's fine.'

Fran came in through the French windows.

'DCI Connell would like a word with you, Faith,' she said, holding out the phone.

Faith stared at it nervously for a moment, then took it very gingerly from Fran's hand. 'Hello?' she said. Fran gestured for her to go out on the balcony and she edged round the table. Fran sat down again, and she, Andrew and Libby all looked at each other.

'Did you call Ian direct?' asked Libby.

'No, I called the police station. When I said who I was and what information I had, I was patched straight through. I don't even know where he is.'

'Wasn't he cross?'

'No, because the station had put me through. He was interested, but didn't say a lot to me.'

Faith came back through the door looking a little shell-shocked.

'What did he say?' asked Andrew.

'He wants to meet me. A statement, or something.'

'Does that mean the police station?' said Libby.

'Well – no. Actually, he seemed to think I was staying with you. One of you.' She shared a smile between Libby and Fran. 'Seemed surprised when I said I wasn't.

188

Anyway, he said he would interview me at my hotel later today. Which is a nuisance.'

'Why?' asked Fran.

'I was going to check out and find somewhere a bit cheaper. And I don't feel at home in those big anonymous hotels.'

'The pub,' said Fran, Libby and Andrew together.

'The pub?' echoed Faith.

'In Steeple Martin,' said Libby, 'where I live. Comes highly recommended. Shall I give them a ring now?'

Faith was still looking bewildered.

'It's probably best,' said Fran. 'You'll be nearer the Notbourne Estate. And if it should become part of the investigation ...'

'I don't see how I could be part of it,' said Faith.

'But are you planning on staying around for a little while?' asked Andrew.

'Well, yes ...'

'It's nice and quiet, it's only got three rooms and I'm round the corner,' said Libby.

'All right,' said Faith. 'I suppose it makes sense.' She gave Fran back her phone. 'I'd better go and check out of the hotel, hadn't I? Will you let me know how to get to your village?'

'Are you driving?' asked Libby.

'Yes – I hired a car.'

'Satnav?'

'That's how I got here.'

'Right, give me your mobile number and I'll send you the postcode,' said Libby. 'Mind you, you'll go through the village on your way back to Maidstone.'

Numbers were exchanged, Andrew was thanked by all parties who then left to go their separate ways. Andrew leant over his balcony, waving as they all drove off. Fran was following Libby back to Steeple Martin, where they both intended to wait for Faith to relocate.

As they parked opposite number 17 Allhallow's Lane, they were both taken aback to see Ian Connell just turning away from Libby's front door.

'You were together this morning?' Ian said as they crossed the road.

'Yes.' Fran said. 'Why?'

'I suppose I assumed that you were with this Mrs Conway in Nethergate and Libby was here.'

'And?' prompted Libby as she unlocked the front door.

'I wanted to ask a few questions before I met her, and I thought you'd know.'

'Were you in the area?' asked Fran.

'I was.'

They both waited for more, but Ian wasn't saying.

'Well, go and sit down, then,' said Libby. 'Do you want tea or anything?'

'No thanks,' said Ian. 'What can you tell me about this lady?'

'I told you when I rang,' said Fran. 'She came over from Ireland because she was looking for Rowena Harris, who it appears is – or was – the owner of Notbourne Court.'

'And it was your friend Professor Wylie who found her? Tell me how.'

Fran looked at Libby. Libby sighed. 'We asked him if he knew anything about Notbourne Court. He knew about the seventh-century building that had been there, but said he'd enjoy going and looking through the archives at Maidstone.' Libby went on to tell the story of how Andrew had then found Faith. 'Terrific coincidence,' she finished.

'Too much of a coincidence?' suggested Ian.

'How could that be?' gasped Libby.

'Nonsense, Ian,' said Fran.

'Anyway, she's moving from Maidstone to the pub here this afternoon, so you can talk to her there,' said Libby.

'I knew it. I thought she must already be holed up with one of you,' said Ian. 'Please don't interfere any more. I'm sure you feel she needs protecting, but I repeat: *don't interfere.*'

He stood up. 'I'll speak to you later.'

'He can't honestly suspect Faith!' Libby said, as she shut the door behind him.

'It does look odd her turning up right at this time, you must admit,' said Fran. 'Although what she could have to do with Lisa I don't know.'

'At least we know who owns the Court now.' Libby went through to the kitchen to see if she had anything for lunch hidden away in the fridge.

'It makes what Roly told you even more suspect, though, doesn't it?' Fran followed her. 'Rowena certainly wasn't the person Roly was referring to.'

'So either Lisa was lying when she told the tale to Roly, or Roly was lying when he talked to me.' Libby shut the fridge door. 'I could make soup again?'

'Why did Roly ring you up, then, if he was lying?'

'I don't know. It's all beyond me. Ian's got everything we know, now, so it's up to him.'

'Hmm.' Fran was frowning. 'Come on, let's go and have a sandwich for lunch at the pub.'

'Then we could wait for Faith to book in,' said Libby.

'If she does,' said Fran. 'She might have changed her mind by the time she gets back to Maidstone. She'd never met us before, after all.'

'Shall I ring her? I've got her number.'

'No, that's pushy. If she arrives at the pub, we'll see her, but we don't want her to feel uncomfortable.'

But just as they finished their sandwiches and Fran was ordering a lemonade for herself and a half of lager for Libby, Faith appeared in the bar.

'Everything all right?' Libby asked her.

'Yes, thank you.' Faith sat down at their table. 'The manager told me you were here. I've ordered a sandwich, but you've finished yours. Don't let me keep you.'

'We've got drinks to finish,' said Libby. 'And it's horrible eating on your own in a place like this.'

'Faith,' Fran said, sitting down beside her, 'you didn't tell us where Rowena was living. Presumably not anywhere near the Court? And when exactly did she go missing?'

'Well, I don't know, *exactly*, I only know when I received her last email. She lived in London, and she'd been talking about coming down to Kent to make an inspection visit, which she did every now and then, although the running of the estate, or what was left of it, was left to someone else. A firm of lawyers, I think she said.'

'Yes, the police found that out, although they were told it was some kind of trust. We told you that, and you said she'd said nothing about a trust, but that must have been the posse of snotty lawyers.' said Libby. 'And you say she was coming down for an inspection? When had she last done that?'

'A few years, she said,' said Faith. 'Why?'

'Because somebody definitely didn't want her to come down again.'

Chapter Twenty-four

'You must tell Ian that when he talks to you,' said Fran. 'It's very important.'

'Is it?' Faith was looking bewildered again.

'Somebody – Lisa Harwood – was staying in Chestnut Cottage, and she shouldn't have been there. Somebody else had let her in. If your Rowena had come down, the game would've been up, wouldn't it?'

'I'll take your word for it,' said Faith tiredly. 'I can't follow all this really. I think I just ought to go back to Ireland and forget all about it.'

'If you think so,' said Libby doubtfully, 'but talk to Ian first – the policeman, you know – and let us show you what's left of the Court. You can have a quiet few days' holiday, and then go home.'

'All right.' Faith gave them a tired smile. 'Will you be here when the policeman comes to talk to me?'

'I don't suppose he'd let us stay,' said Fran, 'but he really isn't frightening at all.'

Faith's sandwich arrived, and by mutual and tacit consent, they changed the subject, until a shadow fell across their table.

'Good afternoon, ladies,' said Ian. 'May we join you? This is DC Turnbull.'

The woman standing just behind Ian nodded her sleek blonde head.

Libby raised her eyebrows, eyes wide.

'Shall we leave you?' asked Fran.

'Not at all,' said Ian, holding out a hand to Faith. 'Mrs Conway, I presume?'

He pulled up two more chairs for himself and Turnbull, and they all shuffled round to make room. Faith looked scared.

'Now, Mrs Conway, perhaps you could tell me again what you told me on the phone? And anything else you can remember? DC Turnbull will make notes if you don't mind.'

'Um – Ian,' said Libby. 'I don't think Fran and I should be here, really.'

Ian gave her a wry smile. 'It's unorthodox, I know, but I have the feeling Mrs Conway will feel a lot happier if you stay.'

Faith nodded and Libby subsided.

Faith's story coincided exactly with what she'd told Ian before, and included the information Libby and Fran had just heard.

'And you thought what?' Ian turned to Fran and Libby. They looked at each other.

'Lisa wasn't supposed to be in Chestnut Cottage and Rowena was coming down to have a look round,' said Fran.

'Which means we must start looking for Mrs Harris, now,' said Ian. He let out a frustrated breath. 'I don't know how it is, but you two manage to make every case more complicated than it was at the start.'

Fran and Libby simultaneously gasped in outrage.

'It isn't us!' said Libby. 'We had nothing to do with it.'

'I'm sorry. I put it badly.' Ian nodded to DC Turnbull and she closed her notebook. 'I'm grateful that you brought this to my attention.'

'It links the cases, doesn't it?' said Fran. 'And makes

Lisa's death slightly easier to understand.'

'I wouldn't say that,' said Ian. 'I can understand that Mrs Harris might have had to disappear, but that was well before Mrs Harwood's death, so why was she killed?'

DC Turnbull was looking faintly shocked. Libby leant towards her. 'Don't worry about it. We've known each other for a long time.'

Turnbull coloured and Ian smiled at her. 'Yes, I'm afraid these two are known to the police. And occasionally, known to be useful.'

'Or annoying,' said Libby. 'What shall we do now?'

'You will do nothing,' said Ian, standing up. 'At some point, we'll ask Mrs Conway to sign a statement, and that is all we shall need from her for the moment. Meanwhile, ladies, just stay out of trouble.'

'Of course,' said Fran serenely. 'See you tomorrow?'

Faith and DC Turnbull both looked surprised. Ian coloured, very slightly.

'Possibly,' he said. 'Thank you all for your help.'

'He's a friend,' Libby explained to Faith as Ian practically hustled Turnbull out of the door. 'We usually see him on Wednesday evenings here at the pub.'

'Oh,' said Faith, not looking as though she understood. 'He's very good-looking.'

'He is, isn't he,' said Libby, avoiding Fran's eye.

'There's something I forgot to tell him, though.' Faith frowned down at her empty plate.

'What's that?' asked Libby.

'What Rowena Harris's married name was, I should think,' said Fran. 'He kept referring to her as Mrs Harris. I wondered why you didn't correct him.'

'I didn't think. I've never been questioned by the police before.'

'We'll leave a message at the police station,' said Fran.

'I don't want to risk Ian's personal phones again!'

Fran was put through to CID and gave her message to the person who answered the phone.

'Oh – what was her name, Faith?' She held her hand over the phone. 'Samuels,' she repeated into it after Faith told her. 'Thank you.'

'So,' said Libby, 'Rowena Samuels. The daughter of Mr and Mrs Harris, who inherited the house from the Hays family. And who thinks it should go back to them.'

'There really isn't much there,' said Fran. 'Two cottages, is it? Chestnut and another one, I think.'

'Maple Cottage,' said Faith. 'Not far from Chestnut, Rowena said.'

'We didn't come across that, did we?' said Libby.

Fran shook her head. 'Maybe we'll find it when we take Faith over for a look.'

'Do you mind if we don't go today?' asked Faith. Her voice, always quiet, was almost inaudible now.

'You've had quite a day, haven't you?' said Libby. 'We'll leave you to settle in, now. Is there anything you want?'

Faith smiled timidly. 'No, thank you. I can call you if I need to, can I?'

'Of course.' Libby stood up.

'It's been nice meeting you.' Faith stood and turned to Fran. 'And thank you.'

'Will she be all right, do you think?' asked Libby, as she and Fran walked back to Allhallow's Lane. 'After all, we did bulldoze her a bit.'

'I think she'll be fine,' said Fran. 'And she's not as frail as she makes out. She came over here from Ireland on her own, hired a car and started making enquiries. I should say she's quite resourceful. And it wouldn't surprise me a bit if our Prof Wylie comes beetling over to make sure she's all right.'

'Really? Well, if he does, I hope it works out better than his romance with Rosie.'

'He's old enough to look after himself,' said Fran. 'Now. I shall come up tomorrow evening, as I've told Ian I would. Is there anything we can do at the theatre?'

'No, but if you're coming up, shall we see if Harry's got room for us all at the caff?'

'That would be nice,' said Fran. 'And I'll try and find out from Sophie if any of the Harriers has the surname Samuels.'

'Or Harris or Hays, I suppose,' said Libby. 'Do you really think it's got something to do with Notbourne Court? Lisa's death, I mean.'

'It looks like it,' said Fran. 'I'm sure Ian will find something.'

Neither Fran nor Libby heard anything from either the police or Faith Conway over the next twenty-four hours. Libby resisted the urge to call Faith to see if she was all right, and Fran to see if she'd found anything out. She concentrated ferociously hard on a painting for Guy's gallery, and roughed out a few sketches for future paintings. She was surprised to see that the last two were rather impressionistic images of the remaining wall of Notbourne Court.

When she and Ben arrived at the Pink Geranium, they found Fran and Guy already at a table with the Rev. Patti and Anne Douglas and, surprisingly, Faith Conway and Andrew Wylie on the sofa in the left-hand window. Faith smiled hesitantly, but Andrew beamed and stood up.

'I've already said hello to the others,' he said, waving a hand in the direction of the other table. 'Nice to see you again, Ben.'

'And you,' said Ben politely, shaking hands. 'And you

must be Mrs Conway.'

'Faith, please,' said Faith in her fading voice.

'We'll see you later,' said Libby, moving as fast as she could to their own table.

'You were right,' she said to Fran as she sat down. 'That Andrew's a fast mover.'

'He hasn't got any time to waste,' said Anne. 'Sorry, was that bad taste?'

'You're terrible, you know that?' said Patti. 'Fran's been bringing us up to date with everything that's been happening, Libby. How on earth do you get yourselves mixed up in these things?'

'Not on purpose,' said Libby. 'Let's talk about something else or it will look as if we're talking about *them*.' She turned to Guy. 'I've just finished a painting for you. I would have brought it over tonight, but it's not dry yet. And I've done a couple of little studies, as well.'

They continued to talk art for most of the meal, a subject Patti and Anne were both interested in. They had been on a painting holiday in Italy only a couple of years ago, which they had loved.

'Do we,' Libby asked her table after Harry had presented them with the bill, 'ask *them* to join us at the pub?'

'They'll be going there anyway,' said Fran. 'Faith's staying there. We can hardly ignore them.'

'What about when Ian comes in – if he does?' asked Ben. 'She's a witness in his case.'

'Let him decide,' said Fran. 'They're not finished yet, anyway.'

They all filed past Andrew and Faith saying goodbye.

'I expect we'll see you in the bar later,' Andrew sang out, just as Patti was getting Anne's chair unstuck from the doorway.

'Right,' said Libby. 'Bother.'

Patti, Anne and Libby all emerged into the street, flustered. Harry came up behind them.

'What happened there?' he asked. 'Has my doorway shrunk?'

'No, I got myself at an awkward angle by being nosy,' said Anne. 'I was trying to look over my shoulder.'

'Good job you haven't got a chair, me old trout.' Harry patted Libby's shoulder. 'You'd be stuck forever.'

By the time Libby, Patti and Anne arrived in the pub, they found Fran, Guy and Ben already ensconced at a table with Ian.

'You're in mufti!' said Libby in surprise.

Ian laughed. 'I'm in disguise, actually.'

'No, you don't look like you.' Libby surveyed him from top to toe. 'I've never seen you in a T-shirt before, have I?'

'I don't know,' said Ian. 'Have you?'

'Stop it, you two,' said Fran. 'Have the lovebirds emerged yet, Lib?'

'No, but Andrew said he'd probably see us in here,' said Libby.

'If he's not predated first,' said Ian.

Patti looked shocked. 'That little woman?'

Ian looked serious. 'That little woman has already seen off two husbands,' he said. 'Let's hope Andrew doesn't become the third.'

Chapter Twenty-five

There was a chorus of protest.

'I don't believe it,' said Libby. 'She seems too wet and weedy to be a predatory female.'

'And what do you mean by "seen off"?' asked Fran.

'They both died,' said Ian.

'That's not her fault – it's bad luck,' said Patti.

'I hope so,' said Ian dubiously. 'I've asked for details.'

'Did you find anything else?' asked Libby.

'As far as I could see, everything she told you is true. She's another one with a fairly limited online footprint, but at least we've now got a line on Rowena Harris – or Samuels, as we now know she is.'

'And is *she* active online?' asked Fran.

'Not hugely, but more than Mrs Conway. Nothing at all for several months, though, which doesn't look good.'

'And how does the young woman who died here fit in with her?' asked Anne. 'I think I've got a bit lost.'

Ian looked guilty. 'I shouldn't be discussing it with any of you.'

'No, but you know perfectly well Libby will tell us everything she and Fran know, so you might as well,' said Anne, with a mischievous grin.

'I can't help thinking we've strayed an awful long way from Lisa's death and disappearance,' mused Libby.

'To reassure you,' said an amused Ian, 'the police haven't.'

'I suppose we can't ask?' said Libby wistfully.

'You can ask, but I won't tell you.' Ian swivelled in his chair. 'And here comes Professor Wylie.'

Libby looked up quickly. 'And Faith Conway.'

Andrew waved a hand as he escorted Faith to the bar.

'Not sure what the etiquette is here,' Fran whispered to Libby. 'Do we ask them to join us? Will they expect to join us?'

'I don't know, but I don't think Ian wants them to join us,' Libby whispered back. 'Very awkward. If he's sensible – which he sometimes isn't, as we know – Andrew will see that it's inappropriate.' She risked a look at the couple by the bar. 'Faith's shaking her head, so perhaps she doesn't want to join us.'

Luckily, Ben, Guy and Patti kept up a flow of conversation, or the silence round the table would have been noticeable. At last, Libby let out a breath and leant back in her chair. 'They've gone into the other bar. What a relief.'

Ian grinned. 'I wasn't looking forward to sharing a drink with a suspect.'

'Suspect? How can she be a suspect?' asked Fran. 'She only arrived in the country a few days ago.'

'Person of interest, then,' said Ian. 'You're the ones who introduced her to me, you should know.'

'Only because she had information which would be useful,' said Libby. 'Not as a sus – person of interest.'

'What I would like to ask Andrew, though,' said Fran, 'is what he found out about the history of Notbourne Court. Neither he or Faith told us much, did they? We don't know much about the history further back than the Edwardian era.'

'It doesn't have anything to do with the current situation, does it?' asked Libby.

'No, I was just interested. It seems so odd that a

centuries-old house should be destroyed. I know they did it a lot after the Second World War because of death duties, but I didn't know it happened earlier than that.'

'I expect it's always happened,' said Libby. 'You hear of houses being left to rot away after the Civil Wars, too, don't you?'

'That's true,' said Fran. 'I could still bear to hear the history of this one, though.'

'That should keep you out of mischief,' said Ian.

Fran bristled. 'Don't patronise.'

Ian held up his hands. 'I wasn't! Simply saying it would keep you occupied while Kent Police are diligently investigating the death of Lisa Harwood, and the possible disappearance of Rowena Samuels.'

'So you've already linked them,' said Libby, unable to keep a note of triumph out of her voice.

'Mrs Samuels' name, as you know, has come up during the investigation process. You brought it up.' Ian fixed them with a minatory eye. 'And that's as far as you go.'

Anne laughed. 'I think he means it, girls. Tell you what, I'll have a look in our archives too and see if I can find anything.'

Anne worked at the library in Canterbury.

'Thanks, Anne.' Libby turned to her with a smile.

'Pleasure. Much as I love my job, it's good to have something different to do now and then.'

'That's it, then,' said Fran. 'No more involvement.'

'Interfering,' said Libby. 'No, perhaps not, but I still feel guilty about Roly. Dare I ask?'

Ian was now deep in conversation with Ben and Guy.

'No.' Fran sighed. 'He'll tell us if he thinks we ought to know.'

The door opened and Peter and Harry came in. Room

was made at the table and Ben went with Harry to the bar.

'Ian – I'm glad to see you,' said Peter. 'You remember my young brother James?'

'Of course.' Ian nodded.

'He knows Roly Johnson. I don't know how he knows him, but he was with us when your query came in on Sunday and mentioned it. So he's been checking his social media pages and there's been nothing since Saturday morning.'

Ian nodded again. 'So have we, Pete, but do thank James for me. His parents have no idea where he could be and have tried everyone they can think of. If you think of anywhere, or who might know, would you ask and let me know?'

'I'll pass it on to James now, if you'll excuse me?' Peter stood up, pulling his phone out of his pocket. 'Whatever did we do without these things?'

'So Roly really has disappeared,' said Libby. 'I feel so guilty about that.'

'Don't,' said Ian. 'Why should you feel guilty? He not only told you his story of his own accord, he admitted to making threatening phone calls.'

'Suppose he hasn't run away, but someone's – well, done something,' Libby finished lamely.

'There are an awful lot of vanishing people in this case, aren't there?' said Anne.

'Oh, sorry, Anne, we must sound awful, going on and on about everything,' said Fran. 'But we are worried about the poor boy.'

'Leave the worrying to me,' said Ian. 'Right now I've got two missing persons investigations to run alongside a murder. I do *not* need to be worrying about you two as well.'

'No, Ian,' they chorused.

'All the same,' said Libby, when Ian had gone back to his conversation about cricket, 'I can't help worrying. I mean when you go back to the beginning.'

'How do you mean?' Patti inched her chair closer to the women and further away from the men.

'Well, first Lisa disappears on the run. Then they find a cup, or whatever it was with dregs of some kind of a heart stimulant in it.'

'And,' said Fran, 'it turns out that nobody knew about her heart defect.'

'Except Roly,' said Libby.

'So, anyway, she's dragged off to a car and loaded in, then her body's kept somewhere for a week. And whoever the killer is, he then dumps her in a farmyard gateway just outside Steeple Martin. Presumably for someone to find her.'

'So it looks like Roly, if he was the only one who knew about her defect,' said Anne.

'Or the husband,' said Libby. 'He's the one who told the police about the heart defect.'

'How did she get the drink?' asked Patti.

'They had stewards along the route handing them out,' said Fran. 'Anyone could have borrowed a hi-vis jacket and mingled. Except you would have thought she'd have recognised them.'

'But even if she did,' said Anne, 'would that have mattered? She'd just think "Oh, what's he or she doing here?" and run on. Under the circumstances she wouldn't stop to chat, would she?'

'That's true,' acknowledged Libby. 'But I think if it had been Roly she'd have said something because he was supposed to be running with her, not prancing about in a hi-vis jacket. She'd be surprised if her husband was there, but maybe he regularly tried to get back with her, so it wouldn't be that odd.'

'Following that line of reasoning,' said Patti, 'it could be that she did recognise the person who gave her the drink, and trusted them. She wouldn't even think there was anything odd about it. And the murderer wouldn't care, because he or she knew that Lisa would be dead before she could say anything.' She shuddered. 'Horrible.'

'So that leaves the field wide open to everyone except the members of the Harriers,' said Fran.

'Heavens above!' said Libby. 'Anyone in the world!'

'So then we go back to Roly,' said Anne. 'You said earlier that you thought his story sounded a bit made up.'

'Yes, did Lisa make it up to impress him, or did he make it up to impress me,' said Libby. 'Obviously there's something he thinks he knows, or he wouldn't have bothered with the phone calls to me. Is he genuinely frightened of something – or someone – and has he run away to hide?'

'If he is genuinely frightened,' said Fran, 'then it's of the murderer. It's got to be someone Roly knows.'

'And their only mutual acquaintances were the running club!' said Anne triumphantly. 'There! It all makes sense.'

'Well, not quite,' said Fran. 'There's still the matter of Chestnut Cottage. Why was Lisa allowed to live there? And why does Roly believe it was the owner who installed her there, when it now turns out that the owner is an elderly lady who lives in London.'

'Who has, it appears, also vanished into thin air,' said Libby.

They sat in silence for a moment.

'How's this for a theory,' said Patti eventually. 'Speaking as someone who knows nothing about any of the characters, you understand. Someone, male presumably, but not definitely, wants to get Lisa into Chestnut Cottage for some reason as yet unknown.'

'Roly said sex parties,' muttered Libby.

'OK, for sex parties. He has access to it, so in she goes. Then the real owner tells him or her that she's coming down to do an inventory, or something, because she's thinking of handing it back to the original owners. So he agrees to meet elderly lady and bumps her off. Then Lisa finds out what he's done, so he bumps *her* off. And then, somehow, young Roly lets on that he knows all about it – or at least part of it – so he has to be bumped off, too.'

The other women were watching her with open mouths.

'Very good, Reverend.' Ian's amused voice broke the spell. 'Yes, sorry,' he said, as Patti looked round embarrassed, 'we were all spellbound.'

'It's clever though, Ian,' said Ben.

'It is, and very much what we've thought out ourselves, except that we're all hoping that neither the elderly owner nor young Roly – why does everyone call him "young Roly"? – have been – er – bumped off.'

Patti's cheeks had turned a delicate shade of pink. 'Sorry,' she said.

'What for?' Ian grinned at her. 'It was a logical piece of thinking, and I shall be very surprised if we don't find that the truth is along those lines. We just have to find the person who let Lisa Harwood have the cottage.'

'So we assume that this person was also aware of the heart defect?' said Libby.

'You can assume what you like, Lib.'

'Sorry,' said Libby. 'I'll keep out of it.'

'Don't get huffy, petal.' Harry leant across the table and patted her hand. 'Just because your mate figured it out and you didn't –'

'I wasn't!' Libby was horrified, and felt colour burning up her neck and into her face. 'Oh, God, I wasn't!' She looked at Patti. 'Oh, God, Patti, I'm sorry! I shouldn't be saying Oh, God …'

Libby subsided because everyone was laughing.

'It's Harry who should be sorry,' said Patti, standing up and coming round to kiss Libby and give her a hug.

'Sorry, petal,' said an unrepentant Harry, with a grin. 'Now, who wants another drink?'

Chapter Twenty-six

A rather subdued Libby spent Thursday morning finishing a couple of small sketches for Guy, and loading them and the painting finished last week into the silver bullet ready to take to Nethergate. On the way, she planned to call in on Farthing's Plants and see if Mike had heard anything in the village.

However, when she arrived she was surprised to see her cousin Cassandra's car parked on the forecourt. Cassandra herself she found in one of the huge greenhouses, wielding a small paintbrush.

'What are you doing?' asked Libby, peering across the bench.

'Don't breathe,' whispered Cass, 'or you'll blow the pollen off.'

Libby watched, fascinated, as Cassandra carefully transferred pollen on the tip of the brush to another bloom, then covered that with a small paper bag.

'Breeding,' Cass said succinctly. 'Never quite sure what will emerge, but always a great surprise and sense of achievement. What can I do for you, Lib? Did you come to see Mike?'

'Yes, I just wondered if he'd heard anything in the village about our latest murder.'

Cass looked amused as she pulled off her plastic gloves. 'Yes, he said you were in here last week. How you do fall over murders, little coz.'

'Not my fault,' said Libby, 'and we aren't involved really.'

'I bet.' Cass put away her tools. 'Do you want coffee? Or tea? I've got both in the office.'

'I won't if you don't mind, Cass. I'm on my way to deliver a couple of pictures to Guy. I don't know, sometimes I feel like a production line.'

'OK, but come in anyway, Mike's in there going cross-eyed over spreadsheets.'

Mike looked up gratefully when they walked in to the office.

'Libby! Staying for coffee?'

'No, she's delivering paintings,' said Cass. 'She just wanted to know if you'd heard anything in the village about the murder.'

Mike stood up and came round the counter.

'There was a lot of talk about it in The Poacher at the weekend. No one seems to know anything about the owner.'

'Oh, we know that, now,' said Libby. 'Only she's disappeared, too.' She thought for a moment. 'I don't suppose I should have told you that.'

'Probably not.' Cass tucked an escaping grey lock behind her ear. Tall and patrician-looking, she appeared for all the world like the headmistress of a rather up-market school – which, in fact, she had been. 'Who is she, then?'

Deciding that it was a matter of record, Libby recounted the story of the Hays family, the Harrises and Rowena Samuels. She didn't mention Faith Conway.

'Well,' said Cass when she'd finished. 'Looks as though someone was doing something at Chestnut Cottage that they shouldn't and put this Samuels woman out of the way.'

'That sounds very cold-blooded,' said Libby.

Cass shrugged. 'Cold-blooded thing to do.'

'Yes.' Libby hitched her bag onto her shoulder and began to turn to the door. 'Oh – and you know you told me a young man used to run with Lisa? Well – he's disappeared, too.'

'Really?' Mike's shaggy eyebrows shot up. 'When was that?'

Libby frowned. 'Last seen on Saturday afternoon. By me. Why?'

'Oh, I've seen him since then,' said Mike.

'What? When? Where?' said Libby.

'Um ...' Mike drew his brows together. 'Tuesday, it must have been. I thought it was odd. I was down at the bottom of the field, where it backs on to the Notbourne land, you know? I keep the compost bins down there. Anyway, I saw him in the field. Running along the hedge line. That's how I recognised him – because he was running.'

'You're sure?' gasped Libby, reaching for her phone.

'Yes, I'm sure,' said Mike, eyeing her phone suspiciously. 'What are you doing?'

'Telling the police of course,' said Cass with some asperity. 'This is presumably an official missing person, right, Lib?'

Libby nodded, by now already speaking into her phone.

'I know, I know, Ian, and I'm really sorry to disturb you, but I've got news about Roly Johnson.'

'This had better be good.' Ian did not sound as though he was in a very good mood. He also sounded as though he was outside in a high wind.

'You remember Mike Farthing, of Farthing's Plants?'

'Yes, yes. Get on with it.'

211

'He saw Roly on Tuesday in the field backing on to his property.'

'Alive?'

'Yes, running. Along the hedge line.'

'Where are you now?'

'At Mike's. I came over to see Cass.' Libby crossed her fingers and grinned at Mike and Cass. 'I was on my way to Guy's to –'

'All right. Stay there. I'll be with you shortly. Five minutes.'

'Five – where are you?'

'Maple Cottage.' Ian ended the call.

'Well!' said Libby. 'Ian's on his way.'

Mike looked uncomfortable. 'Oh.'

'Look, I know you had a bad experience with the police, but it was all sorted out, wasn't it? Ian will be really grateful, honestly.'

However, when he arrived, followed by a squad car, he didn't look grateful.

'I don't know how you do it,' he muttered to Libby as he strode past her. 'Mr Farthing. Thank you for this information. Now, could you take me to where you saw Mr Johnson?'

'Roly,' put in Libby.

'Roly,' repeated Ian, sounding as though he was building up a nice head of steam.

Mike led the way out of the office, followed by Ian and two uniformed officers, while Cass and Libby kept a safe distance behind.

At the bottom of the field behind the greenhouses stood the three huge compost bins. Libby wrinkled her nose.

'It doesn't smell,' said Cassandra. 'You're imagining it.'

'Really?' Libby looked doubtful.

'If it smells, you're doing something wrong. Go on, have a sniff.'

Libby sniffed. Nothing assaulted her nostrils other than a whiff of far-away cows.

'Right,' she said. 'I'm surprised, but you're right. What are they doing?'

Cassandra peered across at the four men, not being challenged, as Libby was, in the height department.

'I think one of the officers is trying to climb into the field. Your Ian is talking into his phone and Mike – well, Mike's just looking miserable.'

At that moment, Mike turned and shambled back to them.

'I'm not sure they believe me.'

'Yes, they do,' said Libby. 'Look, that officer's got over the hedge now. And Ian will be summoning reinforcements.'

'Come on,' said Cassandra. 'Back to the office. We might as well have that coffee now.'

'I ought to get on to Nethergate,' said Libby, torn between not wanting to risk Ian's wrath and wanting to know what was going on.

'The DCI will want you to stay, I should think,' said Cass.

'Oh. Well, OK then.' Libby followed Mike and Cassandra into the office and perched on the visitor's chair. Cass had just poured them all coffee when Ian came in.

'Libby, you don't have to stay, you know.' He passed a hand over his face.

'We didn't know –' began Cass.

'No, of course. This came as a bit of a surprise.' Ian looked hopefully at the coffee machine in the corner. Cass

213

held up a mug in enquiry and he nodded gratefully.

'I nearly didn't mention it,' said Libby suddenly.

'Mention what?' said Ian, accepting his coffee mug.

'Roly. I was just leaving, and I turned round to mention that he was missing, because Mike told me last week that he used to see Lisa and Roly running together. You remember? When we told you about Lisa and the tubs?'

Ian nodded. 'That was lucky. We've got a team inside Chestnut Cottage and a team in the garden, but we haven't found your tubs,' he said to Mike. 'Which is very odd.'

Mike frowned. 'But they were huge.'

'Yes. Anyway, we're now looking at Maple Cottage just further up the lane, and I'll have to get back there soon. When backup arrives here, I'll go.' He took a mouthful of coffee. 'I'm very grateful, Mr Farthing – and Mrs –'

'Just call me Cass,' said Cass. 'But it's Libby you should be grateful to.'

'I know.' He gave Libby a tired smile. 'I am.'

Libby beamed.

'I'd better get off to deliver my paintings,' she said, and stood up. 'Thanks for the coffee, Cass. I'll see you soon. Why don't we all go to the caff one evening? Haven't seen you socially for ages.'

They both smiled and agreed, while Ian held the door of the office open for her.

'I'll walk you to your car,' he said.

'It's only a couple of yards,' said Libby.

'I know, but I needed to say something that I didn't want Mike and Cass to hear.'

'You were very formal towards them in there.'

'Because they – or Mike, at any rate – is a witness. Now, did you see anything more of Mrs Conway yesterday evening after I left?'

'Not properly. We looked into the other bar to say goodnight, that was it.'

'And she and Professor Wylie were still there?'

'Oh, yes.' Libby was surprised. 'Why?'

'Just checking. The reason we're starting to go over Maple Cottage is that someone reported seeing a light in there last night.'

'Who reported the light?'

'A shift worker from the hospital coming home. He lives just beyond Maple Cottage and says it's been locked up for years.'

'As Chestnut was,' said Libby.

'Yes. So is it the same someone who tidied up Chestnut and let Lisa Harwood use it who is now using Maple Cottage?'

'Odd that a light was seen,' said Libby with a frown. 'The electricity would have been switched off for ages, wouldn't it?'

'A torch, probably.'

'So that was why you asked about Faith?' said Libby. 'In case it was her over there? What time was this light seen?'

'About two o'clock,' said Ian.

'Well, then, she could have gone over there after the pub closed. Except that she doesn't know her way, and it would have been pitch black. No street lighting in Itching and Shott.'

Ian nodded slowly. 'Don't say anything, will you? I'll be over to see her later this afternoon.'

'Can I tell Fran?'

Ian patted her shoulder. 'I wouldn't expect anything less.'

Libby turned the silver bullet round very carefully,

avoiding Ian's sleek saloon, the squad car and Cass's sensible vehicle. She drove to Nethergate, her mind going over all the surprising things she'd been told in the last hour or so. When she arrived in Harbour Street, she was gratified to find a parking space close to the shop.

'Libby?' Guy looked up in surprise. 'Is Fran expecting you?'

'No, I've brought you that painting I mentioned and a couple of sketches. Shall I fetch them in?'

'I'll give Fran a ring and let her know you're here.'

Libby went back to the car and collected the pieces. She was met at the door of the shop by Fran, also looking surprised.

'You didn't say anything about coming over today?' she said, holding the door open.

'No, but I didn't know what to do with myself, and I'm really glad I did.'

'Oh, why?'

Guy took the painting and the sketches and propped them up behind the counter.

'Nice,' he said. 'The sketches are a bit different. We'll see how they go, shall we?'

'Yes, thanks,' said Libby.

'Now,' said Fran. 'Stop getting distracted and tell us what's happened.'

Libby recounted her visit to Mike and Cass and how she'd nearly missed the news about Roly.

'Just think if you hadn't thought to mention it,' said Fran.

'I know. But even stranger than that, when Ian came over …' She told them about the search of Maple Cottage and the light seen inside.

'Roly?' suggested Guy.

'It would make sense, I suppose,' said Libby. 'I'm just

surprised that he's stayed so close to home. If he was that scared of someone, wouldn't he have gone a long way away?'

'Shall I make us some tea?' asked Guy.

'No, thanks,' said Libby. 'I'm awash with Cass's strong coffee.' She turned to Fran. 'You know, Ian was really grateful today. Do you think he might keep us up to date now?'

Half an hour later, Libby was driving back into Steeple Martin. She had just come down the hill when she trod sharply on the brake. Outside the pub was a squad car and Ian's saloon. And the blue lights were flashing.

Chapter Twenty-seven

Checking traffic, Libby pulled in to the Manor drive and switched off the engine. She didn't know whether to go into the pub or not. After all, Ian might be after someone else – it might have nothing to do with Faith. But then again …

She got out of the car and trotted down to The Pink Geranium. Harry was standing by the door peering out.

'What's going on?' she asked, when he opened the door.

'No idea. The squad car arrived and a minute later Ian did. Must be something to do with that Faith, mustn't it?'

'I assume so, especially after …' she trailed off. 'Well, I had a bit of a surprise this afternoon.'

'Go on.' Harry leant against the door frame, arms folded.

Libby told him of her surprising afternoon.

'And Ian was going off to the other cottage,' she finished.

'So you think they found something pointing to Faith as the murderer then?'

'I don't know. How could she be?'

Harry shrugged. 'Have to wait and see, won't we? But I don't think you'd better go barging in there now.'

'No.' Libby nodded reluctantly. 'I'd better go home. Or into the eight-til-late, at any rate. I think I've forgotten dinner again.'

It was as Libby was returning to the car after

provisioning herself from the eight-til-late and Nella and Joe's Cattlegreen Nursery shop that she heard someone calling her name.

'What are you doing here?' asked Ian.

Libby raised her eyebrows. 'I live here. What are you doing here?'

'I wondered why you were walking towards the drive.'

Libby held up her two shopping bags. 'Dinner. I stopped on the way home from Fran's.'

'And what did Fran have to say about the revelations of earlier today?'

Libby scowled at him. 'Surprised. What do you expect? Can I go now?'

Ian sighed and stepped back. 'Sorry. And you haven't even asked me a question.'

'I did. I said "What are you doing here?" And you didn't answer.'

'I was speaking to Mrs Conway.'

'Why the squad car?'

'Look, if you want to know, come back to the pub and I'll explain.'

Libby gaped. 'You'll what?'

Ian took her elbow. 'Come on.'

'What about my food?'

Ian gave her a look.

In the pub, she was unsurprised to be led to the rear of the entrance hall and into the manager's office.

'He's letting me use it while I'm here,' said Ian, settling himself behind the desk.

'All right, stop being mysterious and tell me just why you're here,' said Libby. 'Is it Faith?'

Ian looked down at his hands clasped together on the desk.

'You remember we were going over Maple Cottage

when I saw you at Mike Farthing's place?'

'Yes?'

'I'm afraid we made a rather unpleasant discovery.'

Libby felt the same rush of adrenalin that comes from a near miss in a car.

'We found what we believe to be Rowena Samuels.'

Libby swallowed. 'You believe?'

'We had no idea what she looked like. We had to ask Mrs Conway.'

Libby looked horrified. 'But ...?'

'It's all right – it wasn't horrific. Mrs Samuels had been kept in a freezer.'

Now Libby felt the blood drain from her face.

'So Patti was right,' she whispered.

'Not quite. Young Roly appears to be still around, if Farthing is to be believed.'

'It isn't him,' said Libby instantly.

'It isn't?'

'He isn't the killer.'

Ian supressed a smile. 'How do you know?'

Libby looked down. 'I just do,' she mumbled.

'We are, however, still continuing to look for him,' said Ian. 'He has questions to answer at the very least. Now, if you want to, you can see if Mrs Conway needs anything. She was very shocked.'

Libby nodded and stood up as a thought occurred to her.

'What about electricity?' she said. 'Surely it had been turned off. That's what I couldn't understand about the light that the neighbour saw.'

'The electricity was still on, amazingly,' said Ian. We're checking with the solicitors who are supposed to manage the estate. Now Mrs Samuels is dead, perhaps we can persuade them to open up a bit.'

'How much am I allowed to say and to whom?' Libby asked.

Ian regarded her speculatively. 'I shouldn't say this, but apart from the media, and that includes your friend Jane, you can talk about it to most people. In particular, the Harriers.'

'Really?' Libby narrowed her eyes at him. 'You suspect one of them?'

Ian shrugged. 'Maybe. But it was Lisa Harwood's connection to them that seemed to lead to this whole chain of events.'

'OK.' Libby nodded. 'Let things slip, sort of?'

'That's it.' Ian stood up. 'Do you want me to take you up to Mrs Conway?'

'Do you think you ought to? Just to say it's all right with you?'

Ian gave her an odd look. 'When did that ever matter to you?'

'It always does,' said Libby, affronted, as she stalked ahead of him to the stairs. 'I gather she's in her room?'

Faith was sitting in a chair by the window, while a uniformed officer, looking almost as unhappy as she did, stood by the door trying to be inconspicuous.

'Mrs Conway,' said Ian, going over to Faith, 'Mrs Sarjeant is here. Would you like to see her?'

'Oh, Libby.' Faith raised a lacklustre face. 'Yes, of course. Andrew's coming over as soon as he can.'

Ian and Libby exchanged an interested look.

'We can go now, officer,' said Ian. 'Thank you, Mrs Conway. I'm sorry to have been the bearer of bad news. We'll be in touch.' He passed Libby in the doorway. 'And I'll be in touch with you, too.'

When the door closed behind the two men, Libby crossed the room to Faith.

'I'm so sorry,' she said. 'What horrible news.'

Faith nodded, her eyes turning to the street outside. 'But I think that's why I came over in the first place. I think I was sure that something had happened to her.'

Libby frowned. 'Did she ever give you any indication that something might happen to her?'

'Not really. I believe she'd talked to some family members about returning the estate to my family, but I don't know what their opinion was, or who they were. But I can't think she'd be in danger from family.'

You'd be surprised, thought Libby.

'Did Ian – DCI Connell – give you any idea of when she might have been killed?'

Faith shuddered. 'No. He said she'd been in a freezer.'

'Yes.' Libby shifted from one foot to the other, wondering what she ought to do next.

'Oh, look.' Faith pointed. 'There's Andrew.'

'Right,' said Libby with relief. 'I'll go, then, and meet him in the hall. I hope everything's – ah – all right.'

She escaped down the stairs and met Andrew with his foot on the bottom step.

'She's waiting for you,' said Libby.

'Why are you here?' Andrew looked suspicious.

'Ian asked me in because he thought Faith needed someone with her.'

'Oh, well, I'm here now,' said Andrew.

'Yes, thank goodness,' said Libby. 'See you soon.'

She just stopped herself from telling him to be careful. She loaded her shopping into the car and drove slowly home, trying to work out what it was Ian wanted her to do. Spread the news of Rowena Samuels' death? That Roly was still missing but believed to be hale and hearty?

The shopping put away, she called Fran.

'If you're asking me,' said Fran, when she'd heard the

latest news, 'I think we should tell Sophie. Then she can work out what to say to her members.'

'Don't you think Ian wants to get our impressions? Personally, I mean.'

'Short of calling a meeting of all interested parties, I can't see how we could. I've had an idea, though. I'm pretty sure they keep in touch via their Facebook page. I'll see if she can get us on there. If I do, you mustn't post there, just watch and listen.'

'That's brilliant, Fran. Let me know later.'

She called Ben to update him on the dinner situation, then Cassandra.

'I guessed it was important because they all shot off from here a little while after you left,' said Cass. 'I don't suppose they found Roly, too?'

'No, from what Ian said, he's not top priority, so presumably they don't think he had anything to do with either of the deaths.'

'Oh, well, thanks for telling us. If we see him again we'll let you know, of course.'

'I should let the police know first,' said Libby. 'And I doubt you'll see him again if he was aware of the police presence this afternoon.'

'That's true,' said Cass. 'How are your pots doing?'

Libby thought guiltily of the beautifully planted pots Cass and Mike had given her a year or so ago, now lurking, unloved, at the bottom of the garden.

'Oh, OK,' she said. 'You know.'

'Hmm,' said Cass. 'I'll have to come over and have a look.'

'Yes!' said Libby brightly. 'Well, look, I've got to go. I'm expecting calls from Ian and Fran.'

Well, she said to herself as she ended the call, she was expecting a call from Fran, and from what he'd said, she would be surprised if Ian didn't call, too.

Fran called while she and Ben were watching the news before dinner.

'Sophie has added us both to the Facebook page,' she said, 'although she thought we ought to go and talk to them again.'

'Good idea!' said Libby.

'I don't think so,' said Fran. 'I think it would look a bit odd. Much better to let the news – such as it is – slip out.'

'That's what I said to Ian, actually.' Libby thought for a moment. 'And he, or his officers, have already got access to the Harriers' page, so he can look at the conversations. Oh – that's the drawback. They know about that, because they all posted their GPS results and talked to the police about them, so they won't speak freely. Or write freely.'

'I hadn't thought of that.' Fran went quiet for a moment. 'I'll speak to Sophie again, but I think she's already leaked some of the news.'

'I'll keep an eye on the page, then,' said Libby.

'This,' said Ben, when she told him what had happened, 'is when you need a smart phone. You'll have to keep your laptop open on your lap all the time.'

'I don't mind,' said Libby. 'I'll go and start dinner now, then I'll come and have a look.'

There was a brief mention of the discovery of Rowena Samuels' body, although no details, and certainly not connecting it in any way to the death of Lisa Harwood. Libby dished up her risotto and took her computer to the kitchen table.

'You don't mind, do you?' she asked, as Ben took a seat opposite her.

'No. Especially as you appear to have Ian's permission to go ferreting.'

Sophie had posted on the Harriers' page: "Heard today that Roly has been sighted, although not found yet. Fingers crossed."

"Can't understand why he's gone in the first place." commented Kirsty Trent.

"Well that's something. Silly boy," said someone else.

"Who saw him?" asked Steve Reid.

"And where?" asked Nick Heap.

Libby jumped in her chair. 'Don't tell them, Sophie!' she said aloud.

Chapter Twenty-eight

'What?' Ben almost choked on a mouthful of risotto.

'Sorry.' Libby put down her fork. 'I just realised something. I don't think we should have put this on Facebook. Someone's just asked where Roly was seen.'

'Natural enough question, I would have thought,' said Ben, recovering.

'Yes, but Ian particularly wanted to gauge reaction among the Harriers, which means, although he didn't actually come out and say it, he suspects the murderer is one of them. And if Roly is scared of someone and has run away to hide, then to give his whereabouts away is signing a death sentence.'

Ben looked dubious. 'That's a lot of leaps into the unknown.'

'But logical,' said Libby. She looked back at the screen and was relieved to see that Sophie hadn't answered the question.

'I'm phoning Sophie,' she said and went to fetch her mobile. However, Sophie was engaged. Libby, frustrated, sat down and began to eat her cooling risotto while keeping an eye on the screen. After a few moments a new comment appeared.

Sophie: "Don't know exactly where. I expect the police don't want to give that information out."

Nick Heap: "You got that information from the police? How come?"

Steve Reid: "Got connections, has our Soph!

Remember the two women who came to see us at the pub? Her stepmother and the other one? They do stuff with the police. They've been in the paper."

Kirsty Trent: "They're looking for Roly?"

Sophie: "I don't know. That's all I've been told."

Libby's mobile rang.

'I guessed it was you, Libby. I was on the phone to Fran.'

'I gather from the Facebook page she told you the same thing I was going to. Don't tell them where he was seen.'

'Exactly. I don't think I intended to, but just as well she warned me. I'm not going back on the page for a bit. I'll let it stew.'

'Good idea – and well done, Sophie.' Libby ended the call and showed Ben the page. There were a few more comments from other members of the Harriers, but nothing of immediate interest.

'I feel quite drained,' said Libby, pushing both plate and laptop away from her. 'So much has happened.'

'A quiet night in, that's what we need,' said Ben. 'Go on, you go and sit down and I'll clear up. See what's on the TV.'

To Libby's relief, they were undisturbed on Thursday night. On Friday evening there was to be a meeting of the prospective cast of The End Of The Pier Show, to which Susannah would be coming, and apart from that, the day was her own. Not for the first time she wondered if she really ought to get a proper job. Selling the odd picture wasn't exactly a regular income, neither was the occasional royalty payment from the sale of pantomime scripts.

'A parasite, that's what I am,' she told Sidney. 'Living off Ben.'

Although, she admitted to herself, that wasn't true, either. Number 17 was hers, mortgage-free, and the remainder of the lump sum settled on her at the divorce had been invested wisely and produced a decent enough amount every month. She was very lucky, really. But – bored.

And that was the problem. That was why she got involved in all these cases. Each time, she could have walked away, but she hadn't, although every time she said she would. So, of course, people expected her to take an interest now. But Fran wasn't bored. She'd married Guy and had an interest in his gallery and shop. As Libby had had an interest in turning the Manor into an arts training centre, a venture that had failed in its second attempt – due, naturally, to a murder.

No amount of deep and introverted thinking was going to change the fact, however, that Libby was bored. Last autumn they'd actually had the Manor full of dancers, while they rehearsed and then performed Max's *Pendle*. Then she'd had plenty to do. She wondered again if it would be worth trying to revive the writing and painting courses at the Manor, but reluctantly decided against it. Hetty was getting on, after all, and it wouldn't be fair on her.

Just as she'd decided to look up Open University courses online, the landline rang.

'Libby, it's Andrew Wylie.'

'Oh, hello, Andrew. How's Faith?'

Andrew paused. 'All right, I think. I haven't seen her today, of course.'

'Oh.' For some reason, Libby had been sure he would stay overnight at the pub. Just shows, she thought, you shouldn't jump to conclusions.

'No, what I'm ringing about is Notbourne Court.'

'Oh,' said Libby again. 'But that does concern Faith, doesn't it?'

'Only if the estate somehow comes back to her, and personally, I don't see how it could. Stephanie Hays willed it quite specifically to Christobel Harris, Rowena's mother. But that's nothing to do with why I'm ringing. I'm testing the water, you see.'

'You are?'

'Well, yes. You see, I've found a couple of mentions in the archives which intrigue me. And I don't know if I should mention them to Ian Connell or not.'

Libby's boredom vanished.

'What are they? And where are you?'

'I'm in Maidstone. I can't take any of this away – so I wondered – I don't suppose you'd be free to come over and have a look, would you? It doesn't matter if you can't –'

'I'll be there as soon as I can,' said Libby.

The new purpose-built Kent History and Library Centre wasn't far from the old building, and when Libby had parked she found Andrew waiting for her outside.

'What is it that's so important?' she asked, as she followed him inside.

'I'll show you,' he said, 'but first we've got to be frisked!'

The security was understandable, Libby thought, as there were priceless documents held here, and heaven help anyone who took in a pen and tried to deface them.

Andrew led her to a workstation, nodded to a librarian, or curator, perhaps, and opened a large and venerable ledger. At first Libby had no idea what she was looking at.

'I almost missed it,' said Andrew pulling on white

gloves. 'There. See?'

'Er – no.'

'The caves. Dug out at the end of the eighteenth century.'

Eventually Libby managed to see what he was talking about. The old document, some sort of land register, spoke of the mining of tunnels and the creation of a dining room.

'Dining room? Is that what it says?'

'A touch euphemistically, yes.' Andrew smiled at her. 'Remind you of anything?'

Libby shook her head. 'Not unless it's the tunnels we found before.'

'This is old Lord Cheveley's idea. When the Court was rebuilt.'

'Oh, yes! I remember when I looked it up online, it said it had been rebuilt in 1790. There was a painting of it in its heyday. Gorgeous.'

'Right.' Andrew pulled out another document, much faded, but with a seal still intact. 'And this.'

Again, Libby tried to read it, but was defeated. 'Tell me what it is, Andrew. I'll never read that.'

'This is asserting that these chambers belong to the Abbey of Notbourne.' He raised an eyebrow at her.

'But there isn't an Abbey ...' Libby stopped, her eyes widening. 'No! I don't believe it!'

'Oh, yes. In fact, further on in these documents, it asserts that Lord Cheveley wished to keep up the traditions inaugurated by Sir Francis Dashwood, and there are sketches of some of the decoration used inside.'

'I don't think I want to see.'

'No, they are pretty – er – ripe. Anyway, it appears that like several others, they carried on some form of the Hellfire Club for most of the nineteenth century, mostly underground – in both senses – in defiance of the puritan on the throne. Whether they were still going on into the early twentieth, I can't find out. However, there is one last thing.' He moved the book and other papers aside and brought out a document Libby had seen before.

'Oh, this is the auction notice, isn't it?'

'It is. I'd already found this in my original searches – so had Faith – but further than Chestnut Cottage I hadn't really looked. But ...' he turned over two more pages. 'Here.'

'"Tunnels and dining room purported to belong to the former Notbourne Abbey,"' she read. 'So they're still there?'

'I've no idea. This was over a hundred years ago, remember.'

'We've got to find out.'

'I knew you'd say that. But I think we'd be better telling Ian. That's why I wanted your opinion.'

'I suppose so.' Libby bit her lip. 'It's amazing, isn't it? These organisations going on down the centuries. You didn't know about our last adventure, did you?'

'With the dancers? Not really. Why, they didn't have Mad Medmenham Monks too, did they?'

'No, but someone connected to them had belonged to a similar organisation in the sixties.'

'I believe there are still similar things going on today,' said Andrew. 'I even heard of something connected to the grotto at Steeple Mount.'

'Oh, I've seen that. Really? But that's a fake, isn't it?'

'I don't suppose it matters. It's the atmosphere that counts,' said Andrew. 'After all, these tunnels are fake, aren't they? A fake Abbey.'

'So they are. Oh, Lord!' She looked up suddenly.

'What?'

'I've just remembered – sex parties.'

'Eh?' Startled, Andrew stepped back.

'Someone said our first victim was mixed up with sex parties.' Libby looked at Andrew in horror. 'You don't think …?'

'It's a coincidence,' said Andrew. 'I definitely think I must tell Ian. Or someone.'

'Ian, definitely,' said Libby. 'Not Faith.'

He eyed her oddly. 'No, not Faith.'

He went to ask if he could photograph relevant passages of the document, then tidily cleared them away.

'I'll buy you a coffee, and we can ring Ian.' He led the way outside. 'Where *can* we get coffee?'

They found somewhere towards the centre of town, and picked a table outside. Libby went in to order coffee, while Andrew sat outside with his list of phone numbers. By the time she returned, he was talking animatedly into the phone.

'Yes, of course. I took some pictures. No, you wouldn't be able to take any of them away. No, I haven't told Mrs Conway. Libby's here with me, though. She saw them, too.' He paused, listening, and smiled at Libby. 'I know, but she thought I ought to tell you too, even though she's dying to find those tunnels herself. No, I'll tell her.' He paused again, then nodded. 'Right. We'll wait to hear from you.'

'What did he say?' asked Libby. 'Was he annoyed at me being here?'

'Amused, I think. But in general, rather pleased. He's getting a warrant to search the grounds.'

'Goodness! I wonder if Roly's been hiding in the tunnels?'

Andrew frowned. 'Didn't you say he was frightened of someone? If that someone was the person who killed your first body, and she was involved in sex parties, it's quite likely the tunnels are still in use – that's what you think, isn't it?'

'Yes – oh, I see. So Roly wouldn't hide there. No, not if he knows what's been going on – and he told me he did.'

'Well, now, I don't think there's anything more you or I can do except to wait until the police have searched the tunnels. If they're still there.'

'No. I'm surprised, if they are still there, that they weren't used in the Second World War, though. Lots of others were, weren't they?'

'Certainly were,' said Andrew, looking interested. 'I don't think that would have come up within the parameters I'd set for research. I'll have to look into it when I get home.'

'I can't believe the last couple of days,' said Libby, leaning back in her chair. 'So much has happened. How was Faith last night?'

'Shocked,' said Andrew. 'Yet not as much, somehow, as I would have thought. I don't really know why she wanted to see me.'

'Don't you?' Libby grinned at him. 'Perhaps you're a candidate for husband number three! Take care, Andrew.'

Chapter Twenty-nine

Libby called Fran, then drove straight from Maidstone to Nethergate. Fran greeted her at the door of Coastguard Cottage.

'Shall we go and get a sandwich at Mavis's?' she suggested.

'Good idea – I've parked behind there, anyway,' said Libby.

'Come on, then, tell me all about these amazing discoveries,' said Fran as they walked back towards the cafe.

By the time Libby had finished, they were seated at one of the outside tables and the current waitress had taken their order.

'What I don't understand,' said Fran with a frown, 'is why this hasn't come up anywhere before. Rowena must have known about the tunnels. I mean, when her parents inherited the estate from Stephanie Hays, there must have been title deeds that mention them. After all, they're mentioned in the auction catalogue, so they'd be on the deeds.'

'How do we know they weren't sold, though?' said Libby. 'I can't remember if they were in a separate lot. The cottages were, I seem to remember.'

'And they weren't sold. In fact, it doesn't look as if much of the estate was sold. We know the Court was knocked down.'

'Oh, well, we'll soon know. Ian will have got his

search warrant by now, so they'll go over the place with a toothcomb. They might even find Roly in the process.'

'That's another thing I don't understand,' said Fran. 'If Roly's scared of someone connected to Lisa's death, why is he hanging around so close to Chestnut Cottage?'

'That's what Andrew said.' Libby rested her chin on her hand. 'Roly said he knew who the owner was, didn't he?'

'No – you said he *didn't* know. Just that it was the owner of Chestnut Cottage who had her working for him. Which it patently wasn't.'

'No. Poor Rowena.'

'But he had connected Chestnut Cottage to the whole scenario, which was why he made the phone calls to you, so it seems odd that he should still be around, as I said.'

'Perhaps he isn't,' said Libby. 'Perhaps he was just paying a flying visit? Oh, here are our sandwiches.'

'Have you had a look at the Harriers' page this morning?' she asked a little later, her mouth full of tuna sandwich.

'Briefly,' said Fran. 'No new postings or comments. But I suppose they're all at work.'

'Do you really think it's one of the members?'

'Ian does. Mind you, he probably knows a lot more about them all than we do.'

'And the reasoning is that Lisa started running when she was in Canterbury, then joined the Harriers – why, I wonder? – and was offered Chestnut Cottage. By one of the members?'

'I think that's it. No one's been able to say why she joined the Harriers when she lived in Canterbury, have they?'

'No.' Libby finished her sandwich and wiped her mouth. 'We don't know where she worked, either, do we?

Again, none of the members knew, and assumed she worked in an office – Roly did, didn't he? But she couldn't have been working from home – at least not at the same sort of thing – when she lived at home with her husband and children. I wonder if the husband's been asked.'

'Bound to have been,' said Fran. 'I should think his whole life has been turned inside out by the police.'

'Of course. The things we don't know about an investigation.'

'That's as it should be.' Fran pushed back her chair. 'Do you want anything else? Only I ought to get back and relieve Guy for lunch.'

'No, I'll pootle off home. I've got some stuff to sort out for tonight. You are coming, aren't you?'

'Yes, I'm giving Susannah a lift.'

They paid their bill and wandered back down the street. Libby bought an ice cream from the kiosk and sat on the wall to eat it while Fran went into the shop. A few minutes later, Guy joined her on the wall.

'I hear you've been busy.'

Libby finished her ice cream and nodded.

'I don't know how it happened. We're not connected to this at all.'

'In a way by Sophie and Adam.' Guy looked out to sea. 'And Fran's had a feeling about it from the start.'

'She did seem interested at first,' said Libby cautiously. Guy could be even more unhappy about his other half's exploits than Ben could with hers.

'She still is. She won't – or can't – explain why.'

'I expect she can't,' said Libby. 'She still doesn't understand her strange brain after all these years.'

Guy swung himself off the wall. 'I know. It makes married life difficult sometimes.'

'Oh, dear, does it?' Libby looked up at him, worried.

He grinned. 'Interesting, let's say. I'm off to get some lunch.'

Libby watched him let himself into Coastguard Cottage, then stood up and walked slowly back down Harbour Street to fetch her car from behind The Blue Anchor.

Back in Steeple Martin, she made herself tea, then sat down with piles of music and sheaves of paper to work on the programme for The End Of The Pier Show. She was quite surprised when the phone rang to find that a couple of hours had passed without her even thinking about Lisa, Roly or the Notbourne Estate.

'It's me, Andrew!' said a breathless voice. 'I'm over in Shott – and we've found the tunnels!'

'You've what? How?'

'Your Ian got a warrant and various other bits of information and invited me over with my copies of the documents I showed you this morning. Somehow, they worked out where the tunnels were most likely to be – and here they are!'

'That's quick work,' said Libby. 'I can't quite believe it.'

'I think the urgency was in case your missing young man was there,' said Andrew. 'But the ironic thing is, now that we've located them, no one can go inside. They've got to be inspected by a specialist team first.'

'I suppose they would,' said Libby. 'But when you see archaeologists' digs and they find tunnels, they don't have anyone go in and inspect them first, do they?'

'But this is the police. I expect they might need an archaeologist to go in first. I don't know. I just thought I'd tell you. I knew you'd want to know.'

'It's brilliant, Andrew. Do you think there'll be

anything left?'

'I doubt it. We don't know when they wound it up, do we?'

'I wish we could find out more,' said Libby. 'I think it's odd that there isn't more information out there.'

'There are probably specialist local historians who know more. There usually are.'

'I wonder how we could find one?'

'I'll ask at the university. They usually know these people. Right, I'm being moved on. I'll keep you informed.'

Libby went into the kitchen to find something for supper, taking the phone with her. While she investigated the fridge she rang Fran.

'I can't believe it's so quick! Everything seems to be moving at lightning speed.'

'When will they be able to get in there?' asked Fran.

'I don't know. I expect Ian will be agitating for it to be as soon as possible, don't you? But they won't do it tonight.'

'No. First thing in the morning then, when they've got the equipment.'

'I expect so. I wonder if they'll find Roly there?'

'They won't,' said Fran. 'If he is there, he will have heard them and he'll make a bolt during the night.'

'But they'll have left a copper on duty overnight, surely?'

'I think that might be stretching their resources.'

'Hmm. But suppose the tunnels are being used – perhaps something's stored there – the murderer or whoever could come back tonight to get rid of the evidence,' Libby argued.

'There is that,' Fran conceded. 'But they won't find Roly, anyway. Not there.'

Libby didn't bother to ask how she knew.

'Right, I've got to go and rustle up supper,' she said instead. 'I'll see you at the theatre later.'

Ben was gratifyingly impressed with her day of surprises.

'And now you'd better get off to the theatre,' he said, when they'd finished their meal. 'I'll come up a bit later, if you need me to.'

'Yes, please,' said Libby. 'I probably will.'

Fran and Susannah arrived first.

'Fran's been telling me all about the murders and Notbourne Court. Have you asked Jane about it?'

'Jane?' repeated Libby.

'She could have a look in the archives of the paper,' said Susannah. 'I don't suppose everything goes online.'

'Good idea,' said Fran. 'I'll ring her tomorrow.'

'Andrew said what we need is a local historian – you know, one of those people who study the area and appear on documentary shows on TV,' said Libby.

'Where would we find one of those?' asked Fran.

'That's what I said. Andrew said he'd ask at the university.'

'I know one,' said Susannah surprisingly. 'So does your Sophie, Fran. He's one of her Harriers.'

'Really?' said Fran and Libby together.

'Who?' said Libby.

'Fellow called Nick. Nick Heap. He went to Imogen's school once for a history event. Immie was too young for it, but we went along anyway.'

'What was the event about?' asked Fran.

'The history of the area, right back to pre-Roman. Very simplified, obviously for primary school kids, but there were an astonishing number in the higher classes who were really interested. I think it was called something like "Marks we leave behind us" – something like that.'

'So, do we speak to him ourselves or tell Ian?' said Libby. 'Thanks, Susannah, that's really great.'

'I suggest we tell Andrew,' said Fran. 'Ian seems to be treating him as an expert witness, and it would come better from him.'

Libby pulled out her mobile.

'Not now!' said Susannah and Fran together.

The meeting went as well as could be expected. Most of the cast had done the show before and much of the material was recycled, although Libby tried to find new things to put in each year. Susannah took them through a few of the chorus numbers, and a few people were allotted a new solo piece. Ben came in and had a discussion with Bob the butcher about the seaside set they built between them, which had to be portable, as the show itself was staged at The Alexandria in Nethergate. One of Libby's fantasies was to come true this year, of having a "live" Punch and Judy show acted out – rather, over-acted – in a huge Punch and Judy booth on stage. There seemed to her to be limitless comedy opportunities in having real people playing dog Toby, the sausages and the Crocodile, as well as an oversized Baby.

By ten o'clock Libby declared herself satisfied.

'Drink?' suggested Ben.

Several people including Libby and Bob agreed, but Fran and Susannah declined.

'Susannah has to get back and I have to drive,' said Fran. 'I'll speak to you tomorrow.'

In the pub, Libby asked if anyone knew anything about Notbourne Court, as it appeared to lie at the heart of the whole Lisa Harwood/Rowena Samuels/Roly Johnson mystery.

Most people who had lived in the area all their lives

had heard of it, but not much more than that.

'Wait a minute,' piped up a voice from the back. 'I've heard something about it. You remember that bloke that came and stayed here when you were mixed up in that murder over at – where was it? – Keeper's Cob, that's it.'

All eyes turned to look at Olivia, former principal boy and now concert party soubrette.

'You mean that black bloke?' said someone.

'Edward Hall?' said Libby. 'You talked to him?'

'Yes.' Olivia blushed. 'He was nice.'

'Yes, he is,' said Libby. 'But what did he say? He wasn't from around here.'

'No, but you know he was interested in the Civil War period? He was telling me about some of the other places locally that were involved. And one of them was Notbourne Court. Apparently they built themselves escape tunnels.'

Chapter Thirty

Libby turned to Ben. 'That's amazing. Who shall we tell?'

'Andrew again,' said Ben. 'Olivia, that's really interesting news. Thank you for remembering it.'

''s OK,' said Olivia, and blushed again.

'Sorry,' said Libby, 'I'm just going to have to send Andrew a text. I can't believe so much is coming together.'

'Don't count your chickens,' said Ben. 'Neither this Nick person nor Edward Hall may have anything for us.'

'But they might,' said Libby, laboriously sending Andrew a text message. 'Andrew's got Edward's number, hasn't he? They got on quite well last time he was here.' She pressed send. 'Done now. Either he'll phone back now or in the morning.'

But Andrew was obviously too impatient to wait until morning, and a few moments later Libby's phone warbled. She excused herself and left the table.

'Sorry – am I interrupting anything?'

'No, we're in the pub with some of the theatre people.'

'Tell me what's happened.'

Libby related the conversations with both Susannah and Olivia. 'And I assume you still have Edward's number?' she concluded.

'Yes, I have. Good sort, Edward. But what about this other person? What's his number?'

'Not the faintest. We can ask Fran's step-daughter Sophie, but I think she'd be wary of giving out members' details to anyone else. The dreaded Data Protection Act.'

'I expect Ian will have a way of tracking him down,' said Andrew. 'I hope I can meet him.'

'And you'll tell Ian, will you? And get in touch with Edward?'

'Yes, yes. I think I'm supposed to be accompanying them in the morning.'

'As an expert witness?' asked Libby.

'Sounds silly, doesn't it? But yes. I'll keep you informed.'

Libby went back to the table. 'Your news has gone down well,' she said to Olivia. 'Thank you.'

Olivia mumbled something and took refuge in her drink.

Libby wasn't surprised to receive an early phone call from Edward Hall, a historian they had met while looking into possible treasure from the Civil Wars.

'Lovely to hear from you, Edward, but I suspect you've heard from Andrew?'

'He left me a text message quite early this morning. Presumably didn't want to wake me on a Saturday.' Edward laughed.

'Kind of him. How much did he say?'

'I'll read it. "Do you know anything about Notbourne Court and tunnels?" So, yes, I do, and what's it all about?'

Libby went back over the whole story, from Lisa Harwood's disappearance to the discovery of Rowena Samuels' body.

'I think I got most of that,' said Edward. 'How do you come into it this time?'

'I'm not sure. Fran's stepdaughter Sophie and my son Adam – do you remember him? – were running with Lisa

Harwood when she disappeared, and they are – were – all members of the same running club. So was the boy who's disappeared, but we don't think he's dead.'

'So it's this club that's under suspicion?'

'Not exactly,' said Libby. 'Anyway, you apparently told one of our theatre company all about the tunnels when you were staying here.'

'Ah, the pretty, tall girl who was in the pantomime? Yes, I remember. She seemed very interested.'

'She was,' said Libby, with a grin.

'Right, so what do you want me to do? Will I meet your handsome detective again?'

'If you could give Andrew a quick ring on his mobile, I think they – he and the police – are at the site now. And how did you know about Notbourne Court and the tunnels in the first place? No one here seems to know anything about them.'

'You remember I was particularly interested in that period? While we were investigating the smuggling tunnels, I just looked up some of the other references out of interest. I expect a local historian in your neck of the woods will know all about it. I'm surprised Andrew didn't.'

'He found out about it when we asked him to look up Notbourne Court at the county archives.'

'Well, well. I'll give him a ring now, then. Shame I can't get down to give them a hand.'

'Are you still in Birmingham?'

'Only until the end of this term. Then I'm moving.'

'Oh, where?'

Edward gave a mysterious giggle. 'Wouldn't you like to know!'

'Yes, I would,' said Libby. 'Don't be childish.'

'Sorry, miss. But it's a bit top secret at the moment.

I'll let you all know when I can.'

'And that's that,' Libby said to Ben when she had recounted the phone call. 'I suppose we sit and wait for somebody to pass us a titbit of information.'

'Meanwhile, you'd better update Fran with the information, hadn't you?'

'So I had!' Libby picked up the phone again.

'I was just going to call you,' said Fran, answering on the first ring.

'Oh, why?'

'Something odd's happened.'

'It has? What?'

'When I got home last night, it turned out that Guy was with Sophie in The Swan, so I went and joined them and told them about Nick Heap. So Sophie said she'd ask him when she saw him this morning.'

'That doesn't sound very odd.'

'No, but she's just rung and said that Nick denied all knowledge.'

'Really? This early?'

'Well, they do their training run, then they join the public for the Park Run, which they act as stewards for, so they start early.'

'OK, that mostly sounds like Greek, but I get the gist. And what happened?'

'Well, she asked Nick what he knew about Notbourne Court and he said nothing. So she pursued it a bit, said she'd been told he was a local historian, talked about the event at Imogen's school, that sort of thing, and he said yes, that was him, but sorry, he knew nothing about Notbourne Court.'

Libby frowned.

'It's even odder,' she said, 'because listen to this.

Remember young Olivia who played the prince in Cinderella?'

'She's in the show, isn't she?'

'Yes, she is, but when she was the prince, apparently she got talking to Edward Hall when he was at the pub.'

'You did say he was attractive. A dish, was the expression used, I believe.'

'Yes, well. And in the pub last night I just tossed out a remark about the Court and asked if anyone knew anything about it. And up pops Olivia saying Edward does, and told her about the tunnels.'

'Good grief!' said Fran.

'So Andrew left him a text and he phoned me just now. He got interested in the tunnels after those ones we found, and started looking them up. He was surprised Andrew didn't know about them already, and said a local historian would be sure to know.'

'Only ours didn't,' said Fran. 'You're right – odder and odder.'

'There'll be a local history society, won't there? I wonder if Ian or one of his minions has smoked them out yet?'

'Andrew should have thought of that,' said Fran, 'and of course, there's the Kent Archaeological Trust. They'd know, too, wouldn't they?'

'Yes, they would, because Andrew had heard of a dig there.'

'All right. I'm going to look up history societies.'

'So am I.'

Libby brought the laptop to the kitchen table and started a search. It didn't take her long to find that Shott, Itching and Bishop's Bottom all came within the remit of the Felling Local History Society.

247

'Should I ring the number?' Libby asked Ben, who was busy making a fresh pot of tea.

'Shouldn't you check with the police first? Or Andrew, at least.'

'Yes, I suppose I should.' The phone rang again.

'It's Fran. I just found the Felling Local History Society –'

'So did I.'

'Did you ring them?'

'No, why?'

'I did, and they aren't too happy. They've had several phone calls over the last day or so about the same thing, including one yesterday from the police.'

'Oh.' Libby sat back in her chair and stared at the ceiling. 'So what does that mean?'

'That someone else is looking into it apart from us and the police.'

'And he or she didn't say who the calls were from?'

'She, and no. She said the police had told her not to say anything about it to anyone. And she finished up, with quite a snap, I must say, by saying that it wouldn't be any good because she didn't know anything, anyway.'

'Cor blimey! It is indeed odder and odder, isn't it?'

'It's annoying because I wanted to ask her if she knew Nick Heap, but I didn't get the chance, and anyway, the fact that she – or the society – don't know anything about the tunnels, backs up what Heap said.'

'It really is very odd,' said Libby. 'Even Andrew didn't know until he went to the archives, yet Edward found them ages ago, obviously not hidden in any way.'

'I wish we could talk to Edward,' said Fran. 'Find out where he found them.'

'There's nothing to stop you phoning him.'

'It's not the same. And I suppose we can't interrupt

Andrew and Ian if they're on site.'

'I don't think we'd be too popular,' said Libby with a sigh.

The sunshine tempted Libby into the garden to refresh her pots. Sending Ben off to buy more compost from Nella at the nursery shop, she began re-planting some of the plants that had survived winter.

Ben reappeared lugging a large sack of compost and the landline phone, which he held out.

'Andrew,' he said, raising an eyebrow.

Libby took it with a muddy hand.

'Andrew? What is it?'

'Oh, all sorts of things! Look, can I come over when we have a lunch break here? Ian has given me permission to talk to you.'

'That sounds exciting. Yes, of course you can come. Shall I ask Fran, too?'

'If she's prepared to make the journey from Nethergate, yes.'

'I'll see,' said Libby. 'The trouble is, it's Saturday and the shop gets busy.'

'Ask her anyway, or she'll feel left out.'

Libby laughed. 'I will. What time will you be here?'

'About twelve thirty, I imagine. See you later.'

Assuming that Andrew would require lunch, Libby made soup and dug some rolls out of the freezer to crisp up in the oven.

'Lovely,' said Andrew, when he came into the kitchen later. 'Now – I really must tell you what's been going on. It's all very mysterious.'

'First of all – did you tell Ian about Nick Heap and Edward?'

'I did. And he told me that his team had been enquiring among the local history societies.'

'Ah. Fran rang one of those this morning. They said they'd had the police on, but they didn't know anything.'

'That's what they all said. Some of them knew a bit about it – what appears on websites, basically – you know, the auction and so on, but very little detail about the family.'

'What about the Hellfire Club angle?'

'Nothing, although they may have been clamming up about that, but Ian says his officers went about the matter very delicately I didn't know policemen could be delicate.'

'Well, our local historian we told you about last night doesn't know anything, either. Sophie asked him this morning.'

'Oh, dear. Ian was having someone track him down and ask him today. That doesn't sound promising.'

'So what about Edward?'

'Our one ray of hope,' said Andrew with a smile. 'He's going to try and look up his sources, which he thinks will relate to the previous case, and he's coming down!'

'He said it was a pity he couldn't come down,' said Libby. 'What changed his mind?'

'Ian did.'

'How?'

'By tempting him with treasure. Now, can I have some of that soup?'

Chapter Thirty-one

'Treasure?' gasped Libby.

'You'll remember we looked for treasure before?' Andrew accepted more soup.

'The Civil War connection,' said Libby. 'But your documents said the tunnels at Notbourne were dug in the – what was it – 1790s? The others were much earlier.'

'Yes, but what else did we find – or you find?'

'Smugglers and French prisoners of war,' said Ben.

'And these are –?' Libby shook her head. 'I don't believe it.'

'I should have thought of it myself,' said Andrew, 'and I'm surprised that none of us made the connection.'

'You only found out about the tunnels yesterday for goodness sake,' said Libby. 'Perhaps we might have done, in time. Are they smugglers' tunnels, then?'

'They've found nineteenth-century items in there, but they haven't got very far yet. They're doing a geo-physics survey and a GPR, but the work is going rather slowly.'

'GPR – is that ground penetrating radar?' asked Libby.

Andrew nodded, busy with his soup.

'Hmm.' Libby leant her chin on her hand, thinking. 'If they haven't got very far yet, it means the tunnel is blocked, doesn't it?'

'Not entirely,' said Andrew.

'But even if it's only partially blocked, that means it hasn't been in use recently, surely?'

'That's what I was thinking,' said Ben.

'You said Ian tempted Edward down here with treasure,' said Libby. 'But his period is the Civil Wars and the Restoration. He wouldn't be interested in the later stuff.'

'But he discovered the tunnels when he was looking into houses from his period, so they must have been there then,' said Andrew. 'It's beginning to look as if they were possibly dug out during the Civil War – or earlier, perhaps during Elizabeth's reign – and then utilised by the so-called Abbey of Notbourne, and possibly by smugglers and prisoners of war too.'

'It's all very interesting,' said Ben, 'but what does it have to do with the murders? And young Roly?'

'I don't know,' said Andrew. 'Ian isn't on site any more, and I think I was only really there as a courtesy, so I don't have to go back. And I don't think anyone would tell me anything if I did.'

'Are you not going back, then?' asked Libby.

'I might pop in on my way home – it's only a short diversion. If I find out anything else, I'll let you know.'

'Do you know when Edward's coming down?'

'No, but Ian seemed to think as soon as possible.'

'Do you think he'll stay at the pub again?'

'He might stay over at Shott,' said Ben. 'What's the name of the pub there?'

'The Poacher. Can't remember if it's got any rooms, though,' said Libby. 'I would have thought he'd come here.'

'If you're worried about seeing him,' said Ben, 'I'm sure he'll be in touch.'

'I'm not worried,' said Libby, lifting her chin, and both Ben and Andrew laughed.

Shortly afterwards, Andrew left.

'I thought there was going to be some kind of huge revelation,' said Libby, putting plates in the dishwasher, 'and it was really only about Edward coming down.'

'There was more to it than that,' said Ben. 'The fact that the tunnels have been there for a lot longer than you thought, and were used for far more, too. In fact, has it occurred to you that they might not even have been used as a Hellfire Club?'

'But Andrew found evidence –' began Libby.

'Did he really? Or did he make inferences? Draw conclusions?'

'No.' Libby shook her head firmly. 'I remember him saying that it actually stated in the documents somewhere that the Lord Cheveley who was supposed to have dug the tunnels wanted to uphold Sir Francis Dashwood's traditions, and there were sketches of decorations that were supposed to be found in the so-called dining room. I didn't look at those.'

'Even so, it might have been a bit pie in the sky. Lord Cheveley might have wanted to have grand and uninhibited gatherings in his underground lair and made plans for it, but it might never have come off.'

'What are you saying?' Libby watched him with a puzzled look on her face. 'That it's all made up?'

'It could be, couldn't it?'

'I suppose so,' she said slowly. 'But in that case, what about the stuff Edward found out?'

'I don't expect it's got anything to do with your story,' said Ben. 'And I still can't see that it's got anything to do with the murders. Or Roly.'

'Oh, I can, but I don't know what.' Libby wandered out into the garden and stared at the pots she'd been working with that morning.

'Do you know,' she said after a moment, turning back

to Ben, 'I think I need some more bedding plants for these pots.'

'You do?' Ben raised his eyebrows. 'Why – all of a sudden?'

'I thought we could drive up to the nursery,' she said slyly.

'I wish you'd thought of that before I dragged the compost halfway down the high street.'

'Ah, but I hadn't thought of it then.'

Ben frowned. 'Thought of what?'

'Joe.'

'Joe?' Joe ran the Cattlegreen Nursery just outside the village, while his wife Nella ran the farm shop in the high street.

'Yes. Remember when we found out he knew all about the smuggling routes and all the great houses because he said local people always know?'

'But you said the local history groups didn't know?'

'Local history groups aren't always made up of local people, are they? Not the real, down-to-earth, lived-here-for-generations locals.'

'Hmm.' Ben narrowed his eyes at her. 'So I suppose I drive?'

'I can go on my own,' said Libby.

He laughed. 'But you don't want to. Come on, then. We'd better take my car if you're going to buy masses of plants.'

Cattlegreen Nursery was busy. Libby could see young Owen, the "boy", busy with something in among the rows of plants, and Joe inside by the till serving customers.

'Bit early for the Christmas tree,' he said with a grin as he came out to speak to them.

'Bedding plants, Joe,' said Libby. 'Begonias and geraniums.'

Joe's eyebrows rose. 'I thought you got all that sort of thing from Mike Farthing.'

'He doesn't supply mere mortals, Joe, you know that.'

'But I thought – with your cousin –'

'Not even then,' said Ben. 'Besides, you know Libby. She has an agenda.'

'Might have known,' said Joe, with a chuckle. 'I wondered if you actually knew what to do with bedding plants! What it is this time?'

'I genuinely need plants,' said Libby with a rueful grin. 'That cousin you just mentioned gave me two beautifully planted pots last year ...'

'And you've let them go,' said Joe. 'Come on, then, I'll help you choose. And what was it you wanted to ask me?'

'Do you remember telling us a couple of years ago that all the big houses round here had tunnels?'

'Most of 'em.'

'Well, what do you know about Notbourne Court? Nobody seems to know anything about that.'

Joe stopped by the pelargonium section.

'Notbourne? There's only an old ruin there, now.'

'Yes, but do you know anything about the estate?'

'Bad reputation.'

Libby looked expectant.

'Old boy was a bad payer. Couldn't sell up's what I heard, so pulled the place down.'

'Yes, we knew about that,' said Libby. 'What about tunnels?'

'Not that I heard,' said Joe. 'Leastways, not in living memory.'

'The smugglers weren't in living memory and you knew about those,' said Libby.

Joe grinned. 'You know what I mean. Course, there

may have been all sorts up there nobody knew about. Strange family. Old man used to go about in monk's robes.'

'Monk's robes?' Libby's voice rose, and Owen looked across. His face cleared when he saw Libby.

'Yes.' Joe looked surprised. 'Now, everyone knew about that. Not that I was around o'course. Rowed with his family, they said.'

'With one of them, certainly,' said Libby.

'And old Stephanie died – oh, back in the eighties. Left it to someone else.'

'Yes.' Libby stared down at the plants which had somehow accumulated in her trolley. 'We knew all that. And we've met the last of the Hays line.'

'Last? I thought Stephanie was the last?'

'The family she left it to did some research and discovered there was another descendent. She's staying in Steeple Martin now,' said Ben.

'Well, well,' said Joe, shaking his head. 'Lost sight of it all over the years, I s'pose. Thought there was only a bit of a ruin left. Cottages were all shut up, weren't they?'

'There were only two of them,' said Libby, deciding not to say too much about Chestnut Cottage.

'Right, well, sorry I couldn't be more help,' said Joe, adding a large and showy plant to the trolley. 'Tunnels, eh? More treasure, I s'pose?'

'I don't think so, Joe,' said Libby, looking down at the increased number of plants and wondering how she was going to fit them all in. 'I don't think I'd better buy any more.'

'Oh, you can't refuse Owen,' said Ben, as Owen, beaming as usual, arrived bearing a large scarlet pelargonium which appeared to be climbing up a support.

'I didn't think they did that,' said Libby, taken aback.

'Course they do.' Owen nodded vigorously. 'Climb up your fence, it will.'

'Right.' Libby took the heavy pot while Ben made room for it in the trolley. 'Thank you, Owen. I shall take great care of it.'

Owen and Ben loaded the trays of plants into the Range Rover while Libby paid for them.

'Let me know about them tunnels,' said Joe. 'Got me interested, now!'

'Mad Monks again,' Libby said to Ben as they drove back towards the village. 'And I've just had a thought. Andrew had heard of Notbourne because there'd been a dig there – Roman and Romano-British finds, I think he said. And Fran and I did think about the Kent Archaeological Trust – they'd know about it. I'm just wondering if that's where Edward heard about the tunnels.'

'They aren't *that* old,' said Ben, rounding the bend into Steeple Martin and waiting to turn right into Allhallow's Lane.

'No, but it may mention them. In an archaeological report or something.'

'I should imagine both Andrew and Ian's team have gone through every possible source by now,' said Ben, pulling the Range Rover in behind the silver bullet opposite number 17. 'And why are you bothered? Have you gone back to not trusting Edward again?'

'Of course not. I just wondered how he knew about those tunnels back when we were looking into Dark House.'

'Because,' said Ben, exasperated, 'we were looking into tunnels! For goodness' sake, woman! Get that door open!'

Libby wisely shut up.

Plants unloaded and tea made, they both went to sit under the cherry tree.

'There are too many for the pots,' said Libby.

Ben's face darkened. 'I am *not* going back to buy pots!'

'No, no!' Libby hastened to reassure him. 'I was going to say, I can fill up the beds with the overflow. And that climbing one can go against the trellis on the fence.'

'Are you turning into a gardener?'

'No, of course not. I don't know anything about it,' said Libby. 'I just think it will look pretty.'

'Well, let's do it in the morning, not now,' said Ben. 'I think we ought to be thinking about dinner.'

'Dinner? It's too early for dinner!'

'No, I thought we might go over to The Dragon. You and the boys have been over there recently, but I haven't. I've a fancy for one of the tagines.'

'Oh!' said Libby in surprise. 'That would be lovely. Hadn't we better book?'

Ben grinned. 'I've already done it. While you were making the tea.'

'Sneaky wotsit,' said Libby. 'Shall I drive?'

'No, thanks,' said Ben. 'Not that I don't trust you …'

Libby thumped him on the arm.

Chapter Thirty-two

The Dragon was packed, but still the chef managed to come out and have a word with them and sent his regards to Harry.

'It is gorgeous food,' said Libby at length, laying down her fork. 'I can't even manage a dessert.'

'Neither can I,' said Ben. 'Do you want coffee, or shall we head back so that I can have a drink?'

'Good idea.' Libby reached down into her bag. 'Pub or home?'

'Pub,' said Ben. 'I need a pint.'

'We might see Faith,' warned Libby.

'For the sake of a pint I really don't mind.' Ben gestured to the waiter and asked for the bill.

Ben parked outside the cottage once more and they strolled back to the pub.

'You go in,' said Ben. 'I'll just put my head round the door of the caff, see if they can join us.'

Libby pushed open the pub door and went into the bar, where she stopped dead. Sitting at a table by the empty fireplace sat Faith Conway, deep in conversation with Edward Hall.

'Edward!'

He looked up, his face breaking into his huge, white smile.

'Libby!' He came forward to give her a hug.

'I see you've met Faith,' she said, when she emerged.

'Yes – but no coincidence. Andrew told me to ask for her when he heard I'd booked in here.'

'I thought he might have come over himself,' said Faith, sounding, Libby thought, slightly plaintive.

'No, we'll see each other tomorrow,' said Edward, blithely unconscious of any undercurrent. 'I called you, Libby, in case you wanted to meet for dinner. Where's Ben?'

'On his way,' said Libby. 'We went over to The Dragon for dinner. Remember it?'

'Gorgeous tagines,' said Edward, then turned back to Faith, sitting looking melancholy. 'Sorry, Faith, we've got a lot of catching up to do.' Libby could have sworn she saw the ghost of a wink as he said this.

Faith, however, stayed exactly where she was.

Ben appeared, with Peter behind him, and Edward darted over to greet them.

'Do you know everybody?' asked Faith, in a flat voice.

'It just so happens,' said Libby, 'that all these people are concerned about what happened at your old family home, which you were also looking into.'

'What's Edward got to do with it? He said he's a Professor of History.'

Bandying titles about, was he? Hmm, thought Libby. Not said anything about the tunnels, then.

'Andrew asked his opinion on something to do with the estate,' she said out loud. 'Did Andrew not tell you?'

'I haven't spoken to him today. I tried to call him yesterday, but he didn't answer.' Faith twisted her hands together. 'Actually, I was thinking of going home. There isn't anything I can do here, and now they've found Rowena ...' She looked down at her twisting hands.

'I suppose there isn't,' said Libby. 'Except that you

might find out more about your old home and your family.'

'It was never my home,' said Faith.

'About your family, then,' persisted Libby.

'I don't think there's anything much to find out. They don't seem very respectable, do they?'

You don't know the half of it, thought Libby.

'I suppose, now you know what happened to Rowena,' she said out loud, 'you've achieved what you wanted to do here.'

'But I haven't – I don't know what happened. All I know is she's dead.'

Libby's brow wrinkled. 'That's true.'

Edward, Ben and Peter joined them at the table.

'Quite like old times, isn't it?' said Edward, sending his beaming white smile round the company.

'Let's hope not quite like that,' said Ben. 'Hello, Faith.'

Faith essayed a small smile and Edward looked embarrassed.

'Actually,' said Peter, 'I came with Ben to ask if Edward would like to come and have a drink in the caff.' He flicked an invisible speck of dust from his shirt without looking at any of them, and Libby marvelled, not only at his immediate grasp of the situation, but his considerable aplomb in dealing with it.

'What a good idea,' she said, and turned to Faith. 'Sorry to leave you alone, Faith, but as Edward said, we've all got a lot of catching up to do.'

Faith shrugged. 'I'm going up to read, anyway.'

'Let us know what you intend to do.' Libby stood up, followed by the three men. 'Goodnight.'

With murmured "goodnights" all round, they left the pub.

'That was quick thinking, Pete.' Libby tucked her arm into her friend's.

'It was fairly obvious that she was going to stick like a burr, and you couldn't talk to Edward while she was there,' said Peter.

'Yes, Edward had already given her a hint, but she stayed put. She seems a bit fed up.'

'She was expecting Andrew,' said Edward. 'I gather she's after him?'

'We think so,' said Libby, 'but they've only just met.'

'It's more than that, though,' continued Edward. 'From what she said to me, I think she was hoping to claim this Notbourne Estate. But then she said it wasn't worth it. I think somebody had better explain this more thoroughly to me.'

Inside the Pink Geranium, after Harry greeted Edward effusively, and had his own invitation explained to him, they sat in the left-hand window round the coffee table, while the last of the diners finished their meals.

Ben and Libby between them told Edward the whole story, including Faith's involvement.

'Ah, that's what she meant.' Edward held up his brandy glass to the light and twirled it appreciatively. 'I couldn't understand what she was talking about. I suppose she assumed the estate was worth more than it is?'

'Must have done,' said Harry, who had joined them, sitting astride a chair with his arms resting along the back. 'Same as she was sure she had the Prof on a hook when they had dinner in here.'

'Was she awful?' asked Libby. 'We were doing our best to ignore them.'

'Fluttery and flirty,' said Harry. 'At her age. Honestly.'

'Watch it, sunshine,' said Libby.

Harry grinned. 'You aren't fluttery and flirty, flower. You're more like a busy bee, nosing into everything.'

Peter and Ben laughed, and Edward snorted.

'I'm glad you all think that's funny,' said Libby, 'but on the whole, I'd prefer to be a bee. I like bees.'

'Now you know the whole story,' said Ben, 'Libby and Fran were desperate to know where you found out about the tunnels when you were here before, because they can't find out anything about them.'

'As far as I can remember it was in a private collection. They were mentioned in conjunction with the smuggling tunnels, but went back to the Elizabethan period.'

'So Lord Cheveley didn't dig them out in the 1790s, as it said in the archives,' said Libby.

'You have to be very careful with historical documentation,' said Edward. 'I'm sure Andrew will have told you, but you often get different versions, and especially if the document was written after the event – sometimes years after.'

'The Venerable Bede.' Libby nodded wisely.

'An extreme example,' said Edward.

'I was going to give another example,' said Harry, 'but if I did, Patti wouldn't love me any more.'

Libby smiled. 'Do you remember our friend Patti, Edward? The vicar?'

'Ah, yes.' Edward grinned at Harry. 'I get the reference now. Anyway, these tunnels, or at least parts of them, were there back in the sixteenth century. It's thought they were in use during the Civil Wars, and I have no doubt that if this Lord Cheveley was hell bent, if you'll pardon the pun, on following in Francis Dashwood's footsteps, he could have started using them again.'

'I expect he enlarged them, don't you?' said Libby. 'To make them into his temple, or whatever it was.'

'It's all very intriguing,' said Peter, leaning back and stretching out his long legs, 'but I'm still struggling to find out what any of this has to do with the disappearance and death of Lisa Harwood.'

'Or Rowena Thing?' said Harry.

'She owned the estate, such as it was,' said Libby, 'and it looks as if she didn't know she also owned tunnels.'

'I'd quite like to own tunnels,' said Harry, a faraway look in his eye. Peter gave him a jab in the ribs.

'Andrew said you were tempted down here by treasure,' said Libby, turning back to Edward. 'Is that true?'

'In a way.' Edward leant forward, elbows on knees. 'Andrew found out that the Lord Cheveley of 1648 was another who fought at the Battle of Maidstone. Your DCI Connell put two and two together, came up with seventeen, and called me.'

'Andrew didn't tell us that,' said Libby.

'I don't think he thought it was relevant,' said Edward. 'Anyway, Inspector Connell wondered if there might be any artefacts in the tunnels from that time and asked if I'd like to come and have a look. How could I resist?'

'As you said, just like old times,' said Ben wryly.

'Why did Ian want to know, though?' asked Libby, with a puzzled frown. 'It doesn't matter when the tunnels were dug. I mean, I know we were interested, but it doesn't have any bearing on the case, does it?'

'I don't know, but I think he's being thorough. If this woman – the first one – was living on the estate in a highly secretive manner, there must be a reason for it, and perhaps it's in the tunnels.'

'More treasure left behind for the family, you mean?'

Edward shrugged. 'It's possible. Unlikely, but possible.'

'Well, I still can't see what it has to do with the murders,' said Ben.

'As I said, I think Inspector Connell is just being thorough. If I knew about the tunnels, someone else must have done, and was that the reason for keeping quiet? If someone was using them for criminal purposes, perhaps.'

'Like the sex parties?' said Harry. 'Except that I didn't think sex was illegal – yet.'

'There must be more to it than sex, then,' said Ben. 'Is it still illegal to keep a brothel? Would they be organising prostitution?'

'Oh, heavens, I don't know,' said Libby. 'It looks as though Faith's thinking about going home, so that complication might be gone, and if the police can find Roly …'

'Are you going through one of your "giving up" phases?' asked Peter.

'Yes.' Libby pulled down the corners of her mouth. 'I think the tunnels are a distraction. And I can't see any connection to the deaths of two women – and it's none of my business anyway.'

Everyone laughed.

'Libby's Loonies can't function without their leader,' said Edward.

Libby gave a tired smile. 'But the police can. And Ian knows what he's doing. If he's got a reason for looking at the tunnels, that's good enough, but I'm not going to worry my head about it.'

'But you were so excited about the tunnels yesterday,' said Ben, looking puzzled. 'And you dragged us up to see Joe this afternoon.'

'Who's Joe?' asked Edward.

'Owns a plant nursery and his family have lived in the area for ever,' said Harry. 'Good bloke.'

'And he knows all about the old tunnels,' said Libby, 'and when you were here before he told us that loads of the country houses had tunnels. So I wanted to ask if he knew about Notbourne. All he told us was that the last Lord Cheveley went around in a monk's habit.'

Edward raised his eyebrows. 'Isn't that significant?'

'Is it?'

'Andrew said that the Cheveleys – or the Hays – referred to the tunnels as the Abbey of Notbourne.'

'Yes.'

'So ...'

'Oh, I don't know,' said Libby. 'It looked like it to me at first, but would an Edwardian Lord Cheveley still be carrying on Francis Dashwood's legacy?'

'Are you going on about Mad Monks again?' said Harry.

'It's a possibility,' said Edward, 'although as Libby said, unlikely. And nothing to do with the current problems.'

'Unless Ian unearths the tunnels and discovers it's all still going on,' said Harry.

Chapter Thirty-three

'But it's so far-fetched!' said Libby to Ben as they walked home, leaving Edward still demolishing brandy in The Pink Geranium.

'The whole thing is a bit far-fetched,' said Ben, 'starting with that girl disappearing from the Nethergate 5K. Which isn't very long, actually, is it? Why did they make such a thing of it? They do that every week on their Park Run, don't they?'

'I think it's a fun run, like our 10K one. There were lots of people in fancy dress, weren't there? Running for charity.'

'So why do serious runners do it?' asked Ben. 'She was a serious runner, wasn't she?'

'Why not?' said Libby. 'Every opportunity, I suppose.'

'I don't understand it,' said Ben. 'Do you know Adam told me he'd got a PB this morning.'

'A what?'

'PB. It means Personal Best, apparently.'

'Ah. That's why they do fun runs and everything. It all has to be authenticated and timed and stuff,' said Libby. 'I suppose running round the lanes like Lisa did with young Roly doesn't count.'

'Except that they put all the times and distances up on the social media pages with their various devices,' said Ben.

'Yes, but I expect that wouldn't be taken as gospel.'

'Why not? It's technology. More accurate than human

timekeeping, I would have thought. Did you ever find out about Lisa's data on that Saturday?'

'No, I don't think so.' Libby frowned. 'I can't remember. Anyway that's pointless now – she's dead.'

Ben gave her a sharp look. 'She is.'

The next morning Libby surprised Ben by announcing that she was going to church.

'Church?' he echoed. 'Why?'

'I fancied it,' said Libby. 'It's very calming.'

'Oh.' He eyed her suspiciously. 'Do you want me to come with you?'

'No, I'll be fine. I'm just going to sit at the back and sing if I know any of the hymns.'

Ben wasn't the only one to be surprised. Flo, wrapped in a floral quilted housecoat, appeared at her door in Maltby Close as she passed, mouth open to ask a question, but Libby simply waved and passed on. Bethany Cole, regal in her white surplice and stole, smiled delightedly as Libby approached.

'Good Lord! To what do we owe this pleasure?' she asked, shaking Libby's hand.

'The need for a bit of peace,' said Libby, shamefaced. 'You don't mind me using you, do you?'

'Lord love you, that's what we're here for!' said Beth. 'Anybody we can include in our prayers this morning?'

'Well, yes, actually.' Libby moved slightly away from the door of the church. 'You remember the girl who was found murdered during the Fun Run?'

'Yes,' said the vicar, making a face. 'How could I forget.'

'Her name was Lisa Harwood,' said Libby. 'And another victim was found this week. Rowena Samuels, the owner of the Notbourne Estate and the cottage where the murdered girl had been living.'

'How terrible.' Bethany looked at her feet. 'I shall write them down and we'll include them both.'

'Thank you. It's not much, but I feel I need to make some sort of gesture.'

Bethany looked up. 'Did you know them, Libby?'

'No. Just – as usual – a set of unfortunate coincidences.'

The vicar smiled. 'But that's usually what leads you to the truth, isn't it?'

'It's usually the police, if truth be told.' Libby smiled back ruefully. 'And someone's looking for you.'

Beth turned back to the church to appease the irritated looking churchwarden who had come to find her.

The small congregation paid little attention to Libby sitting in the back pew, despite efforts to move her forward. She noticed a stir among the bent heads when the names of Lisa and Rowena were read out, but nothing more. At the end of the service, as soon as Bethany had passed down the aisle and out to the porch to greet her parishioners, Libby was out of her pew.

'Thanks, Beth.'

The vicar drew her forward to kiss her cheek. 'You look a bit frazzled. Do you feel any better?' she asked.

'I do, actually. Very settling. I ought to try it more.' Libby stepped back. 'I'd better let you talk to your flock.'

Just as she turned away, a voice said 'It's Mrs Sarjeant, isn't it?'

She turned round to see a small woman in an unsuitably thick tweed coat and a pale blue fluffy beret smiling at her nervously.

'Yes, that's me. Libby Sarjeant.' Libby put on her friendliest smile.

'You investigate things, don't you?' The woman's voice shook slightly.

'Well – not really …' Libby let it hang.

'I just wondered if you were anything to do with Mrs Samuels.'

'Mrs – oh! Rowena Samuels. Well, I have been involved a little. Mrs –?'

'Janet Dory. I live in Lendle Lane.'

'Mrs Dory. Can I help you somehow?'

'I just wondered …' Janet Dory hesitated, her wrinkled face crumpling. 'I knew her, you see. When she was Rowena Harris.'

'Really? I – I'm sorry.' Libby didn't know what to say. Janet Dory gave another small smile.

'Oh, we hadn't kept in touch. I just wondered …' She stopped.

'Yes?'

'I wondered if she'd come back to live.' Mrs Dory looked up into Libby's face. 'Do you know?'

Libby shook her head. 'I think she was planning something different, Mrs Dory. But can you tell me something else? When her parents inherited Notbourne Court, where did they live? After all, the Court itself had been demolished by then.'

'They actually lived in Canterbury before Miss Hays left them the estate. But then they moved to Maple Cottage. That's one of the cottages left on the estate.'

'I know,' said Libby, slightly appalled at the coincidence of Rowena's final resting place. 'Look – would you like a cup of tea? They serve tea in the narthex, don't they?'

'Well …' Janet Dory hesitated, clutching her handbag tighter to her chest. 'All right. That would be nice.'

Libby led the way back into the church and noticed Bethany's raised eyebrow.

'How do you like the Reverend Cole?' she asked as

they collected two white mugs of tea.

'She took a bit of getting used to,' said Janet, 'but most of us came round to her. A few didn't.'

'Yes, I know.'

'Oh, of course!' Janet laid a hand on Libby's sleeve. 'I'm so sorry! Of course you know all about that. You were attacked, weren't you?'

'I was,' said Libby grimly, remembering a previous adventure, not so long ago.

'I'm sorry.' Janet sat down on one of the chairs Libby had found for them.

'It's fine.' Libby pasted on a bright smile. 'Now tell me how you knew Rowena.'

'We both taught at the village school in Steeple Mount. Closed now, of course. She was younger than I was, but we became friends.'

'When was this – before Notbourne or after?'

'Both.' Janet smiled. 'She started at the school in – when was it – must have been 1982 or 1983. She still lived at home with her parents then.'

'So she wasn't married?'

'Not then. But after they all moved to Maple Cottage she began seeing Derek Samuels ...' The corners of Janet's mouth turned down.

'You didn't like him?'

'No.' Janet sat up straight, looking defiant. 'He seemed to enjoy telling her what to do – how to behave. You know?'

'Controlling and manipulative?' suggested Libby.

Janet nodded. 'Exactly. Of course, things weren't quite as – as – as *modern*,' she came up with triumphantly, 'as they are today, and women were still a little bit dependent on men. It seems very odd now, in today's society.'

'It does. It still amazes me – the progress in society

and technology that has been made in the last twenty, or even ten years. So they married, Derek and Rowena?'

'Yes. And went to live in Chestnut Cottage.'

'Ah. But they moved away?'

'Later, yes. Rowena continued to teach for a few years after the marriage, but she left – quite suddenly – and none of us heard from her again. I tried calling at both Chestnut and Maple Cottage, but I got no reply at Chestnut, and at Maple Mrs Harris said she'd give her a message.' Janet shook her head. 'But she seemed worried.'

'Mrs Harris did? And you never saw Derek Samuels?'

'No. I went round a couple of times, in the early evenings, when I thought he would be home from work, but I never got an answer.' She shook her head. 'To be honest, I wouldn't have been surprised to have heard she was dead back then.'

'You were that worried?'

'I was. But then – oh, it must have been ten years later – she wrote to me. Luckily, I was still at the same address.'

'Golly. What did she say?'

'She said Derek had died and she was living in London and wasn't sure what to do about the Court. She said Derek had been much more fond of it than she was, but now he was dead, she thought it ought to go back to the family it originally belonged to, and what did I remember about them.'

'Yes, that's just what she wanted to do,' agreed Libby.

Janet nodded. 'Well, I wrote back, you know, saying how lovely it was to hear from her and so on, and told her as much as I knew about Miss Hays and the family. I remembered stories of old Lord Cheveley who demolished the house going round in a monk's habit.'

'Yes, we heard about that,' said Libby.

'Well, I found out that there was nobody living in either of the cottages and the remaining land was very overgrown, and she asked me to find a local firm to clear the ground and let her have the details.'

'So did she tidy up the cottages?'

'I'm not sure. She said she was putting everything in the hands of a firm of solicitors and they would look after everything until she'd decided what to do. And then the letters stopped.'

'That doesn't seem very fair. She was using you,' said Libby indignantly.

Janet smiled. 'Oh, I didn't mind. I'd retired by then, and my husband was always off doing his golf or up at the allotment, so I had time to fill, and Rowena and I would never have had much in common.'

Libby regarded the little woman with her head on one side. The she made up her mind.

'She found the family, you know.'

'The Hays?' Janet gaped.

'The last living member of the family, descended from the son who went off to Ireland.'

'No! And then the poor soul died. Did she hand over the estate?'

'No, she didn't. But the lady she found is here in Steeple Martin now. She came to try and find out why Rowena had stopped writing to her.'

'Goodness.' Janet frowned. 'Do you think Rowena was killed – she was killed, wasn't she? – because she was going to give away the estate?'

'It's possible,' said Libby, 'but it's not worth much, is it? The building itself is gone.'

'The two cottages must both be worth something.' She smiled. 'And then, of course, there was the treasure.'

Libby jumped. 'The treasure?'

'Oh, it was only an old story. There's a story like it in all the old families up and down the country. I love them, history was my specialism, as they say today, although I taught primary school, so there was a bit of everything. But no, this is a story that you find everywhere. Especially in great old houses where the family has been for centuries.'

'Yes, I suppose so. There have been dozens of detective stories about exactly that, haven't there? My friends and I knew a house like that, although it wasn't an especially large house or estate, but it belonged to someone who fought in the Civil Wars and was supposed to have left treasure behind to take care of his family.'

Janet turned surprised eyes on her. 'Yes, dear, exactly. That's exactly what Lord Cheveley was supposed to have done in 1648. Hid his gold in his private chapel.'

Chapter Thirty-four

Libby sat back in her chair and simply stared until Janet Dory became uncomfortable.

'What is it, dear? What have I said?'

Libby pulled herself together. 'I'm sorry, Janet. It's just that the police have been trying to find out about the history of the Court, and no one seemed to know anything. Even the local history expert didn't.'

'What were you asking about?' Janet's eyes narrowed.

'The tunnels. We heard there were tunnels. Everyone said there weren't.'

Janet smiled. 'The chapel was dug underground.'

'Dug – oh. You mean it was a Catholic chapel?'

'Of course, dear.'

Libby remembered someone saying it could date back to Elizabethan times. Edward, she supposed. She frowned.

'You say it was an old story. Do you mean that a lot of people knew it?'

'Oh, yes. But it was always "The gold in the chapel" that people talked about. They didn't mention tunnels.'

'So that's why no one knew anything. But when they were asked, why didn't they mention the chapel?'

Janet shrugged. 'Because it was only an old story. I shouldn't think anyone knows for sure if there was a chapel, except that the Cheveleys – or Hays – were a Catholic family, and that was a dangerous thing to be at one time. And then, they were King's Men. That Lord Cheveley and his son fought at the Battle of Maidstone.'

'Yes, I know about that,' said Libby, and Janet nodded approval.

'Do the police think it's true, then? The story of the gold in the chapel?'

'I don't know, but the tunnels were mentioned and they thought it was worth looking into.

'Well, if it was there, I would bet it isn't now. That Derek Samuels would have found it and taken it.' Janet's mouth thinned in disapproval.

'Really?'

'A greedy businessman, that's what he was. And his sister, too. No feeling for anybody else. Kick you out on the street as soon as look at you, the pair of them.'

Surprised at the venom in gentle Janet's voice, Libby leant back to stare at her.

'Landlords, were they?'

'Among other things.' Janet paused. 'In fact, I often wondered what Derek saw in Rowena. Not that she wasn't a pretty young woman, but she didn't seem to have anything that a man like Derek would want. If the Court had been still a valuable property, I could have understood it.'

Libby felt a hand on her shoulder.

'Sorry, Libby, but the ladies want to clear up now.' Bethany glanced curiously at Janet. 'All right, Mrs Dory?'

'Yes, I'm fine, Vicar.' Janet gave a bright smile and stood up. 'Talking to – ah – Libby has been most interesting.'

'It usually is,' said Bethany.

Libby grinned and stood up. 'Thank you for talking to me about Rowena, Mrs Dory. If I hear anything else, I'll let Beth know and she can pass it on.'

Janet Dory stuck out her hand. 'No, thank *you*, Libby. And please, call me Janet.' She smiled at Libby and

Bethany and turning, scuttled out.

'Well, that was a turn-up for the books,' said Libby, as Bethany walked her to the door.

'About the murder was it?' asked Bethany.

'Murders, plural. Yes. She knew one of the victims.'

'Really? This place never ceases to surprise me.'

'Most small communities are like that. And all the villages know each other, too. You've only got to think of Patti's extended parishes. What are yours? Just the Steeples?'

'And that's more than enough,' said Bethany. 'Although Steeple Cross hasn't got its own church, we meet in the village hall once a month. Steeple Mount's is quite pretty, though. Nice congregation.'

'Isn't this one?' Libby grinned slyly.

'That's a leading question, as you know!' Bethany laughed. 'Look I've got to go. Nice to see you here today.'

'It was nice to be here,' said Libby, 'but don't count on me becoming a regular.'

She walked slowly home, thinking about what Janet had told her.

'Does it make any difference?' asked Ben when she relayed the conversation.

'Well, it looks as if the police were asking the wrong question, doesn't it? Should have been asking about the gold in the chapel, apparently.'

'Are you going to tell Ian?' Ben asked innocently.

Libby snorted. 'You obviously think I shouldn't.'

'You keep saying you don't want to be involved.'

'I'll tell Fran. She can decide.' Libby pulled out her phone. 'Then we'd better get off to the Manor or we'll be late for lunch.'

'I'm in the car, Lib,' said Fran when she answered.

'What is it?'

'You're not driving?' said Libby.

'Of course not! Guy's taking Sophie and me out for lunch. We're going over to The Dragon.'

'Oh, lovely. Well, listen. I need your opinion.'

Fran was silent for a moment when Janet Dory's story had been concluded.

'I think Sophie's meeting some of the Harriers tonight at their pub –'

There was a muffled 'Yes,' in the background.

'So I'll ask her to ask Nick Heap about the gold in the chapel instead. And depending on what he says, we'll tell Ian tomorrow. There's quite a bit of new information there.'

'Unless the police have already found out all about it.'

'They might have. I'm surprised these stories didn't come up in their own investigations. Or in Andrew's.'

'We didn't know what we were looking for, I suppose,' said Libby. 'And it still leaves the reason both the women were killed unsolved.'

'From what this woman told you, I'd be inclined to suspect this Samuels person, if he wasn't already dead.'

'Me, too. She did say he had a sister. I wonder if she's still around?'

'If she is, she hasn't got a connection to any of this,' said Fran. 'Look, we're just driving into the car park. I'll let you know if Sophie hears anything from Nick Heap.'

Following their usual routine, after lunch at the Manor, Libby and Ben accompanied Peter back to the cottage he shared with Harry, who arrived, still in his chef's whites, at almost the same time.

'Sunday is a very boozy time, isn't it?' said Harry as he collapsed on the saggy sofa and accepted a glass from

Peter. 'Mind you, your life is a very boozy time, isn't it, petal?'

'I don't drink any more than the rest of you,' said Libby indignantly.

'There just seem to be so many more opportunities for the odd glass of wine,' teased Harry, eying her over the rim of his glass.

'You can talk! You work in a restaurant. And who is it who hands out free drinks, eh?'

'Children, children!' said Peter peaceably. 'Now, Libby. You were dying to say something at lunchtime, but sensibly restrained yourself. What is it? Have you solved Ian's murder for him?'

'No, I went to church.'

Harry choked on his wine.

'I did. I wanted to clear my head, and I was fed up with the whole thing.' Libby sent a warning look to them all. 'And I met a little old lady called Janet Dory.'

'Did she know Flo?' asked Peter.

'Oh! I never thought to ask! Do you think she's part of their knitting circle or whatever it is? Flo and Dolly Webley and Una in Steeple Lane?'

The elderly ladies were a mine of information on the village and its inhabitants past and present. And future, too, if Libby knew anything about it.

'Flo knows what's been going on and she's never mentioned knowing anything about the Court or the Hays family,' she said.

'But Flo's a "newcomer" like my mum,' said Ben. 'They haven't lived here all their lives like the others. She might not know.'

'That's true,' said Libby. 'But I could ask her to ask them.'

'Just tell us what this old lady told you,' said Peter.

So she did.

'I don't see where it gets you,' said Harry. 'Why was the first girl killed? What was being protected? Because that's what it looks like, isn't it? She was installed in that cottage to look after something – to stop people seeing it. And for some reason, she was killed, which only had the effect of concentrating attention on the place. That doesn't make any sense.'

'No, it doesn't.' Libby frowned. 'But just suppose the gold in the chapel story is true – no, it still doesn't make any sense. If the gold was being protected, why remove its protection?'

'I think the gold theory is a little far-fetched,' said Peter. 'As your nice old lady said, it's a story that does the rounds of every old house. I bet you've got some up at the Manor, Ben.'

'I remember Hetty's reaction when we told her she might have secret tunnels up there,' said Libby. 'She told us no one was going to dig up her floors.'

'So.' Harry stretched and swung his feet up onto Peter's lap. 'We've given up on the sex party theory, have we?'

'There was really no evidence for them, was there?' said Libby. 'And I really couldn't bring myself to do internet research on them.'

'You're an old prude, ducks,' said Harry.

'I know,' grinned Libby.

'Actually, I doubt if you would have found much,' said Peter. He leant forward over Harry's legs. 'A friend of mine in London was doing an undercover feature on the Dark Web. I think most of the really nasty stuff is on there.'

'I'm not actually sure I know what that is, except that there are loads of scare stories about it.'

'It's all a bit technical, and some of it is quite legal, but there are some very bad places there.' Peter looked solemn.

'I don't want to look then,' said Libby firmly.

'No, you don't. But people do.' He leant back again. 'The worst excesses of human nature.'

Silence fell in the little sitting-room.

'There aren't many worse excesses than murder,' said Libby after a while, in a small voice.

'Oh, there are. You wouldn't believe what some people do.'

'I don't mean war and genocide –' began Libby.

'Neither do I.' Peter looked down at Harry's feet.

'I think we'd better change the subject, my lovely,' said Harry. 'It's upsetting you.'

Peter smiled at him. 'Yes, you're right. And I didn't even look at the sites – I was just told about them. So Libby, don't go looking.'

Libby was by now looking sick.

'I don't think she will,' said Ben. 'Can I get us all another drink?'

Fran didn't call that evening, and Libby managed to contain her soul in patience until Monday morning before calling.

'I couldn't very well call the poor girl at midnight last night, could I? And I wouldn't expect her to call me, either. It was just a casual question she was asking, not life-changing.' Fran sounded nettled.

'No, sorry.'

Fran sighed. 'However, if you hang on for a moment, I'll call up the stairs and ask her.'

'Oh – are you in the shop?'

'Yes, Libby. Hang on.'

A few moments later, Libby heard a scuffling noise

and Sophie came on the line.

'Hello, Libby. Yes, I asked Nick last night about the gold in the chamber and he laughed.'

'He laughed.'

'Yes! He said if that's what everybody had been looking for, he would have put their minds at rest.'

'So he *did* know after all?'

'He knew about that story, anyway. Anyway, look, he said if you and Step-Ma wanted to know more about it, he'd happily tell you.'

'Really? What does Fran think?'

There was an exchange at the other end that Libby couldn't make out.

'Fran's going to ring him and set up a meeting. But this is just for your own interest, isn't it? Not anything to do with the police?' Sophie sounded anxious.

'No, they know nothing about it,' said Libby. 'It's just that I came across this little old lady –'

'Yes, Fran told us,' interrupted Sophie. 'Look I'd better give Fran her phone back. I'll see you soon.'

'Little whirlwind,' Fran said fondly after the handover had been made. 'So, what do you think?'

'I think we go and meet Nick Heap,' said Libby.

Chapter Thirty-five

To Libby's surprise, Nick Heap had suggested they meet at The Red Lion in Heronsbourne, it being roughly halfway between Nethergate and Steeple Martin.

'Does he actually live in Nethergate, then?' she asked Fran, as they met in the car park of the pub. 'I don't know why, but I had the feeling he lived in Canterbury.'

'I'm not sure,' said Fran. 'It was his suggestion, and I didn't question it. It would have made more sense, if he does live in Nethergate, to have met there. Anyway, George will be pleased to see us.'

George Felton, landlord of The Red Lion, was indeed pleased to see them. 'Them murders you're looking into, eh?' he said. 'Chap over there said he was waiting for you two. Who's he, then? Not another copper?'

'No, a local historian,' said Fran. 'Can I have a coffee, George?'

'And one for me, too, please, George,' said Libby, who had never really become accustomed to drinking anything but alcohol in a pub.

'Go on, you go over,' said George. 'I'll bring them.'

They approached the man at the table in the window, and Libby recognised the man from The Sergeant At Arms who told them he had been given a lift by Lisa Harwood.

'Fran Wolfe.' Fran held out her hand.

'We met before.' Nick Heap stood up and shook hands with a friendly smile.

'Sort of,' agreed Libby. 'I'm Libby. Thanks for seeing us.'

'Pleasure.' He sat down. 'Sophie said you'd been asking about the gold in the chapel.'

'We got it all wrong, apparently,' said Fran. 'We'd heard about tunnels on the Notbourne Estate, and we were asking about those. And no one seemed to know anything about them.'

'And then someone told me about this mythical chapel,' said Libby, 'and suddenly everybody knew about that. Local legend, is it?'

'Can I ask why you were interested?' Nick Heap tilted his dark head sideways, eyes wary.

Fran trod on Libby's foot. 'A couple of historian friends knew about tunnels in local houses. We have an interest because we discovered some a couple of years ago.'

'Really?' Now Nick Heap was interested. 'Would I know of your friends?'

'You might know Andrew Wylie. He lives in Nethergate,' said Libby.

'Professor Wylie? Of course – I don't know him personally, but I've heard of him. So he's interested, too, is he?'

'Oh, yes.' Fran paused to thank George for the coffee, which he set down with a wink. 'He discovered the tunnels at Notbourne.'

'He – discovered?'

'In the archives at Maidstone,' said Libby. 'And then no one seemed to know anything about them until, as I said, I was told about the legend of the gold in the chapel.'

'I didn't know about that.' Nick looked slightly disgruntled. 'And I thought I knew most things about the area.'

'Yes, we heard from a friend about the presentation you did at her daughter's school,' said Fran. 'She was most impressed.'

'That's good. It's difficult sometimes to get young people interested in local history.' Nick relaxed. 'So what exactly is it you want to know?'

'If there's any truth in the story of the chapel,' said Libby. 'The lady who told me laughed about it.'

'My reaction exactly,' said Nick. 'There are all sorts of stories of treasure hidden in old houses, as you must have heard.'

'Oh, yes,' said Fran. Libby nodded, but they didn't look at one another.

'But the chapel – is that true?' asked Libby.

'As far as we know it's possible.' Nick looked thoughtful. 'Have you heard of Mad Monk Cheveley?'

'Not by that name, but wasn't he the Lord Cheveley who lost the Court and went round in a habit?'

Nick nodded. 'It was rumoured that he had found a chapel underground, but the general belief was – and is – that he found a priest's hole.'

'Perhaps big enough for a Catholic family to worship in?' suggested Fran.

Nick sent her a quick look. 'I see you're on the same page as I am.'

Fran, who disliked this kind of modern idiom, nodded.

'Built in the time of Elizabeth, perhaps re-used in the Civil Wars?' said Libby.

'Exactly. It's quite possible, although with the Court being knocked down, there's no knowing where it came out. Where the entrance was, I mean. Most probably bricked up.'

'There would be two ends, though, wouldn't there?' said Libby. 'For escape.'

'Logically there would, but again, never found. The family are interesting, though.' Nick went on to describe the Cheveley family's history from Mad Monk backwards, without, significantly, referring once to the allegiance to the Hellfire Club.

Libby finished her coffee. 'Why do you think the Lord Cheveley of 1908 or whenever it was started going round as a Mad Monk?' she said.

Nick looked startled. 'I don't know. He was known as a local character – as witness his demolition of the Court when he couldn't sell it. And of course later, his descendent left it to people quite outside the family.'

'Yes, that's what started all this really,' said Fran, treading on Libby's foot again. 'Our friend Andrew was asked to look into the history by a living descendent of the Cheveleys.'

'Oh –' Nick looked even more startled. 'Really? I thought you'd been looking into the death of Lisa Harwood.'

'You had heard about the other death, though, hadn't you? The one at Maple Cottage?' asked Libby. 'It's been in the news.'

'Yes, I had, but to be honest, I hadn't taken much notice. And I certainly hadn't linked it to our Lisa. Do you know any more about that, yet?'

'No – we're not privy to the police investigation,' said Fran with a smile.

'But the deaths were linked?' He looked worried. 'How do you make that out?'

'We don't know,' said Libby, 'but we know the police have been questioning the descendent of the Cheveleys about it.'

'She's still here, is she?' Nick shook his head. 'Poor woman.'

'Well, if you don't know any more about this chapel, or the tunnels,' said Fran, 'I don't think we can pick your brains any further.'

'I wish there was more I could tell you.' Nick shook his head. 'I feel as helpless as I did about Lisa. All I could add there was that she'd once given me a lift home. She kept herself to herself, as they say.'

'I remember, now,' said Libby. 'Bishop's Bottom! That's where you live, isn't it?'

He smiled. 'Certainly is. Do you know it?'

'Oh, yes. We have a friend who lives there,' said Fran. 'Very small place, isn't it?'

'Yes, we all know each other. Who's your friend?'

'Ron Stewart,' said Libby. 'Do you know him?'

Nick Heap's face changed dramatically. 'Screwball Stewart? You know him?'

'Yes. And Maria.'

'You are well-connected,' said Nick admiringly.

'No – just local. And we've friends in common,' said Fran.

'You seem to have friends in common with everybody.' Nick finished his pint. 'I don't suppose your friend Professor Wylie would let me have a look at his material, would he?'

'We weren't allowed to take it away,' said Libby, 'so he's only got copies, and I think he gave those to the police.'

'Why did the police want them?'

'No idea,' said Libby. 'Perhaps they think there's a link to the dead women.'

'I shall be in a constant state of anticipation now.' Nick grinned at them. 'It all sounds like something out of a television series rather than a simple country murder.'

'I don't think any murder's simple,' said Libby, with a frown.

'Oh, no!' Nick hastily backtracked. 'I'm sorry – I didn't mean to sound heartless. You didn't know either of the victims, did you?'

'No – how could we?' asked Fran. 'Our children knew Lisa, but that was all.'

'And not well, as you said yourself,' said Libby. 'She kept herself to herself.'

'Very wise sometimes,' said Nick with a sigh. 'Gossip can be a terrible thing.'

'Indeed it can,' said Fran, standing up. 'Well, thank you for seeing us Nick, and taking time out of your day.'

'A pleasure.' Nick also stood up. 'If you find anything more about the tunnels, or the mythical chapel, would you let me know?'

'Of course,' said Libby with a smile. 'And thank you.' She took the coffee mugs over to the counter. 'Thanks, George.' She lowered her voice. 'He a regular?'

'No. Once or twice he's been in over the last year, that's all.'

'On his own?'

'No – with a woman.'

'OK, thanks. See you soon.'

'Give my best to your mate Patti when you see her.'

'So,' said Libby when they were out in the car park, 'why didn't we trust him?'

'I'm glad we both felt the same,' said Fran. 'He's a perfectly friendly looking bloke and we know nothing about him, except that he's the treasurer of the Harriers and he lives in Bishop's Bottom.'

'First of all,' said Libby, 'why was he so keen to meet us? I must say that didn't occur to me at first.'

'No, me neither. But he didn't really know anything at

all, so he could have just told Sophie and left it at that. He hasn't really told us anything about the chapel.'

'Just a lot of incidental family history.'

'He was fishing,' said Fran. 'He wanted to know how much we knew.'

'Or how much the police know,' said Libby.

'Let's drive over and see if Sid knows Nick Heap. If he doesn't drink here, he might use The Poacher.'

But Sid wasn't on duty.

'Cash and Carry,' said the young barman. 'Be back later.'

'Suppose we might just as well go home, then,' said Libby as they emerged into the car park.

'Or we could have a wander along here and look at Chestnut Cottage,' said Fran.

'We could. Why?'

'I just felt like it,' said Fran with a shrug.

They strolled along the lane towards Chestnut Cottage, which, when they reached it, still had police tape fluttering outside.

'I wonder where the tunnel search is going on,' said Libby.

'Somewhere between here and the ruin,' said Fran. 'And someone has been looking after it. Remember how smooth the grass was when we went to have a look?'

'Yes, but Faith told us she'd looked up a firm to tidy the grounds, didn't she, and then everything was put in the hands of the solicitors in London. Presumably they're still paying maintenance people.'

'And what are you two doing here?'

Libby and Fran whirled round so fast they bumped into one another and nearly fell over.

'Ian!'

'Well?' He put his head on one side.

'Actually,' said Libby, a bit confused, 'I don't really know. We were – um –'

'We met Nick Heap,' said Fran. 'And we didn't trust him. We came to ask Sid at The Poacher if he knew him.'

'Remind me – Nick Heap?'

'Treasurer of the Harriers and the local historian who didn't know anything about the tunnels,' said Libby.

'So why meet him, and why didn't you trust him?'

It's a long story,' said Libby, with a sigh. 'And where did you pop up from?'

'Never mind that, get on with your long story.' Ian leant against Chestnut Cottage's front fence and crossed his arms as Libby began to tell him about Janet Dory and the gold in the chapel.

'And he suggested meeting us,' said Fran, 'not the other way round. But he didn't know anything other than the old story. And it seemed to us as if he was trying to find out what we – or the police – knew.'

'And there's another thing,' said Libby slowly.

'What?' said Ian and Fran together.

'When we told him that the Cheveleys' descendent was the one who asked Andrew to look into the archives – little white lie, but still – he said "She's still here, is she?" We never mentioned it, so how did he know it was a woman?'

Chapter Thirty-six

Ian regarded them both with amusement.

'Sometimes I wonder how you manage when you aren't involved with a murder investigation.' He levered himself upright. 'First – why do you need to know more about the tunnels? You know we've found them, so all that needs to be known about them – and if they are connected to two murders – will soon be known.

'Second – I really don't know why you don't trust this man who, it seems to me, was only suffering from the same condition as yourselves. Curiosity.'

Libby felt heat creep up her neck and into her cheeks. Fran was looking at the floor.

'As for how he knew the descendent of the Cheveleys – or Hays – was a woman, her presence in the area and in Steeple Martin has been talked about quite freely, I imagine, within your own families and friends? Sophie will have talked about it with the other members of the Harriers, who will naturally have been interested in the investigation into Lisa Harwood's death.'

'But –' began Libby.

'And if you're going to say they wouldn't know the connection with Lisa's murder, you only have to remember that Lisa was, effectively, the murdered woman's tenant, and that Faith Conway was looking for her … Speculation would be as rife within their group as it is between you two.'

Libby couldn't look at Ian or Fran.

Fran cleared her throat. 'We'll – er – get going, then,' she said.

'I thought you wanted to know where I'd popped up from?' The amusement was back in Ian's voice. Libby sneaked a look upwards. He was smiling.

'Um – well, you know ...' she began.

'Come on, I'll show you.' He opened the gate to Chestnut Cottage and Libby's eyes widened. 'Strictly off the record, of course.'

He led them up the path to where it branched off round the side, leading to the high fence which hid the back garden from view, and opened a gate.

The previously hidden garden was, as far as Libby could see, bare. Grass stretched as far as the eye could see, as far, in fact, as the distant ruin of what had been Notbourne Court.

'Have you walked here from over there?' asked Fran.

'No.' Ian opened a back door into Chestnut Cottage, which led into an uninteresting but functional kitchen.

'This was where Lisa lived,' said Libby, looking round with interest.

'It was,' said Ian. 'As keeper of the gate.'

'Keeper ...?'

'We think this is the other end of our tunnel.' He opened what looked like a pantry door.

'Don't you know?' asked Fran.

'We have our suspicions. I came over to have a sniff around. We don't want to stir up any interest if we can help it, so we're hoping to get into it from the other end.'

'What have you found so far?' asked Libby. 'Or aren't you allowed to tell us?'

'I'm afraid not.' Ian held the pantry door wide open. 'Fran, see if you can notice anything in here, would you?'

Fran threw him a suspicious look, but stepped forward

gingerly, then stopped.

'There's earth on the floor.'

'Yes.'

Fran knelt down by the back wall of the pantry, which, oddly, only had shelves on the side walls.

'This is a false back, isn't it?' she said. 'There's a very slight draught.'

'That's what I think,' said Ian. 'If we can't come at it from the other side, we'll have to get the experts in to get it open.'

'Does it matter, if you've already found the tunnel?' said Libby.

'Oh, yes, it matters,' said Ian.

'There are scrape marks on the floor here, too.' Fran was still peering down. 'Something heavy's been dragged.'

Libby shuddered. 'Oh, please, not a body.'

'No, something stone ... I know!' Fran looked up. 'Those pots!'

Ian squatted to look at the marks. 'Yes, you could be right. We really have to get behind this door.'

'Then you'll have to bring in your experts,' said Fran. 'I don't think you'll get into it from the other end.'

Ian and Libby looked at each other, then back at Fran.

'Did you –'

'Was that –' they said together.

Fran looked surprised. 'Yes, I think so.' She stood up. 'So Lisa was guarding the entrance to whatever this is. On behalf of who, though? Not Rowena.'

Ian was frowning. 'We're looking into that. We've got a team at Maple Cottage as well as in the main tunnel. Which, I can tell you, looks as though it hasn't been used for some time.'

'Oh, that's a pity,' said Libby.

Ian laughed. 'Quite!'

Fran looked up at Ian. 'I'm sorry if we were being intrusive, Ian. And you were right. We were seeing shadows where there were none.'

'Some of your shadows have been helpful,' said Ian, ushering them out of the back door.

Libby and Fran were silent as they walked back to The Poacher.

'I suppose he was right,' said Libby eventually.

'Yes.' Fran kept her eyes on the ground.

'And it was nice of him to show us the – um – entrance.'

'A sop,' said Fran. 'He already knew. He didn't need me to look at it.'

Libby sighed. 'Oh, well. At least they've nearly wrapped it up.'

'Have they?' Fran stopped beside her car. 'Do they know what's been going on? Who put Lisa into Chestnut Cottage? And why? And why Rowena Samuels was killed?'

Libby frowned. 'I suppose that was because she was the real owner, and ...' she shrugged. 'I don't know.'

'I'm going home,' said Fran. 'I shall go and cook something really complicated to take my mind off this.'

'I think you should go back to writing,' said Libby. 'Think what a good story this would make.'

Fran had once toyed with writing a novel and taken classes with Amanda George.

'One with no ending,' said Fran, climbing into the car. She gave Libby a small smile. 'Thanks, though.'

Libby drove slowly back to Steeple Martin, trying to work out the story of Lisa Harwood, Rowena Samuels and the mystery of Notbourne Court.

'Unless,' she said to herself, 'it's nothing to do with

the Court at all, but the people. But there's one big hole in the middle. One person missing. The killer.'

She was almost back at number 17 when her phone rang. She let it go to voicemail while pulling in to her parking space on the other side of Allhallow's Lane, then pulled the phone out to see who had called.

"Unknown Number" it told her, but also that there was a message. As she pressed the button to listen, her heart gave a thump.

'Libby, it's Roly. You went to see Chestnut Cottage today, didn't you? Well – listen –' his voice broke, 'I've found a body.' The message cut off abruptly, and Libby frantically called back.

'Answer, answer!' she pleaded silently, and at last, he did.

'Roly, I was driving! Where are you? How did you know –'

'I saw you.' He sounded as if he was in tears. 'I wanted to call out, but you had that policeman with you.'

'You found a body?'

'Yes. It's – it's horrible. I don't know what to do.'

'Tell the police. You must, Roly, please.'

'I can't!' He was practically screaming now. 'You do it! Please, Libby. You do it.'

Libby took a deep, shaky breath. 'Where are you?'

'At Chestnut Cottage. Where do you think? Will you come? Please?'

'Will you stay there?'

'Yes. I promise.' The phone clicked off.

Libby got out of the car, and realised that her whole body was shaking.

She found Ian's work number, and was patched through.

'Libby – what is it? You know I'm busy.'

'I know, but Roly just called me.'

'Roly?' Ian's voice sharpened. 'What is it? Are you all right?'

'You'll never believe it!' She tried a shaky and unsuccessful laugh. 'He's found a body.'

'Where is he? Where? Quickly!'

'He wants me to go. He told me to call you, too.'

'You stay where you are. Where's Ben?'

'At work – I don't know. Look, Ian, I don't think you'll see Roly unless I'm there. He sounded very on the edge.'

'All right. Are you safe to drive? You sound upset.'

'I am upset. But I'm safe, it isn't far.'

'Where?'

'Chestnut Cottage.'

There was a muffled expletive at the other end.

'I'm at Maple still. I'll meet you.'

Libby got back in the car and managed to turn it round. Several times on the journey back to Shott she questioned her ability to drive safely, but by keeping well below the speed limit she arrived outside Chestnut Cottage in one piece and parked, rather drunkenly, on the opposite side of the lane. No other cars were in sight.

She climbed out and looked round, suddenly scared.

'I'm here, don't worry.' Ian's voice spoke softly in her ear. 'I moved everyone down here, very quietly. Now let's go into Chestnut Cottage.'

Now that she knew, Libby could see signs of movement in the undergrowth along the sides of the lane. Ian led the way across the lane and up the path to Chestnut Cottage's front door. As he opened it, they heard a sound from inside, and Ian pushed Libby behind him, pausing before proceeding.

'Do you think he's armed?' Ian whispered.

'Roly? No, of course not! He's scared stiff,' Libby whispered back.

'Speak to him, then. Quietly.'

'Roly? Are you here? It's Libby. Where are you?'

There was silence for a long minute, then a scraping sound.

'Libby? Are you on your own?'

'No, I called the police, like you told me. I've got DCI Connell with me.'

'Just him?'

'Yes, just him and me.'

Libby's heart was thumping so hard she thought she might black out, but Ian took hold of her arm in a firm grip and moved her slightly forward into the kitchen.

There was another scraping sound, and slowly, the pantry door opened. Roly almost fell through it and stayed on the floor. Ian was down beside him immediately.

'Are you hurt?'

'No.' Roly's voice was a thread. 'Passage.'

Ian stood up, turned away and spoke into his phone. Turning back, he said 'I've called for an ambulance and a couple of my men are coming in as well. Will you be all right, Libby?'

Libby, now down on her knees by Roly's head, nodded. Ian went into the pantry.

'Libby?'

'Yes, Roly. I'm here.' Libby tentatively stroked the dirty and matted hair. 'Don't talk yet.'

Two uniformed police officers came into the cottage, followed by DC Tomlinson, looking nervous.

'DCI Connell went in there,' said Libby pointing at the open pantry door. Showing no surprise, the two uniforms, wearing, Libby noticed, body armour, went straight into the pantry and disappeared. Tomlinson came down on his haunches beside her.

'Ambulance is on its way,' he said, in hushed tones.

Roly began to push himself upwards, and Tomlinson tensed. Libby smiled. 'He's not going anywhere, are you, Roly?'

Roly shook his head and leant against Libby. 'Awful,' he whispered, and fainted. Between them, Libby and Tomlinson prevented his head from crashing down on the stone-flagged floor.

The paramedics arrived and took over.

'Should I go with him?' Libby asked doubtfully.

'I should stay here. I expect DCI Connell will want to speak to you,' said Tomlinson. 'I've got to go to hospital with him.'

'Can I sit outside, then?' Libby asked.

'I suppose so.' Tomlinson sounded doubtful himself now, but led the way outside. Shortly, the paramedics carried Roly out and loaded him into an ambulance. Several more officers went into the cottage.

Libby called Ben, to let him know where she was.

'Oh, Lib!' Ben sounded exasperated. 'Why can't you stay out of things?'

'That's not fair. Roly called me, I told Ian and Ian asked me to come over. And everything's all right. I'm just waiting to be told I can go home.'

'You don't want me to come and get you?'

'No, I'm fine. But you might scout around for something for dinner. We can't even go to Hal's – it's Monday.'

'All right. Oh – before you go, someone called Janet Dory just came looking for you.'

'What, to the Manor?'

'Yes. She didn't know our address, so she came here.'

'What did she want?'

'She said it was a terrific coincidence, but yesterday you were talking about Derek Samuels and today she saw his sister in the village getting into a car.'

'She what?' Libby experienced a surge of adrenalin.

'Yes. She said she hadn't seen her for years, thought she'd moved away, but there she was in the high street.'

'Oh, golly.' Libby was frowning. 'Was she driving?'

'No, she said it was driven by a man. Is it important?'

'I think so,' said Libby, pulling pieces together in her mind. 'Look I'd better go and tell Ian. Would you do me a favour and call Fran to tell her what's been going on?'

'This is serious,' said Ben. 'All right. Look after yourself.'

Libby switched off the phone and walked back towards Chestnut Cottage. The uniformed officer on the door looked at her suspiciously.

'I know I can't go in, officer, but could you get an urgent message to DCI Connell, please?'

'What is it, madam?'

Libby repeated what Ben had told her, and the officer, looking bemused, disappeared inside the cottage. Libby returned to the bench in the front garden where she'd been sitting. Ten minutes later, Ian reappeared and sat down beside her, looking weary and slightly dishevelled.

'Find anything?' Libby asked.

'Oh, yes.' Ian's mouth turned down in distaste. 'We've found the body of what used to be the real Faith Conway.'

Chapter Thirty-seven

Libby gaped. 'How do you know?'

'Passport and driving licence. They were still with the body.'

Libby fell silent.

'And we found the tubs.'

'The tubs? Oh, the tubs. What did they have to do with anything?'

'As far as we can tell, they were simply decoration.'

Libby nodded. 'And did you get my message?'

'That Denise Samuels had been seen in Steeple Martin? Yes.'

'Er – would that be the woman we know as Faith?'

'Until we speak to her we can't be sure. And did you recognise the description of the man with her?'

'It sounded like the historian – Nick Heap.'

Ian stood up. 'We'd better start looking for them, then.'

'Do you think any of the story she told us was true? About the family?'

'I think it probably was – it's too easy to check. After all, we're in touch with the solicitors, and they've confirmed that Rowena had set in train the process of returning the estate to the Hays family.'

Libby frowned. 'So it looks as though the Samuels sister didn't want it returned. But why? It can't be worth that much.'

'There are two highly desirable cottages and a sizeable

chunk of land that could probably be redeveloped.'

'Hold on, though.' Libby thought for a moment. 'If the Samuels sister didn't want it returned to the Hays family, all she has to do is continue to pretend to be Faith. Then everything will be handed over to her.'

'But the solicitors would require proof. And believe me, there was no way Denise Samuels could have persuaded anyone she was Faith Conway.'

'Were they so different?'

'Difficult to tell,' said Ian. 'But from the passport photograph, yes. The woman we know as Faith is small, with greying hair. The real Faith is a bigger woman altogether, and has – had – pure white hair.'

'And was it the chapel?'

'Look, Libby, I'm grateful to you for bringing me out here, but I really can't discuss it with you at the moment. If you're all right to drive, I suggest you go home. I'll let you know as much as I can when I can.'

Libby nodded, and watched him go back towards the cottage, his phone already to his ear. Just as she turned to go back to the car, Detective Constable Turnbull appeared.

'Mrs Sarjeant,' she said, 'DCI Connell though you might like an escort back home.'

'That was kind of him,' said Libby, 'but he probably wants to make sure I don't to get into any trouble.'

DC Turnbull offered an ice maiden smile. 'I couldn't say, ma'am.'

'I think I'm safe to drive,' said Libby.

'How about I follow you home, just in case?' suggested DC Turnbull.

'Seems a bit excessive.'

'You're a valuable witness. I'll stay back.'

Libby shrugged. 'All right. Kind of you.'

Another wintry smile. 'Part of the job, ma'am.'

Libby turned the car round and drove back towards The Poacher, noting the unobtrusive black saloon in her mirror. What was Ian really worried about, she wondered?

She drew in to the side of the road just before the turn into Allhallow's Lane and got out of the car.

'That's my road over there,' she told DC Turnbull, who had pulled in behind her and let down her window. 'I stopped here because it's a cul-de-sac and you'd have to turn round to come out again.'

'Thank you,' said the officer, 'but DCI Connell said I was to make sure you got safely inside.'

'Oh, OK.' Libby straightened up and stopped dead. 'DC Turnbull,' she said quietly. 'Over there. That man outside the pub.'

'The tall dark one?'

'Yes. It's someone DCI Connell wants to speak to.'

DC Turnbull was already speaking into a radio. Libby stood irresolute, wondering what she should do, when out of the pub came the woman she knew as Faith Conway.

'That's the fake Faith!' she whispered to DC Turnbull. 'What do I do if she sees me?'

'I'm going over,' said Turnbull, opening the door. 'Stay here.'

Nick Heap and Denise Samuels were now walking towards them on the other side of the high street. DC Turnbull approached casually then stopped right in front of them. Libby saw both Heap and Samuels shake their heads and make as if to move on.

'She can't stop them,' muttered Libby to herself, and set off across the road just as Nick Heap was ushering Denise Samuels round DC Turnbull.

'Hello, Faith!' called Libby, in what she hoped wasn't

a shaky voice. 'I see you've met our local historian. Hello, Nick.'

Denise Samuels looked horrified and Nick Heap furious. Libby wondered if he was going to just charge straight through her, when he jerked to a halt, surprise written all over his face.

'Mr Heap, I must ask you to accompany me to the station.' Turnbull's voice was as icy as her smile. 'And you, Miss Samuels.'

Denise screamed and lashed out. Libby caught a blow on her arm, and made a grab for the woman.

'It's OK – I've got her.' An unruffled Harry peered between Samuels and Heap. 'And anyway, here comes the cavalry.'

Looking relieved, DC Turnbull lifted her free hand to the uniformed officers who were coming towards them. By this time Denise Samuels was sobbing.

Nick Heap swore at Harry. 'Let go of my mother.'

Libby and Harry both looked astonished, as officers relieved Turnbull of her charges and led them towards waiting police cars. She turned to Libby with a much warmer smile.

'Thank you,' she said. 'You shouldn't have done it, but I don't know how I'd have stopped them walking away.'

'As Harry said, the cavalry were coming.' Libby returned the smile. 'Now what happens? Do I need to make a statement?'

'I think you go home, Mrs Sarjeant,' said the officer. 'And I'm sorry sir, I should thank you, too.'

'Harry Price,' said Harry holding out a hand, 'and I don't suppose I should have done it, either. You know, Lib, I never did trust that woman.'

'No,' said Libby thoughtfully, watching the police cars

driving off in the direction of Canterbury. 'Even her Irish accent wasn't convincing.'

'She kept forgetting to use it,' said Harry. 'Come on, let's go into the caff. You look as if you could do with a glass of something. Is that all right, officer?'

DC Turnbull nodded. 'And DCI Connell knows where to find you if he needs to, doesn't he?'

'Oh, yes,' said Libby with a sigh. 'Always.'

Libby and Ben ate at the pub that evening, joined by Peter and Harry. Guy and Fran drove up from Nethergate with Adam and Sophie, and Ian had promised that if he could, he would call in on his way home. Much to everyone's surprise he arrived earlier than usual and ordered champagne.

'What are we celebrating?' Libby asked, eyeing the bottle suspiciously.

'The resolution of a very nasty case,' said Ian. 'Aspects of which we managed to keep from you, I'm afraid to say.'

'Oh. And now will you tell us what was going on?'

'As much as I can. Where would you like me to start? The end, or the beginning.'

'When you and Libby both realised that Faith Conway was really Derek Samuels' sister,' said Ben. 'That took a leap of faith, if you'll pardon the pun.

'The woman calling herself Faith Conway never left this pub, so to hear that she was getting into a car driven by a man, when she claimed not to know anyone, was suspicious. We checked that it wasn't Andrew Wylie, but Mrs Dory described the man as big and with very dark, greying hair.'

'Nick Heap,' said Sophie, wide-eyed.

'As far as we can make out, Nick Heap, who, of

305

course, was Rowena Samuels' nephew, had discovered the tunnels at Notbourne, including the so-called chapel, or "dining room", as described in the archives. He had access to a lot of archive material, including some passed on to Rowena's parents when they inherited the estate, and, of course, he knew all about the so-called Hellfire Club, including the fact that the Lord Cheveley who tried to sell off the estate was continuing the tradition.'

'We guessed that,' said Fran.

'So, Heap, who had connections to all sorts of different spheres of society, shall we say, began to set it up again. Some of the "amusements" on offer, often conducted in a pseudo-religious manner, were, quite frankly, appalling. Young people, particularly very fit young people –'

'Ballet dancers,' breathed Libby.

'Runners,' said Sophie.

Ian nodded. 'And several circus performers – not just human – were recruited. And it was lucrative. A few people died –' there was a gasp from his audience '– but it was all hushed up. What we gather, although he isn't saying much yet, is that Nick Heap recruited Lisa while she was still living in Canterbury and persuaded her to become, quite literally, the gatekeeper at Chestnut Cottage.

'Although he claimed to know nothing about her, she had recruited Roly, too, which was why he was so frightened. Sadly, he'd been tempted into the whole sex games part of the operation, and, of course, his job in financial services brought him into contact with people who could become – er – clients. But he'd become wary and suspicious, and when Lisa disappeared he guessed part of what had happened, although he didn't know why.'

'And why was it?' asked Fran.

'A lot of what Denise Samuels – the mock Faith Conway – told us was true. Rowena had searched for Faith and found her. They had become very friendly and Rowena was determined to hand the estate back to the family. Then she became suspicious about what was going on behind her back and came down to find out for herself. She actually told Faith about it, saying she would be in touch when she got back, but of course she didn't get back.

'Heap was furious that his aunt by marriage was going to take his lucrative and highly illegal business away from him and probably put him inside for a good proportion of his life, so he killed her and put her in the freezer at Maple Cottage while he figured out what to do.'

'Good God,' said Guy.

'Yes.'

'So where does Lisa Harwood come into it?' asked Peter.

'Faith Conway, just as we were told, came over to find out what had happened because she hadn't heard from Rowena. So Heap had to kill her, too. He hid her in the chapel, and, of course, Lisa, who had access to it, found her. Although we don't know for sure, we think she challenged him on the morning of the Nethergate 5K. He had a ready supply of energy drinks – they were used in his, er, ceremonies at the chapel, as were other drugs, along with other things, and he knew Lisa would never touch them because of her condition. I think he expected her to die out there on the cliffside, but she didn't, so he had to get her away very quickly.'

'Why was she dumped here, though?' asked Libby.

'Again, as far as we can tell, because he hasn't told us in so many words, he had one body in Maple Cottage and another not far from Chestnut Cottage. He knew Chestnut would become a focus for investigation when Lisa disappeared, so after a week of keeping her in his boot, he brought her here. He even tried to get into your new car park that night,' he said to Ben and Libby. Libby turned a pale shade of green.

'How was Lisa paid? And did she know about the other deaths? You said there've been deaths,' asked Fran.

'I imagine we're going to find that Nick Heap was raking it in. And of course, he had so much blackmail material, it would have kept him going for years. I don't think she knew the full extent of the operation, but she obviously began to suspect. And she was obviously one of the women on offer.'

'But what about the Samuels woman?' asked Harry. 'Heap's mother. Why was she involved?'

'They – because they were both involved – knew a lot about the estate, but not everything. They also knew that Rowena had handed control to a firm of solicitors, who didn't take any hands-on control, but who had instructions to put in hand the transfer to Mrs Conway. So there had to be a Mrs Conway. And in order to establish her credentials and fill in any gaps in her knowledge, she went to Maidstone Archives and – well, you know the rest. Her son had given her the hire car documents, but not her passport or driving licence, because the picture looked nothing like Denise Samuels and they didn't have the time to do anything about that. They were still with the body when we found her.'

There was a short silence after he finished and topped up their glasses.

'That's one of the nastiest we've been mixed up with,' said Libby eventually. She looked at Fran. 'And you knew there was something right at the start.'

'I wish I'd known what, though,' said Fran, peering

308

gloomily into her glass.

Guy patted her hand. 'Just be grateful that sometimes it helps.'

'You both did,' said Ian, raising his glass.

'And what about poor little Roly?' asked Harry.

'He had been recruited by Lisa, who told him never to have the drinks, because he had a similar condition to her own, and that was the first thing that raised his suspicions. He didn't dare say anything because he was under Heap's eye both as a Harrier and one of the "amusements", and he had seen what happened on occasions in the ceremonies. He was scared stiff, and tried to draw attention to the whole thing by his phone calls to Libby. Then, when she seemed to have got the message, he got even more terrified and went to ground. We'd have found him eventually – he'd made himself a den in the grounds of the estate.'

'Why didn't he get right away?' asked Peter with a frown. 'Why stay in the area?'

'Because he thought if we were looking for him, he'd be found and then Heap would find him. Besides, in his weird way, he still wanted to draw attention to Heap and the Abbey of Notbourne. And then, earlier today, he went down into the chapel from Chestnut Cottage and found Faith Conway's body.'

'How did he get in there? We couldn't make it open,' said Libby.

'Again, we would have done eventually. There was a concealed mechanism – quite common.'

'And why hadn't he been down there before now?'

'He was scared of being found. Today he was getting desperate, and when he saw us he decided he'd have to go for it. He didn't expect to find a body, though.'

'What will happen to him?' asked Fran.

'He hasn't committed any crimes except officially breaking and entering,' said Ian. 'We don't know what went on during the ceremonies – or rather, we do, as they kept recordings of a lot of them –' a concerted expression of disgust rose from the company '– but I doubt we could recognise any individuals. At the moment, he's in hospital, currently refusing to see his parents.'

'Oh, poor people,' said Libby.

'I expect he's ashamed,' said Ben.

'Those tubs,' said Fran. 'What about them?'

'Ian said they were just decoration,' said Libby.

'Sadly they weren't,' said Ian. 'They were covering several graves.'

There was another mass exclamation of disgust.

'We haven't uncovered everything yet, by any means,' he went on, 'and I don't think you would particularly want to hear about any of it, so I'll get someone to take official statements tomorrow and that will be the end of it. Thank you again, for your help, and where's Edward?'

'Gone to stay with Andrew. We'll give them the good news – if it is good news – tomorrow,' said Libby.

'And meanwhile,' Ian said, 'please don't believe either Libby or Fran when they say they won't get involved any more.'

The End